FIGHT TO
THE LAST MAN!

Fenelon yelled to one of his men to work his way over to Captain York and tell him to withdraw to the riverbed. Yelling to another legionnaire, he told him to do the same on the right. He stopped when he saw the eight Rangers stand. They were out of bullets and were taking on the rebels hand to hand with rifle butts and knifes. It was a valiant effort, but the odds were too great. One by one, they went down until all eight were dead. The rebels slashed and stabbed at the bodies after they fell. Finally they raised their rifles in a victory cheer as they began their charge toward the center of the riverbed. Kueddei's tanks were on line again and moving straight for them. Fenelon turned to Jake, "Commander, gather all the men at the west end of the riverbed. Have them remove their belts and hook them through the back loop of their trousers. Quickly, Commander."

Jake stared at the man in total bewilderment. "What are we doing, Pierre? It would take a miracle for us to walk away from this."

Berkley Books by James N. Pruitt

The SPECIAL OPERATIONS COMMAND Series

SPECIAL OPERATIONS COMMAND
#3
DESERT FURY

JAMES N. PRUITT

BERKLEY BOOKS, NEW YORK

SPECIAL OPERATIONS COMMAND #3: DESERT FURY

A Berkley Book / published by arrangement with
the author

PRINTING HISTORY
Berkley edition / April 1991

ISBN: 0-425-12649-8

A BERKLEY BOOK ® TM757,375
Berkley Books are published by The Berkley Publishing Group,
200 Madison Avenue, New York, New York 10016.
The name "BERKLEY" and the "B" logo
are trademarks belonging to Berkley Publishing Corporation.

PRINTED IN THE UNITED STATES OF AMERICA

10 9 8 7 6 5 4 3 2 1

DESERT FURY

CHAPTER 1

The Marine sergeant, positioned beside the door marked Secretary of Defense, stood at parade rest and stared down the long hallway, straining his eyes in an effort to identify the rank of the approaching officer. However, the man was still too far away. There was one thing that did stand out, even at this distance, and that was the man's snow-white hair. The dress uniform was blue with silver buttons, signifying that he was an Air Force officer. Judging from the multicolored rows of ribbons that covered the left side of the uniform, this guy was someone who had been around for a while.

Still at parade rest and not showing the slightest sign of movement, the marine prepared to snap to attention as the officer drew closer. The sergeant caught a glimpse of the three stars of a lieutenant general on the epaulets of each shoulder. That in itself was not an uncommon sight; this was the Pentagon and to the sergeant it seemed that practically everyone in the place had stars on their shoulders. However, there was something distinctively different about this general—he didn't have that over-the-hill walk, nor the specially altered uniform that had been let out at the waist to hide a bulging, overhanging midsection. Quite the contrary, this officer's uniform fit like a glove over wide, broad shoulders and a muscular chest that tapered down neatly to a trim, narrow waist. The sergeant figured the man to be around six feet two and a solid two hundred pounds. The general was closer now.

His white hair stood out even more against the deeply tanned and rugged face of this fifty-nine-year-old man.

The general came straight up to the marine, who waited until the officer was the proper distance in front of him. The marine snapped to attention, his heels clicking together loudly at exactly the same moment the rigidly extended fingers of his hand touched the brim of his hat in a salute. The general halted, returned the salute, then presented his identification card to the guard as he said, "General J. J. Johnson, CG, Special Operations Command. I have an appointment to see the Secretary."

The marine took the card as he said, "One moment, sir."

Stepping away from the door he moved to a small booth near the far wall. Another marine sat enclosed in a bulletproof glass cubicle that contained a control panel and television monitors for the remote-controlled cameras that made continuous sweeps of the entranceways and corridors that led to the Secretary's office. The sergeant inserted the ID card through a small slot at the front of the cubicle. The marine inside checked it against a list on his desk, then leaned forward and spoke into an intercom system linked with the Secretary's office. After announcing the general's arrival, he slid the card back out and nodded that the general was cleared to enter.

The sergeant handed Johnson back his ID card, then stepped in front of the door. He placed his hand on the doorknob and looked back over his shoulder to the man at the control panel. There was a muffled sound of a sliding bolt, followed by a low buzzing sound as the electrical locking system was temporarily disengaged. The sergeant pulled on the handle and opened the door as he said, "Please go in, General—and have a nice day."

"Thank you, Sergeant, you, too," said Johnson with a smile as he entered the the outer office of Clinton Bowers, the United States Secretary of Defense. The sergeant closed the door behind the general and walked back to the cube. The man inside the glass structure motioned for him to come over.

"Hey, Sarge, is that old guy really the head of Special Operations Command? I mean, I know what it says here on the list, but he must be in his sixties?"

"Yeah, I was thinking the same thing, then I remembered some of the Force Recon Marines talking about this Johnson guy. That's him all right. Ya see that snow-white hair? The

Special Ops people call him, 'Q-Tip.' Supposed to be one hell of a flier. Did some time in the Nam. Flew everything from Spectre gunships and F-4s to Cobras. Even got some gunship time in over Grenada during the invasion. Guy might be old, but he sure as hell ain't no phony. Q-Tip is one of them rare officers who talks the talk, and walks the walk. Too bad he ain't a marine—that would make him the perfect officer."

An attractive young woman in her mid-twenties sat at her desk typing as he entered. Looking up from her typewriter, she gave him a pleasant smile as she said, "Please go right in, General Johnson. The Secretary is expecting you."

Johnson nodded his thanks and went in. Clinton Bowers stood up from behind his desk as Johnson entered and closed the door. Coming around the desk, Bowers extended his hand as he said, "Jonathan, it's so good to see you again."

The two old friends shook hands, then Bowers waved to a chair in front of his desk. "Sit down, Jonathan. Would you like something to drink?"

"No, thank you, Clinton, maybe later," replied the general as he settled comfortably into the overstuffed leather chair. Bowers returned to the chair behind his desk and leaned forward, crossing his hands on the top of the highly polished mahogany.

"You're looking fit and trim as usual, Jonathan. How long has it been now? Almost two months, hasn't it?"

"Closer to three, Clinton."

"That's right. How could I forget that? It was right after your rescue of Senator Kendell and his party from that Chinese warlord in Burma. Hell, Jonathan, the Congress and the Senate were ready to make you the Chief of Staff on the spot when you brought those people home. You and your boys did a great job. Everyone, especially the President, was grateful."

A frown worked its way across Johnson's face as he stared across the desk. The friendly atmosphere of only moments ago suddenly vanished as he said, "Mr. Secretary, I would prefer not to discuss that matter if you don't mind."

Bowers averted the general's glare. Quickly looking down at his hands, he cursed himself for mentioning Kendell's name in Johnson's presence. The rescue of the senator and his party had cost the 75th Rangers of the Special Operations Command twenty-three dead, ten wounded, and four missing. Casualties

among the Burmese friendlies had been three times higher. It
had been a successful rescue marred by the discovery that
Senator Kendell was deeply involved in the drug business and
had even sanctioned the killing of a young congressman in his
party who had discovered his secret.

A congressional investigation into the affair was white-
washed by an election-year-conscious panel of Kendell's peers.
This action had sent General Johnson stomping out of the
hearings. The criminal implications would have netted the
average drug dealer up to 150 years of hard time, but not
Kendell. Through back-room discussions and political deals
that reached into the very chambers of the Justice Department,
the man received a sentence of only ten years, his time to be
served at the minimum security prison in Florida—complete
with its tennis courts, pool, fine food, and television in every
room. It was a VIP facility, hardly what one could call doing
hard time.

For Johnson and the men of SOCOM, the great American
system, for which they risked their lives daily, had made a
mockery of the memory of their dead comrades. The fact that
Kendell would be eligible for parole in eighteen months had
only served to widen the rift of resentment and bitterness
between SOCOM personnel and the people at the top. It was
obviously a bitterness that would last a long time.

Bowers, his voice low and apologetic, said, "Sorry, Jonathan,
I didn't mean to open up old wounds." Looking up again, he
tried to force a smile as he asked, "So, tell me, where are the
M and M boys these days? You know some people were trying
to figure out a way to give those boys the Medal of Honor for
engineering that rescue, but it wasn't really a war, and there are
all of those congressional provisions and red tape. They
couldn't come up with a way to do it. You know what I mean?"

Johnson shifted slightly in his chair. The room suddenly
became stuffy and uncomfortable. "Yeah, I know, Clinton.
Arlington Cemetery is full of fucked-up provisions and backward policies," replied Johnson with a tone of animosity.
"Unfortunately, Major Mattson and Commander Mortimer
survived, therefore, no Medal of Honor. However, I don't
think they really mind—at least they saved the government the
trouble of having to dig two more holes out there."

"Jonathan, I know you and your people are still bitter about . . ."

Johnson cut off his friend who he had known since their college days together at Oklahoma University. "To answer your question, Mr. Secretary, Major Mattson is on a well-deserved leave, and Commander Mortimer should be landing in Chad, Africa, right about now."

Bowers sat upright in his chair, a hint of concern rose in his voice as he repeated the name, "Chad! Why is he there?"

"Hell, Clinton, you know our military support policy with Chad. We rotate one twelve-man A-Team in and out of that country every six months. Commander Mortimer requested that he be allowed to accompany a team from the 5th Group for the changeover. He'll spend a month with them and evaluate their training procedures as a part of his job when he isn't getting his ass shot off. Why? Is there a problem with that?" asked Johnson.

Bowers leaned back in his chair and rubbed his chin a few times as if he were carefully considering his next move. He made his decision; sitting up in his chair, he reached across the desk and pressed the intercom to the outer office. "Miss Craig, please hold all my calls. I do not wish to be disturbed for the next half hour, thank you." Releasing the switch, he stared across at Johnson. "Jonathan, you were going to be brought in on this at tomorrow's staff meeting. As of right now, I doubt if there are five people in Washington who are aware of what I am about to tell you, and for God's sake, don't let this information leave this room. You know how the President feels about leaks in this administration."

The Secretary had the white-haired commander's full attention now.

"What's going down, Clinton?" asked Johnson.

Bowers reached down and unlocked a small safe that was concealed in the right, lower corner of his desk. Removing a manila folder with the bright red "Top Secret" cover sheet attached to the front, he passed it to Johnson.

"Five days ago, the French government began the clandestine removal of troops and civilian personnel, along with all of their high-tech equipment, from the Republic of Chad."

Johnson stared up from the unopened document in disbelief.

"You can't be serious! Do you know what that means, Clinton?"

"I'd better, Jonathan. After all, I am the Secretary of Defense."

"French forces, along with French and American financing, are all that's kept Colonel Qaddafi from taking over that country. The son of a bitch has already tried to take out the government three times and damn near pulled it off in '86—if it hadn't been for intervention by French and Zairian military forces, he would have. There has to be some mistake here, Clinton. France intervened to show the other former French African colonies that they could be depended on for support when predators like the colonel crossed those tenuous African borders."

Bowers nodded in agreement as he said, "We know that, Jonathan, but I'm afraid there is no mistake. The file you are holding is a list of units and equipment that moved from Chad to the shipping ports in Cameroon. The information comes directly from our CIA operatives in both countries. We are expecting the official notification from the French government within the next four or five days. Our ambassador in France is pressuring their government for more details, but so far, nothing. They want to be sure they have at least ninety percent of their people and equipment out of there before anyone has a chance to try to talk them into staying."

Johnson read through the folder, flipping page after page that itemized equipment, personnel, the numbers, and their disposition.

"Jesus," said Johnson as he closed the file and looked up, "they're even stripping their embassy. They're pulling out for good, Clinton."

"Looks that way, Jonathan."

"But why? Chad is one of the last strongholds of French influence in the region. They've always come to the aid of President Tombaye and the Chad government when there's been trouble. Hell, Tombaye is the only man in the last fifty years who has accomplished anything in that oversize sandbox. He brought them international recognition and managed to reconcile his party's differences with former political and armed opponents that ended a thirty-year civil war. The only threat he faces now is that damn traitor and butcher, General

Hissen Kueddei, and a two-thousand-man army of fanatical rebels armed to the teeth by our boy in Libya."

"We all agree on that, Jonathan. We couldn't find a more pro-western ally than President Habre Tombaye. What worries this administration is what Qaddafi and Kueddei will do when they find out the French are pulling out."

Johnson shook his head a moment, then said, "Are you asking me for a professional military opinion, Clinton, or just a friendly analysis?"

"Friendly analysis," smiled Bowers.

"OK, first of all, if we have this information, you can bet Qaddafi does, too. He may be considered a full-fledged whacko, but the man has one of the best intelligence networks in that part of the world. It was set up by the Russian KGB and operates under the direction of East German operatives. They probably have equipment and numbers on their list that our boys missed. Second, you have a world that is under the misconception that Chad is nothing more than just another third-world country sunk in poverty and surrounded by worthless sand, but that is not the case. There are large deposits of uranium in the northern mountain regions of the Tibesti Mountains. You can bet your next month's paycheck that Qaddafi likes the sound of that. Imagine the colonel having his hands on a key element used in the making of atomic bombs. Scary, isn't it? Throw in a former Chad general with an Idi Amin attitude toward his own people, add a few thousand well-armed rebels backed by Libyan tanks and air power, and what have you got? A little war that was nowheresville is suddenly going to be somewhere. Without the French, General Kueddei and his rebels could launch an all-out attack on a Monday and be in the capital of N'Djamena drinking tea by Friday."

Bowers leaned back in his chair with a worried look on his face. The President had definitely chosen the right man to head the Special Operations Command. Johnson was not only a highly qualified officer, but also a man who obviously made it a point to keep himself up-to-date on possible low intensity conflict areas that may require the deployment of his personnel. Unfortunately, everything he had just said was correct. Without the French, Tombaye's government was doomed.

"Isn't there some way the President can convince the French

that they have to reverse their decision, Clinton?" asked Johnson.

"Afraid not, Jonathan. France is in serious trouble at home with civil discontent, unemployment, and an inflation rate that has bread going for about ten dollars a loaf. The French people have had it; they want something done, and they want it now, not later. Crime is rampant all over the country; it's practically killed the tourist business. People are rioting in the streets and looting stores just for the basic necessities of clothes and food. The pullout in Chad came about for two reasons, money and the consolidation of military forces in case of an attempted overthrow of the government. To put it simply, Jonathan, Chad has become a fifty-million-dollar-a-year liability that France can no longer afford."

The general tossed the folder back onto Bowers's desk as he leaned back and said, "So I take it, good old Uncle Sugar is left holding the proverbial well-known bag. Now, let me guess what's in that bag. A shit load of outstanding debts and responsibility for the security of the whole fucking country, right?"

Bowers laughed as he replied, "Never one to look at the world through rose-colored glasses were you, Jonathan? The money part is probably right; but as far as security of the region, that's still up in the air. The President's advisors have suggested that we withhold our annual payment to the United Nations until we get a guarantee that they will place a unilateral peacekeeping force in there to monitor Qaddafi's actions."

"That's not going to do much for the President's popularity," said Johnson.

"Hell, you know how he is. He could give a shit what anybody thinks when it comes to the security of the United States. Besides, after the plastering he got for not aiding that attempted coup in Panama, a little bad press about withholding a few bucks from the UN will seem like nothing. I'll tell you one thing, Jonathan, Mr. Noriega better not push the old man too far. He's not some peanut farmer that'll sit in the corner and wring his hands worrying about what to do next. He'll try all the diplomatic bullshit first, but if Manuel Noriega starts getting too froggy down there, he'll jump on him with both feet. You mark my words, one more incident in Panama, and the shit's going to hit the fan."

Johnson glanced down at his watch, then back to Bowers. "I think you're right on that one, Clinton. Now, on this Chad business, do you think I need to recall Mortimer and the A-Team?"

"No, I'd rather you wait a few days, Jonathan. We are conducting some back-room discussions with Zaire and a group of representatives from Nigeria. Neither one of those countries have any great love for Qaddafi. We may be able to work out a joint resolution with them to support President Tombaye militarily. If we do, we'll need to place more advisors in Chad to provide them with the latest training and equipment. I think Commander Mortimer and the team will be all right for now. The French still have two companies of legionnaires stationed in the capital, as well as a small contingent of French pilots and F-5 Mirage fighters based at the Abeche airfield if something should happen and they need air support. I would, however, suggest that following the meeting in the morning, you contact your people personally and advise of them of the situation. Our embassy will be alerted, but you know how that goes, Jonathan—that doesn't guarantee that Commander Mortimer and your people will know what's going on."

Johnson raised his six-foot-two frame from the chair and nodded in agreement. Bureaucracies and their self-induced tons of paperwork had a way of getting lost, forgotten, or simply ignored. A fact that had been proven in Vietnam on a day-by-day basis.

"Thank you for taking me into your confidence, Clinton. I just hope the old man can get Zaire and Nigeria to go along with us on this. If they don't, we could be looking at a situation that may necessitate a permanent buildup of American troops in Chad, and you know what that means."

"God forbid," said Bowers as he came from behind his desk to walk Johnson to the door. "I can hear Iran and Qaddafi screaming warnings about 'The Great Satan' already."

"It wouldn't be pretty, that's for sure."

Bowers opened the door as he said, "Jonathan, if you want to wait around for another hour or so, I'll be free, and we can grab some lunch."

"Thanks, Clinton, but I thought I might pick up some

flowers and stop by Arlington. It's been a while since I visited
Paul's grave."

Bowers noted the sadness in the man's voice at the end. J. J.
Johnson had not only given thirty years of his life to his
country, but a son as well. Captain Paul Johnson's helicopter
was shot down during the Grenada invasion, not by Cubans,
but rather by friendly fire, making the loss even more difficult
to accept. Johnson was a strong man and the years had slowly
healed the broken heart of this old warrior and had driven him
with an unbridled passion as the SOCOM commander to insure
that such an accident would never happen again during a joint
special operation. He had lost one son, but he had gained three
thousand more.

"Of course, Jonathan, I understand. I'll see you in the
morning then at the staff briefing," said Bowers as the two men
shook hands, and the general left.

The Secretary of Defense went back to his desk and stared
down at the yellow pad he had been doodling on. Three things
stood out, Qaddafi, uranium, and atomic bomb. He felt a
sudden chill go down his back. J. J. Johnson was right; it was
a scary thought!

The first thing a visitor to Arlington National Cemetery
senses is the perfect silence that seems to surround the
best-known military cemetery in the United States. It is as if an
invisible soundproof dome encircles the final resting place of
those fallen warriors who lay beneath the rows of bright white
headstones that fan out uniformly across the vast reaches of a
carpet of neatly trimmed green. It is calm and tranquil,
befitting a place of honor that is dedicated to the memory of a
nation's protectors who gave their ultimate.

J. J. Johnson stood silently staring down at the black inlaid
letters of the headstone bearing his son's name. As always,
when he made this trip, a flood of memories flashed before his
eyes. There was young Paul apprehensively learning to ride his
first bicycle while a worried mother stood fretting nervously on
the front porch and his father anxiously pointed the way for his
son's first solo ride. There was that look of pride on the boy's
face when he had successfully met the challenge; he ran and
leaped into the loving arms of his father and hugged him
tightly. There were visions of tossing a football back and forth

among the leaves in the cool evenings of early fall; of watching the small boy all too soon become a man and go away to college; and of that painful time when they had gained strength from each other as they held hands firmly bidding a final farewell to a caring wife and mother.

The same boyish grin of pride was there the day Paul, the man, graduated from flight school. There was no leaping into Daddy's arms that day, but rather the loving embrace that could only be experienced by a father and son.

A small tear began to form in the corner of the general's eye. It seemed they had shared so much time together; yet when the end came, it was as if there had been no time at all. There had been so much more to say.

Johnson's eyes locked onto a word that appeared below his son's name, "Grenada." The letters stirred a deep-rooted bitterness within the man who had known military life and its risks for nearly thirty years. It was a bitterness brought on not so much because his son had died, but rather by the way he had died. The memory of that fateful day would be burnt into his memory forever, for he too had been in Grenada on that morning. Less than twenty-four hours prior to the invasion, father and son had posed for a picture next to Captain Paul Johnson's Cobra gunship, neither realizing that the camera had recorded the last moments they would spend together.

Much to the dislike of the Pentagon staff, General Johnson had ignored their orders that he man a Command and Control desk safely aboard one of the naval ships. Turning that duty over to his adjutant, Johnson had managed to exchange a seat behind a desk for one he was more comfortable with, the pilot's seat of an AC-130 Spectre gunship and its armament of two 20mm Gatling guns, a 40mm cannon, and a 105mm Howitzer. It was the same type aircraft he had flown to provide close air support for troops on the ground in Vietnam.

Operation Urgent Fury had been beset by problems from the very beginning. The size of the island of Grenada and the reported number of enemy forces expected to be encountered provided the perfect opportunity for the deployment of both the Green Berets and the 75th Rangers, small hard-hitting units that were specifically trained for this type of an operation. However, they were both Army units and therein lay the

problem. The marines began to scream their opposition. They
had to be included. They were, after all, America's heroes, and
demanded they share in the glory. The other branches soon
echoed the same demands. Before long, everyone but troop
232 of the Omaha, Nebraska, Girl Scouts were involved in
Urgent Fury. It had become an accident waiting to happen, and
the architects of that accident were not to be disappointed.

Time delays caused the Rangers to parachute onto the
heavily guarded runway in broad daylight, instead of under the
cover of darkness as originally planned. A botched SEAL
insertion on the coastline cost the lives of a four-man team.
Navy gunfire zeroed in on a platoon of marines who had landed
at the wrong end of the island. To make matters worse,
communications between all four elements involved were
nonexistent. In their haste for glory, no one had bothered to
notice that each branch of the service used different types of
radios. The frequencies that had been given before the operation began were either too high or too low for most of the
ground force communications gear. By midmorning, Urgent
Fury had become a blind four-headed dragon, breathing fire in
all directions, and often burning itself in the process.

Captain Paul Johnson was unfortunate enough to be one of
those who had been burnt. He had observed a small group of
Rangers who had parachuted onto the runway being cut off and
surrounded by a large force of Cuban troops just beyond the
runway. Radio contact was useless. The Rangers had been
given the wrong frequencies. Ignoring the storm of bullets that
had begun to ricochet off his gunship from the rifles of the
Cubans below, Paul Johnson swung his Cobra wide and began
making devastating rocket and mini-gun runs on the Cubans in
an attempt to open an avenue of escape for the trapped
Rangers. His third run did the trick. The Rangers, carrying
their wounded, had paused long enough to wave their thanks
before breaking out of the encirclement.

The general could only imagine the satisfaction his son had
felt at having saved the small group from annihilation as he
tipped the wings of his ship in a salute to the Rangers below.
Thirty seconds later, Paul Johnson was blown out of the sky.
Someone, somewhere, they never found out who, had called
naval gunfire on the area. The Cobra had flown straight into a

barrage fired broadside by the USS *Independence*. The blind dragon had roared and its fire had consumed one of its own.

The bitterness J. J. Johnson felt that day slowly, painstakingly, faded with time, as did the sorrow. His son had died a soldier's death, but not before saving the lives of others. It had brought to mind a verse of Scripture from the Bible: John 15:13—"Greater love hath no man than this, that a man lay down his life for his friends." Although hardly what one would consider compensation for the loss of a son, it had provided J. J. Johnson with a small amount of comfort in those dark days and weeks following the funeral.

A tear now made its way from the corner of his eye and down his leathery, weather-worn cheek. The tear was a signal, a warning, that it was time to leave before the loneliness he had known for so long now fanned to life memories best left locked away deep within his soul. Snapping to attention, the old warrior saluted proudly, turned, and walked away. As he crossed to the walkway that led back to the main entrance, he glanced up at the small knoll that rose to his right. The yellow-orange glow of an eternal flame flickered and danced wildly in the evening breeze. It served as a reminder of another time when he had stood in this place of both glory and sadness and, without modesty or shame, openly cried for the loss of a fellow warrior who had survived the terror of war only to lose his life to an assassin's bullet. On that day, the world lost a leader; America, a president; and Special Operations, one of its most avid supporters. "You are in good company, Mr. President. Rest in peace," whispered Johnson as he passed the knoll and the eternal flame that would burn forever at the grave of John F. Kennedy.

Putting the sadness of his visit aside, Johnson's thoughts were now on the problems that were sure to develop in Chad once the French pulled out. What should he do about Mortimer and the A-Team?

"Excuse me, sir, but could I impose on you for a moment? I have a problem."

Johnson had been so deep in thought that he had not noticed the woman who had come up alongside of him. Momentarily startled, he looked up as he said, "Wha—what?"

His eyes encompassed the full beauty of her flawless face,

her dark hair, which was graying slightly along the forehead, and her penetrating almond-brown eyes that seemed so alive.

"Excuse me, madam. I—I . . ." The general was so stunned by her beauty that he was stuttering like a schoolboy. Clearing his throat, he tried again.

"Pardon me, madam, but did you say you needed assistance?"

Her smile caused his heart to skip a beat. Her almond eyes never wavered from his as she spoke in a pleasant, yet confident tone. "I am so sorry to bother you, sir, but there is a problem with my car. I can't seem to get it started and I am afraid I am totally at a loss when it comes to those types of things. Could I possibly impose upon you to take a look at it for me?"

Only one other woman in J. J. Johnson's life had ever made his heart skip like that while managing to take his breath away with only a smile. That woman had been Paul's mother and his wife of thirty years. Since her death, he had resigned himself to the fact that he would never know such feelings again—until now.

"Of course, madam, although, I must warn you, I am far from being an expert on such matters myself."

Her laughter was as fresh as the evening breeze as she replied, "Well, then, General, between the two of us, I would say that automobile doesn't stand a chance."

They walked to the road. The hood was already up on the car as Johnson directed her to get in and try the key again. The motor ground out a strong, but laboring moan as she pumped the gas pedal a few times, but nothing happened. Waving his hand for her to stop a moment, Johnson studied the problem. The battery was fine, but it sounded as if the engine was not getting enough fuel to turn it over. Yet the odor of gas was strong under the hood. Removing the breather from the carburetor, he immediately spotted the problem. The fuel line had worked its way loose from the carburetor. Replacing the line, he put the breather back in place and waved for her to try it again. The engine cranked once, then fired to life. Closing the hood, he stepped to the side of the car. "Fuel line was off. It shouldn't be a problem now."

There was that smile again. "Oh, thank you so much, General. I . . ." The smile suddenly faded as she reached out and touched the sleeve of his uniform. "Oh, no, I am so sorry about that. You have oil on your uniform."

Johnson glanced down at the tiny spot. "It's nothing, really. Don't worry about it."

"Absolutely not. I insist that you allow me to have it cleaned for you."

"Honestly, it's fine. I have other uniforms."

"Why is it men are always so stubborn? Well, at least allow me to drive you to your car," she said.

"I'm afraid I don't have a car here. I had planned to take a taxi back to my hotel."

Her smile broadened as she said, "Wonderful! At last, there is something I can do to repay you for your kindness. Get in, General, I will take you to your hotel."

Johnson started to protest, but she was not about to give him the chance. "Nope, no arguments, General, I insist."

The general knew when he was outgunned, and this time he didn't really mind. Sliding into the car, he regrettable noticed the wedding band on her finger. "Thank you, Mrs— Mrs. . . . ?" For the first time he detected a glint of sadness in her eyes as she stared out across the rows of tombstones before answering.

"Mrs. Cantrell, General. Helen Cantrell. My husband and two sons are . . . out there."

"I'm—I'm sorry, Mrs. Cantrell."

"No, it's quite all right, General. It's been a long time now, I make this trip once a year. My friends tell me I shouldn't subject myself to such a painful ritual every year, but these visits help keep my life in perspective. They—they were my life for so very long." She paused a moment, allowing the sadness that had crept into her tone to fade, before she turned to him and smiled a gentle smile. "Well, enough of that. Now, General . . ." She leaned over to look at the name plate above his right pocket. "General Johnson, which hotel are you staying at?"

Realizing he hadn't introduced himself, the general's face flushed slightly as he said, "Excuse my manners, Mrs. Cantrell. My name is Jonathan—Jonathan J. Johnson. I'm staying at the Holiday Inn near the Pentagon."

"The Holiday Inn it is, then." She laughed as she pointed to his seat belt. "I think I'd put that on if I were you, Jonathan.

I'm not exactly a big-city driver; and before this ride is over you may be wishing you hadn't fixed that fuel line."

Pulling the belt over his shoulder and locking it into place, he returned her smile with a grin as he replied, "I doubt that, Mrs. Cantrell. Even so, I would consider it a risk well worthwhile in order to enjoy such delightful company."

Their eyes were fixed on each other. She had heard the words, but it was the unspoken language of the eyes that now stirred a long-forgotten excitement. This man Jonathan was ruggedly handsome. Placing the car in gear she pulled away from the curb and out into traffic. They rode in silence for a while, each with their own thoughts racing. She, frightened by feelings that she had not known for so long, was appreciative of having this man so obviously admire her. He was worried that he might have said the wrong thing and misread what he had seen in her eyes. They both turned to speak at the same time.

"Jonathan, I . . ."

"Mrs. Cantrell, I . . ."

They both broke out into laughter. "You first, madam," said Johnson.

There was a hint of nervousness in her voice as she said, "Please call me Helen." She paused for a moment, as if debating with herself before she asked, "Would you consider having dinner with me tonight, Jonathan?"

Johnson's face lit up with joy as if a silent prayer had been answered. "Mrs. Ca—I mean, Helen, I can think of nothing that would give me more pleasure."

By the time Helen Cantrell pulled up to the front entrance of the hotel, the two were talking as if they had been old friends for years. Johnson bid her good-bye. She would be back to pick him up at eight. Hardly a person in the lobby could have missed the spectacle of a smiling fifty-nine-year-old man skipping past the desk and taking the stairs three at a time as he whistled a happy tune.

CHAPTER 2

Commander Jacob Winfield Mortimer IV stood at the back ramp of the C-141 Starlifter with Captain Randy York, the team leader of Special Forces Detachment, A-505. Behind them, the team of highly trained NCOs adjusted their Green Berets and stood to stretch out tightened muscles brought on by the long hours of flying. Chief Warrant Officer Two Scott Hileran joined the two officers near the ramp as the plane taxied to a stop at the far end of the N'Djamena airport. The crew chief stepped forward and pressed the switch that set the hydraulics in motion. A high-pitched whining sound filled the enclosed space of the aircraft; the huge tail section began to open; and the ramp was lowered to the concrete tarmac. Hot, humid air rushed into the belly of the plane to greet the new arrivals to the Republic of Chad.

Captain York motioned for Mortimer and Hileran to lead the way as he turned to his team sergeant and yelled, "Sergeant Vickers, make sure everyone has all their gear. This baby is flying back to the States in an hour. If they forget anything, they can kiss it good-bye for the next six months."

Master Sergeant Mike Vickers was a giant of a man standing almost six feet five, close to 230 pounds of rock-solid muscle. He was a twenty-year veteran of Special Forces and had been weaned on Special Operations with the SOG projects in Vietnam. Nodding to the captain, he turned to the team and in a slow, distinct tone, which identified him as a long-time southern boy, said, "OK, girls, rest time is over. Ya heard what

17

the ol' man said; you forget it—you've lost it, so let's double-check our shit before we off load this bird. You boys that like chewin' and dippin' make sure you bring them spit cups with ya—don't wanta be leavin' that mess on these fly-boys' new airplane. Once you've done that, I want a formation fifty yards to the rear of the plane. We'll find out where they want us to break down the pallet with all our gear on it. OK, let's get it done."

Captain York, Mortimer, and Chief Hileran made their way across the runway and into the customs building. A blast of cold air hit them as they stepped into the air-conditioned lobby. Their fatigue shirts were already showing sweat stains from the short walk from the plane to the office. Hileran headed straight for the window with the entry visa and passport sign above the window. Placing his briefcase on the edge of the window ledge, he opened it and handed the black clerk behind the window the team's passports that had been neatly stacked and secured with rubber bands. The official smiled a toothy grin, removed the bands, and began stamping the documents.

Mortimer and York stood near the plate-glass windows of the lobby and watched the team disembark from the plane. A forklift made its way slowly along the outer perimeter of the runway. Once in position, the operator pulled to the rear of the plane and removed the pallet containing all the personnel gear and equipment A-505 had packed for the six months' mission. York kept looking from one end of the airfield to the other, then around the lobby.

"Something wrong, Captain York?" asked Jake Mortimer.

"Naw, not really, Commander. I'm just a little surprised that Captain Tanner and the boys from A-502 are not here to meet us. You'd think after six months in this place, they'd be camped on the runway waiting to mob that bird going back to the States."

Navy Commander Jake Mortimer flexed the strained muscles in his back and broad shoulders as a smile appeared across his ruggedly handsome face. Jake was a Navy SEAL, hand-picked by General J. J. Johnson to work alongside B. J. Mattson, his assistant S-2 at SOCOM. Together they were the general's watchdogs over important missions. He gave them full authority to take whatever actions they deemed necessary to accomplish a mission, as well as investigate and terminate any actions determined to be detrimental to the security of the United States. This mission, however, was more of a break for the commander. With B.J. on leave, Jake grew weary of daily training reports and the humdrum routines at SOCOM headquarters. He recognized the rotation in Chad as an opportunity to get away from the flagpole for a while. For the thirty-three-year-old naval officer, it provided a chance to add Chad to an already long list of countries he had visited in ten years of naval service. A small dimple that drove the girls crazy whenever he grinned suddenly appeared as he said, "They could be moving a little slow this morning, Captain. I understand the French like to throw a party for the departing team the night before they leave."

"Yeah, that thought crossed my mind," said York as he turned back to the window and watched the unloading of the pallet. "It's too bad B.J. couldn't have come along, Commander. I haven't seen that nine-fingered bastard since the CCN SOG reunion in Las Vegas a couple of years ago. He's really one piece of work, isn't he?"

"You can say that again. The man's definitely got his shit together," replied Jake as he glanced over at Hileran still waiting at the passport window. Mortimer's attention was drawn to three men who had just come through the double doors at the main entrance. "Uh-oh, looks like we've got some VIP visitors coming our way," he said as he tapped York on the elbow and motioned toward the doors. Two of the men were tall, middle-aged, with short blond hair. They wore slacks with tan bush jackets, obviously Americans. The third man was a general officer in the Chad Army and was wearing enough medals and battle cords to be classified as a walking Christmas tree. "That must be General Mohammed Gaafar, Commander of the Army of the Republic," whispered York. "He's the guy we work for."

"Jesus, and I thought Idi Amin had bought up all the medals in the PX."

"Now, be nice, Commander, here they come."

General Gaafar stopped a few feet away, allowing his American escorts to advance and proceed with the introductions. The older of the two men extended his hand.

"Captain York, I am Wayne Privett, senior advisor to the defense attaché's office." Shaking York's hand firmly, he nodded to the man with him, "And this is. Mr. Fredrick Calhoun, head of the U.S. Agency for International Development."

Calhoun shook hands with York and cast a suspicious look in Jake's direction as the captain introduced the Navy commander.

More handshakes were exchanged as Privett said, "I'm afraid we weren't expecting you, Commander. Your name was not on the embassy arrival list that we received yesterday."

"Sorry about that, sir. A last-minute change," said Jake. "Excuse me, Mr. Privett, but who is the gentleman with all the color behind you?"

Privett quickly stepped to one side, and in a flurry of elaborate French terms, he gave a full thirty-second introduction before presenting General Gaafar, the commander in chief of Chad's military forces.

Gaafar clicked his heels loudly, took two steps forward, and clicked them together again as he saluted. A host of photographers suddenly appeared from out of nowhere. Cameras flashed from all angles as the general, his chest hyperextended to show all his medals, held the salute. Confident that sufficient pictures had been taken, Gaafar exhaled, lowered his salute, and shooed the cameramen away as he reached out his hand to the new arrivals.

Mortimer gave the general a quick evaluation—height: a little over six feet, not big, but more the wary type; age: somewhere around early to mid-sixties. It was hard to tell. His face was dark and sun-baked, with wrinkled lines and cracks that spread outward from the corners of his eyes like dried leather. A neatly trimmed, but thin mustache rested on his upper lip. His eyes were black and penetrating, like the eyes of a shark, thought Jake, as he pulled his hand back from the general's clammy, halfhearted handshake. Mortimer had taken French in high school, but that had been ages ago. He only managed to catch part of what the general said to Privett; it had something to do with gifts for the President.

Jake glanced over at York, whispered, and asked, "Did you get that?"

The captain shrugged his shoulders. "Nope. Chief Hileran and Doc Blancher are the French experts on the team. You got any idea?"

"Something about gifts for President Tombaye, I think," answered Jake.

Privett rattled off a rapid string of French words and patted the general on the back as he pointed out the window at two large crates that were being unloaded from the tail of the C-141. The general smiled in satisfaction. His large pearly white teeth gave his dark face an almost comical look.

Jake turned to York. "Captain, I think I'll . . ."

Calhoun cut him off. "Gentlemen, there has been a slight delay with the arrival of Captain Tanner and his people, transportation problem or something like that. Captain York, we will go ahead and take you and your officers to the ambassador's residence; they have planned a small luncheon in your honor. Your men can wait here for the trucks."

Chief Hileran strolled up to the group as York answered, "Thank you, sir; but if you don't mind, I'll remain with the team. Besides, I have a few questions for Captain Tanner when he arrives. However, I see no reason why Commander Mortimer and my executive officer cannot take you up on the offer."

"Are you sure, Captain? I could stay with the team, sir," said Hileran.

"No, that's fine, Scotty. You and Jake go ahead. I'll be along shortly."

"Listen, Captain, I could—" Once again Mortimer was abruptly interrupted by Calhoun, who had pulled a huge handkerchief from his pocket and mopped at the sweat on his forehead.

"Well, good, now that's all settled, let's be on our way. By noon the thermometer will hit one hundred and ten. Thank God we have air-conditioning at our facilities."

Jake stood perfectly still, his hands resting on the hips of his six-foot-three frame. His Robert Redford eyes fixed solidly on Calhoun. This AID guy was not only a rude bastard, but a whinning wimp as well. Calhoun's tan safari suit was already soaked through with sweat. The wet material clung to his body forming an outline of his skinny frame. Beads of perspiration were crawling slowly down the sides of his hollow-cheeked face. Calhoun had small, almost oval brown eyes, and he wrinkled his bushy eyebrows constantly, which made it appear as if he were squinting all the time. Jake Mortimer was not the type to make snap judgments about people he had just met, but in Calhoun's case he made an exception; he didn't like the little bastard, and he was about to tell him so when Privett spoke.

"Gentlemen, the general is ready to leave."

Captain York motioned for Jake and the chief to go on.

"What the hell," said Jake. "Let's go, Chief, nothing we can do here anyway. Might as well see how the better half lives."

Privett and his entourage departed the airport. As they exited the building there were two black limousines waiting for them. The drivers, dressed in desert fatigues, raced to the back doors of their vehicles and held them open. Calhoun gestured for Jake to step into the second one with him, while Privett, the general, and Hileran entered the first.

"Nothing personal, ol' chap," said Jake with a smile, "but I think I'll hang with the other boys. Your Right Guard antiperspirant isn't holding up real well." Turning away from a surprised Calhoun, Jake whistled for the driver of the first car to hold the door. Stepping into the roomy, air-conditioned limousine, he scooted in next to the chief who gave him a knowing grin. Hileran had heard Jake's remark to the AID man.

General Gaafar whispered something to Privett who turned to Jake and said, "The general wanted to know if there was a problem with the other car, Commander."

"No, sir, not at all. It's just that Mr. Calhoun has an underarm problem, and his breath isn't something I'd write home about."

Hileran fought back the urge to burst out laughing as Privett stared at Mortimer with a blank look on his face.

"Uh . . . I see," he said.

Jake didn't know what answer Privett gave the general, but it had been too short to be a word-for-word answer.

The cars pulled away from the airport and onto the Rue Commandant Curlu, across Boulevard de Strasbourg, and into the main flow of traffic down Avenue du General de Gaulle. Jake and the chief were immediately aware that the big limos seemed totally out of place as they neared the heart of the city. There were few private vehicles on the streets. Dark yellow taxis filled to overflowing darted in, out, and around pedestrians, bicycles, motorbikes, and donkey-pulled carts of various sizes. Tapping Hileran on the knee, Jake directed his attention toward a row of buildings that were coming up on their right.

The cement and plaster structures were pockmarked with bullet
holes, while others were no more than bombed-out shells.
Noting their curiosity Privett said, "Results of the long and
bitter civil war these people had to endure to get their freedom,
gentlemen. Of course that was before you people began
arriving to provide military training for General Gaafar's
forces. Reconstruction of this area is slated to begin next
month. It was rather a bloody affair, I might add."

"Aren't they all," said Hileran sadly.

As the car swung over one street and onto the Avenue du
Gouverneur Felix Eboue, Privett pointed to the body of water
that appeared out the right window.

"That's the Chari River. The land mass on the other side is
the country of Cameroon. A little farther up you'll see the
bridge we constructed to link the two countries together.
Unfortunately, it was destroyed during the fighting, and as yet,
we have not been able to acquire the necessary funds and
materials to rebuild it; however, Mr. Calhoun is working on
that for us. There is a ferry that makes daily runs back and forth
across the river should you or any of your men feel the need for
a change of scenery."

"I had a chance to read a little of the area study that was
provided the team before they departed, Mr. Privett. There was
mention of a rather shaky, but enduring truce between the Chad
forces and the rebel forces under the command of a General
Hissen Kueddei. Just how shaky are we talking here?" asked
Jake.

General Gaafar had not spoken since leaving the airport. The
mention of the name Kueddei brought an intense glare from the
military leader.

"Yes, it is a rather unstable situation, Commander. Kueddei
is backed by Colonel Qaddafi of Libya, but, of course, I'm
sure you are well aware of that. He has provided Kueddei and
his rebels with a safe haven within the boundaries of the Anzou
Strip, a hotly contested area along the border between Libya
and Chad. Ownership of the area has been in dispute since the
Ottoman days. Qaddafi managed to hold on to the strip
following the 1986 incursion. It was part of a deal cut for his
withdrawal of Libyan forces. In actuality, the country is
divided in half, roughly along the sixteenth parallel, kind of
like an imaginary line drawn in the sand. Qaddafi and Kueddei

control the northern sector, while President Tombaye and General Gaafar's forces control the southern areas. Occasionally someone steps across the line and—well, you've seen the results."

"I wouldn't think the Chadian people, no matter which side they were on, would want anything to do with Qaddafi. They have to know the only reason he wants his hands on this country is to use it as a stepping stone to go after the prize he really wants, and unless I haven't done my homework, I'd say that was Niger," said Hileran.

"That is correct, Mr. Hileran. Chad is the keystone to central Africa. Colonel Qaddafi has stated repeatedly that he has been called upon by Allah to become a great leader within the Arab world. Under Allah's divine guidance, he is to establish an empire that will stretch from Somalia on the Indian Ocean to Liberia on the Atlantic and from the Mediterranean in the north to the Cape of Good Hope in the south."

"The boy doesn't think small, does he?" said Jake.

"No, Commander, he doesn't. The worst mistake anyone can make is underestimating the man. As a youth, Qaddafi saw the results of Italian colonialism and knew the ugly history of the Ottoman occupation. That has played a large part in the shaping of his view of the world. Throw in a little messianic Islam and a romantic quest for power, and you have a man with a vision of himself as the sultan of a Moslem empire. No, Commander, this man should not be taken lightly. Chad is the key to his vision of power, and he knows that. He has to have it as a base of operations and supply before he can make his move on Niger to the west and Sudan on the east."

"So what does Kueddei plan to gain from all this?" asked Hileran. "Even if he were to take over the country, Qaddafi would be the man pulling the strings."

"He will not succeed in his efforts, Mr. Hileran. I can assure you of that," said Gaafar.

Jake and Hileran looked at each other for a moment in surprise. They had assumed that due to his constant use of French that Gaafar knew little or no English. Yet the statement he had just made was clear and precise. Both American officers felt a sudden sense of embarrassment at the fact that they had directed their entire conversation to only Privett.

Hileran, red-faced and glaring at Privett, tried to explain,

"General . . . you'll have to excuse us, we had no idea that you—"

Gaafar raised his hand, "Rest assured, Mr. Hileran, there is no need to apologize. Please, do not hold any animosity toward Mr. Privett. He did not mention my language capabilities to you because I requested that he not do so. I find that such action often provides me an insight into the character of the men who have come here to train my army."

Privett sat back in his seat as he shrugged his shoulders and offered a silent, pained expression as an apology.

"Your English is excellent, General. Where did you study?" asked Jake.

"London and Paris, Commander. However, I must admit, I am partial to French. It flows off the tongue so smoothly, much like silk from a woman's bare breast. So vibrant, so alive, do you know what I mean? I must also ask you to forgive this atrocious display of meaningless regalia upon my uniform, but it is the type of thing my people expect in their military leaders. We must be colorful, virile, and display the courage of the tiger. The medals serve only to consummate their wishes."

Jake and Scott were in awe of this man. It was not unusual to find black generals commanding armies in the improver-ished third-world countries of Africa, but to find one who spoke like a professor from Oxford seemed as out of place as the limo sitting next to the donkey carts at a stoplight.

"To answer your question, Mr. Hileran, General Kueddei has no intention of sharing this country with anyone, especially Colonel Qaddafi. Kueddei is a master of words. He would make a deal with the devil for money and guns in order to reclaim the seat of power he once held in our country. In this case, he has chosen Qaddafi as his devil; but I assure you, should he, by some fate of Allah, succeed in his mission, he will turn on Libya like the venomous snake he is."

"It sounds like you know this Kueddei fellow pretty well, sir," said Hileran.

"I should, Mr. Hileran—he is my brother . . ."

"Your brother!" exclaimed Jake.

"Yes, Commander. Two mothers, but born of the same father; although I must admit, there have been times that I have seriously questioned that fact. We are as different as night and day in our political views. I stand steadfastly by President

Tombaye and his efforts to end this useless civil strife that divides us. This can only be accomplished by restoring our territorial integrity, while at the same time pursuing reconstruction and internal political reconciliation. My brother, Hissen, on the other hand, seeks only to establish himself as the supreme ruler of Chad. It is unfortunate that one must speak so badly of one's own blood, but Hissen would make our people slaves within their own country. He has vowed to succeed in his quest, or die. Allah forgive me, but there is no other way." Gaafar paused, averting his eyes from the Americans to the carpeted floor of the car, there was sadness in his voice as he finished by saying, "Peace will not come to my country until my brother is dead."

Mortimer and Hileran both sat back against the seat in silence. What could they possibly say to this man who they had so misjudged earlier. He was an educated man of values. A man of determined loyalty dedicated to the preservation of his country and its people, no matter what the cost. The price was already set—a brother's life. What could anyone say?

The occupants of the car rode the remaining short distance to the ambassador's residence in silence. It was only as they exited the car that Gaafar said, "Gentlemen, if you will excuse me, I must check in with my headquarters. Mr. Privett will make the introductions. I shall join you later. Commander Mortimer, Mr. Hileran, I am glad you are here. My country and I are grateful." Shaking hands firmly with both officers, Gaafar headed for the side entrance of the residence. He was followed closely by two personal bodyguards. Privett led the way through the front doors and out onto the patio. It was a two-tiered garden affair with a large swimming pool, outdoor bar, dressing rooms, and toilet-shower facilities. A long table set near the bar. It was adorned with a variety of colorful fruits and vegetables, French imported cheeses, wines, and beer. A tall nomad servant dressed in what appeared to be a long white sheet that trailed down to the floor, with a leather belt around his waist and the traditional white, towellike turban wrapped around his head, was turning steaks on a grill. His dark face was fixed on the glowing coals, totally oblivious of the activities around him. Privett motioned for the two officers to join him near the pool. As they made their way across the patio Jake noticed the various nationalities in attendance. They

were from various embassies scattered throughout N'Djamena.
There were Chinese, Egyptians, Germans, Nigerians, and a
few Sudanese. Conspicuously absent was the one country Jake
had figured would dominate the festivities, the French. There
was not one Frenchman present. It was not an observation that
had gone unnoticed by Hileran. He raised an eyebrow to let
Jake know that he had noticed that as well.

There were two men and three women standing with Privett
as they walked up. The elderly gentleman was Horace Frugenson, the ambassador, and his wife. The other man was Charles
Murdock, aide to the ambassador, with his wife, Helen. Jake
shook hands with the men, but his eyes were fixed on the
shapely, strikingly beautiful brunette in the short bright red
cotton dress who stood to Privett's right. She appeared to be in
her mid-thirties. She had the most pleasant blue-green eyes
Jake had ever seen. She smiled at him, her white teeth
contrasting with the golden glow of her tanned face. "And who
might this Venus of the desert be, may I ask?" said Jake as he
stepped past Privett and closed in on the attractive woman.

She answered before Privett could make the introductions.
"Hello, Commander, my name is Sharon Chambers. I am the
contract nurse assigned to the embassy. I'm afraid we don't
have a doctor here. The State Department medical officer is
stationed in Kinshasa and only has three scheduled visits per
year to N'Djamena, so if you should become ill or injured, I'm
afraid I'm it."

Jake looked her up and down. Seeing no wedding ring on her
finger, he smiled and replied, "You certainly are, Ms. Chambers."

The comment brought a slight blush to her cheeks. "Are you
going to be here the entire tour, Commander?" she asked.

"That depends on how long it takes me to do a total evaluation and area study . . . of the training." Jake paused
purposely, his smile widening on his face, and his eyes giving
way to a suggestive seductive glance. "And any other areas of
extensive study that may require my attention."

"I see," she said as she tried to avert her eyes from his, but
found she couldn't. "Well, then, I hope you can find the time
to visit our health unit. It is located in the USAID compound."

"You can be assured that I will, Ms. Chambers."

"Excuse me, Ambassador Frugenson, but I couldn't help

noticing that our French allies are not here today," said Hileran.

At the mention of the French the entire patio seemed to fall into silence. Jake and Hileran glanced around at the staring people who had suddenly stopped talking. Jake whispered, "You get the feeling maybe we're in one of those E. F. Hutton commercials."

Scotty Hileran shrugged. "Hell, either that, or I said something bad about somebody's mama in seven different languages at the same time."

The ambassador turned to Privett. Jake noted an edge of irritation in Frugenson's voice as he said, "Apparently, Mr. Privett, you have not informed our guests of the present situation here. Is that correct?"

Privett was clearly nervous. "No, sir, Captain York, the team commander, is still at the airport with the detachment. I thought it best to wait until we had them all together. That would facilitate matters all the way around."

"Of course, you may be right. Since you have already made that decision, we shall stick with it." Turning back to Jake and Scotty, he said, "Gentlemen, a situation has developed involving our French allies. I believe Mr. Privett's explanation will suffice for the time being. I will, however, have to ask that you refrain from any mention of the French while you are here. I assure you, the situation will be explained in its entirety before the evening is over."

"Of course, sir," said Hileran. Jake nodded in agreement. The silence of the moment was suddenly broken by a round of applause from the guests as General Gaafar came down the steps of the patio. Jake and Scotty moved out of the way as Frugenson pushed past them to greet the general. "Read much Sherlock Holmes when you were a kid, Scotty?" asked Jake.

"Yeah, and I believe you're right, 'The game is afoot.'"

Jake winked as he said, "Right on, Watson. Let's get a beer. Hell, there isn't any rule that says just because we used a dirty word and are being left in the dark like a couple of toadstools, we have to go thirsty."

"I hear you. Boy, the captain's gonna love this shit. We haven't been here two hours and already something is fucked up. Bet he'll wish he was back in Oklahoma on leave with B.J. before this is over. It was Oklahoma, wasn't it?"

"Yeah, B.J.'s probably sitting out on the front porch right now watching the sunset with an ice-cold Bud and not a worry in the world," laughed Jake.

"Ladies and gentlemen, let's hear it for a rough and tumble boy from Texas and a Green Beret officer who knows how to have fun when he's on leave. Let's put those hands together now and have a good ol'-fashioned Oklahoma welcome for Major B. J. Mattson coming out of chute number three on a bull called Widow Maker."

B. J. Mattson shifted his six-foot-four, two-hundred-pound frame astride the one-ton Brahman bull that bowed his huge head and snorted in defiance of the cowboy who had lowered himself onto his back.

"Better make sure ya got a solid wrap 'round that grip hand, partner. Ol' Widow Maker ain't been rode the limit by nobody for four years now. He's a right bad bull," said a young cowhand sitting along the top rail of the next chute. B.J. nodded his thanks and gave the taunt leather strap another wrap around his right hand that held a death grip on the belly band. Crossing over his left hand, he struck the leather-wrapped hand a couple of forceful blows in an attempt to form the two into one tightly uniform unit.

Widow Maker slung his head back toward Mattson. The right eye of the bull rolled back slightly fixing his coal-black gaze onto the would-be rider. Then, as if to demonstrate the futility of the man's effort, he swung the huge head viciously to the left and bucked, lifting his two thousand pounds off the ground effortlessly. The force of the blow shattered two of the rails of the next chute and sent the young cowboy, who had been talking to Mattson, sprawling backward off the top of the fence. "You're a regular bad-ass, aren't you, Widow Maker. Well, you go ahead and wear yourself out. That'll just make it that much easier for me," whispered Mattson.

The chute foreman stared up at Mattson through the railings as he yelled, "You ready, cowboy?"

Adrenaline was pumping wildly through the Green Beret's body as he shook his head that he was and howled, "Let 'er rip!"

The gate swung open and two thousand pounds of pissed-off Brahman bull shot out of the opening with amazing speed. The bull took two loping steps, then sprung upward, all four hooves clearing the ground, treating the two-hundred-pound man on his back as if he were no more than a flea on an elephant. B.J. hung on for dear life as Widow Maker spun right, then left, and leaped again, this time clearing the ground at such an incredible height that it brought a gasp, then a roar from the crowd. Mattson was only vaguely aware of the sound. His mind was concentrating on which way the one-ton devil from hell was going to turn next. He figured Widow Maker would wheel right; if he could only hang on for a few more seconds—B.J. had guessed wrong. The bull faked a motion right as his feet came back down to earth. Then sensing the man's shifting weight on his back, he lowered his head and swung to the left. "Shit!" yelled B.J. as he felt gravity taking him right while the bull went left. His right hand began to slip free from the belly band, and before he knew it, he was airborne. Flying through the air for a few seconds, he came down hard on the arena's dirt-covered floor. The smell of cow and horse manure mixed with straw and dirt filled his nostrils and clung to one side of his face.

Mattson rolled over and found Widow Maker standing a few feet away. His coal-black eyes stared at him mockingly. Bowing his head, the bull began to paw at the ground; now it was his turn. "Oh, shit!" uttered B.J. as he tried to scramble to his feet. A rodeo clown appeared and jerked him to his feet, "Better make for that fence, cowboy, he's coming after you."

"You don't have to say it twice, partner!" yelled B.J. as he took off at a dead run for the wooden pens to his right, with Widow Maker tearing up the dirt only a few feet behind him. Leaping up onto the third rail, B.J. turned and looked down at the bull who now stood only inches from the fence. The bull snorted his defiance as if satisfied that he had demonstrated who was the better of the two, turned away, and pranced off through one of the side gates for a well-deserved rest and something to eat.

B.J. shook his head as he looked up at the scoreboard at one end of the arena. "No Time" read the bright red letters. He hadn't made the eight seconds required to receive a score. Standing high on the rail he scanned the front row of seats on his left searching the crowd for his wife Charlotte and his two kids, Jason, who had just turned sixteen, and his fourteen-year-old daughter, Angela. They were all three standing and waving wildly to him, and the kids held their hands out giving him the thumbs-up signal. Charlotte waved; the tension of the moment still showed slightly on her lovely face.

"Nice-lookin' family," said one of the cowboys next to him on the rail.

"Thanks," said B.J., "they sure do put up with a lot of shit."

"Reckon that comes with the territory, partner, but they get used to it," replied the cowboy as Jake climbed down from the fence without answering. Walking back behind the chutes, he grabbed up his saddle, ropes, and chaps and headed out toward the parking lot. He wanted to store all his gear away before going back inside to watch the finals. "They get used to it," the man had said. Shows how much that guy knows, thought B.J. Take his job with the military, for instance: he loved it; Charlotte hated it. Some things people just can't get used to. For her, the constant moving and long periods of being left alone had reached a breaking point. That was why he was in Oklahoma right now, trying to save a marriage that had lasted nearly eighteen years. He returned home from a mission in Ecuador and found Charlotte and the kids gone. Her message was clear and simple: either the military, or the family, it was his choice. For most people, it might have been an easy choice, but not for B.J. He realized how much he loved it after those first few months in Vietnam. The friends, the people, and even the battles. The military was his life, and he was good at it. No other job could possibly give him the satisfaction that he had found these last fifteen years. Charlotte didn't see it that way. It was a situation that had nearly turned him into an alcoholic, and probably would have if it hadn't been for the help and advice of his partner, Jake Mortimer, and the support of his commander, General J. J. Johnson.

Tossing the gear into the back of a Ford Bronco, he headed back to the arena. B.J. knew he and Charlotte loved each other as much now as they had eighteen years ago when they met at Texas A & M. He was a returning Green Beret medic who had been shot all to hell in Vietnam and lost an index finger off his right hand in the process. It was a wound that had ended his dreams of becoming a surgeon. She was the beautiful head cheerleader and campus sweetheart with all the boys drooling after her body. Somehow, B.J. had always known he would be the one to win her heart. A whirlwind courtship, marriage, and direct commission from the ROTC program had led them to this point in their lives. There had to be a middle ground; some way they could compromise. B.J. loved the military as much as Charlotte hated it. They had been apart for four months now; their only contact was a few phone calls each month to talk with the kids. The leave had been Charlotte's idea, but one that B.J. had been quick to agree to. He stayed at her parent's home. They liked him and were sorry to see that there were problems with the marriage. They refused to say anything one way or the other. It was their daughter's life, and any decisions she made were going to be hers alone.

Stopping to pick up some hot dogs and Cokes for the family, B.J. went up the stairs to join Charlotte and the kids. "Are you all right?" she asked as he passed out the food and sat down next to her.

"Yeah, I'm fine," he answered.

Jason and Angela reached over and hugged their father. "Heck, Dad, you had that ol' Widow Maker on the ropes there for a minute, but he's really a tough one—threw Larry Mahan six different times, and he's the national champion. Ya done good, Dad," smiled Jason.

"Thanks, son," said B.J. as the boy turned his attention back to the next rider coming out of the chutes.

"He's really proud of you, you know," whispered Charlotte with a grin.

"Yeah, makes me feel good, too. Listen, Charlotte, we've got to get this thing back on track. You know this isn't any good for either of us. I love you, and I know you still love me. I want you to come back to Florida with me. I know we can work this out."

Charlotte lowered her head and stared down at her hand that rested on his leg. "I—I just don't know, B.J. I know I still love you; there could never be another man in my life as important as you are to me—but I have to think about the kids. They need more than a part-time father. They're getting older and reaching that age where they know more than I do. I need you with me to help them when those normal crises arise in a teenager's life. They're going to want you there, not crawling around some jungle. Don't you understand, B.J.? It's as much for them as it is for me. They need you, too."

B.J. sat silently staring across the arena at nothing in particular. She was right of course, she always was, and when she put it that way, B.J. had a hard time trying to justify why he was still with SOCOM in particular and the military in general. Hell, he had a degree from Texas A & M. He wouldn't have a problem getting another job, but that wasn't the point. He didn't want another job.

Squeezing his leg gently, she leaned closer to him. "Just consider those things, B.J., that's all I'm asking," she whispered. Placing his hand over hers he kissed her softly on the cheek.

"Maybe you're right, Charla. I guess I have been dumping all the responsibility for the kids off on you. I just never looked at it that way before."

"Are you sure you're all right? You weren't hurt out there?" she asked.

"No, I'm fine. Why?"

A devilish grin spread across her radiant face as she squeezed his leg even tighter and whispered in his ear, "Because I had another kind of ride in mind for you tonight."

B.J. returned her smile. "Honey, I've never been so beat-up I couldn't make that ride." They both laughed as Charlotte excused herself. Taking Angela with her, she left for the ladies' room. Jason sat down next to his father. "Dad, how has Commander Jake been doing? I'll bet he feels kinda lost without you around."

"Yeah, you're probably right, son, but that's something he may have to start getting used to."

CHAPTER 3

It was late afternoon and most of the guests had departed by the time Captain York arrived at the ambassador's residence. MSG Vickers was with him as they came down the patio steps, a look of seriousness etched across both their faces. They headed straight for Privett and the ambassador, who stood near the bar. Jake had been enjoying the company of Sharon Chambers the past hour, while the chief had made the acquaintance of an attractive young secretary on the embassy staff.

Sharon stirred the ice in her drink as she asked, "Mortimer . . . I heard that name before when I worked at Philadelphia Memorial. You wouldn't happen to be related to the law firm of Mortimer and Associates, would you?"

"Yeah, afraid so. The black-sheep son of the Mortimer clan."

"Well, they're very good at their business. They sued the pants off that hospital in a wrongful death suit, and won it hands down. That happened just before I left there three years ago. So why is the son of the richest and most influential families in Philadelphia knocking around the desert sands of Chad with the military?"

Jake hadn't heard the question. She glanced up to see him staring intently across the patio at the two men who had just entered.

"So they cut their balls off and hung them on the lamppost in front of the hospital." Raising her voice slightly, she asked, "Right?"

Jake glanced her way for a second, then back at York and Vickers. "Uh . . . yeah, right."

Chambers laughed as she set her glass down and picked up her purse.

"Well, I see by the old attention meter on the wall that it's time to go. It's been a pleasure, Commander," she said as she extended her hand.

Jake watched York walk straight up to Frugenson. He was standing only inches from the ambassador and staring him straight in the eyes. There was little doubt that the captain was pissed. Privett started to say something, but the burly team sergeant took him by the arm and moved him off to one side and began giving him the same treatment the ambassador was receiving.

Sharon lowered her hand and sighed. "From a queen of the desert to a leper of the evening in only a matter of four hours. That's a new record even for me."

"Wh—what?" said Jake as he turned to her. "Oh, I'm sorry, Sharon. I'm afraid I was so involved in what was going on across the way there that I didn't hear what you said."

"That's quite all right, Commander. I really must be going anyway. I'm sure we'll be bumping into each other on occasion, until then." Sharon nodded and started toward the stairs.

"Offer still hold for me to come by anytime?" asked Jake.

Turning slowly on her well-built legs, she smiled. "Of course, Jake, I'm dying to know what they did with those balls hanging from the lamppost."

Jake gave her a bewildered look. Balls? Lamppost?

She was still laughing as she skipped up the steps and left. Hileran came up beside Jake. "Telling dirty jokes to the local witch doctor, are we?"

"I have absolutely no idea what she was talking about," said Jake as he motioned toward York. "What do you make of that?" he asked.

"Only one way to find out," answered Hileran. "Let's go."

York was talking as the two officers crossed the patio toward the group.

"Well, I've got news for you people! Anybody tries fucking around with my team, and we're outta here."

Frugenson's face was turning a crimson red as he fought to

control the tension in his voice. "You and your team are under my direct supervision, Captain. You will do whatever, wherever, and whenever I say. Those measures were necessary to demonstrate to our Chadian allies our feelings in regard to the French government's decision to abandon them. I will remind you, Captain, you are here for a military purpose, and that purpose is to train the soldiers of General Gaafar, not make policy—that, sir, is my job."

York's expression of anger did not change as he stepped back from the official. "I am perfectly aware of my duties, Mr. Frugenson. You just make sure you and your people stick to your paper shuffling and leave my team alone. They answer only to me—no one else."

Frugenson started to reply, but thought better of it. Pivoting sharply on his heels, he walked directly up the stairs and into the house. York's eyes burned a hole through him every step of the way. Big Mike Vickers was laying it on Privett at the same time.

"And just who the hell are you people to be locking up fucking U.S. military personnel. Been me, I'd of shot my way outta that place just to come here and kick the livin' shit outta all you motherfuckers!"

Privett was visibly trembling as the huge team sergeant towering over him directed the words down onto him like a hailstorm. Privett's eyes caught the ambassador going up the stairs and into the house. God, the last thing he wanted was to be left out here with this giant by himself. Taking a couple of steps back, he raised his hands as he said, "Of course, Sergeant, I understand perfectly. I—I'll express your opinions to the ambassador personally. Ex—excuse me."

Privett saw his chance and walked hurriedly out and around Vickers and disappeared into the house at a rapid pace. Jake and Hileran caught the end of the verbal exchanges. Jake asked York, "What the hell was all that about, Randy?"

York was still upset as he said, "Come on, let's get a drink and I'll tell you a little story." The group headed for the bar. Vickers waved for the Chadian bartender to move out of the way, stepped behind the polished hardwood counter himself, and placed two bottles of whiskey on the bar with four glasses. As he poured the round, York looked at Jake as he said, "The French have been pulling out of here for the last week."

The news had the shock value York figured it would on both the officers.

"You can't be serious, Captain. Hell, I personally did the intell update before we left the States. There wasn't a single line of that report that mentioned anything about a planned pullout."

"That's why we didn't see any French at this little get-together," said Jake. "Are they all pulling out, Randy?"

York downed the shot of whiskey. Vickers refilled the glass. "Lock, stock and fucking barrel, Jake. They've already moved all their troops out, except for a couple of units. One's a small group of French pilots stationed at a place called Abeche, a small air base where they trained the Chad pilots to fly F-5s. Tanner figures they'll be the last ones to come out. When they do, they'll fly out, leaving the Chad Air Force with less than half the planes they have now. They have another group of legionnaires at a place called Mangalme."

"Tanner—Tanner told you about this?" asked Jake.

"Yeah, our policy boys here didn't want me to talk to Tanner, and that's why. These assholes pulled Tanner and his boys in and locked them up in one of the compounds because they refused to stop associating with the French Foreign Legionnaires of the 3rd Infantry Regiment who were stationed down the road from them."

"They locked our guys up for having a drink with the Legion?" asked Scotty.

"That wasn't the main reason, sir," said Vickers from behind the bar. " 'Bout a week ago, the legionnaires had a convoy ambushed outside of camp. Tanner and the team just happened to be out that way and jumped into the middle of the fight. Kicked some ass on them rebels and saved the Frenchy's butt. Course, Captain Tanner had already been instructed by the embassy here to avoid the French boys like the plague. Frugenson went nuts when he heard what Tanner did. Had the Marine guard here go out with some of Gaafar's boys and disarm the whole fuckin' team and bring them back here. That's where they been sittin' for the last two weeks. They just been waitin' for us to get here so they could leave."

"Now, both Tanner and his XO are facing a shit load of charges when they get back to Fort Bragg," said York as he tossed down his second drink.

"Did Tanner try to get in contact with General Johnson about this?" asked Jake.

"Yeah, but Frugenson refused to let them use the communications center. Said the information was too highly classified to go out over the air. And another thing, Tanner said to watch out for that guy Calhoun from the AID outfit. He's a long-time personal friend of General Sweet's. Tanner thinks it was Calhoun who got the ambassador all stirred up over the shoot-out," said York.

General Raymond Sweet was the Special Operations Command's Judas. He had been placed second in command of SOCOM by jealous staff officers at the Pentagon because they considered the use of small effective combat units as a threat to their multimillion-dollar budgets. Talks of cutting troop strengths throughout the different branches of the service had already started making the rumor mill around the Pentagon. It had a lot of generals worried. Sweet's position with SOCOM had been for no other purpose than to disrupt operations and missions assigned the group, preferably by embarrassing the command publicly. So far, Sweet's first two such attempts had embarrassed no one but Sweet himself. Moreover, this business with Tanner bore all the signs of General Sweet's interference.

"Where's the team now, Randy?" asked Jake.

"They're at one of the abandoned French barracks out by the airport. One of Privett's men wanted me to bring them into the embassy, but after hearing what Rick Tanner had to say, I figured, I'd find our own place for tonight anyway. The guy told us about the empty barracks, so I put 'em in there until we found out just what the fuck is going on around here. You know, Jake, this little old training mission could turn into an all-out war once the rebels and Qaddafi find out the French have pulled out."

"Yeah, I know. We better see if we can get in touch with General Johnson and request some adult leadership on this thing."

Vickers broke out in a loud country-boy laugh as he said, "Hey, that's good, Commander, 'adult leadership,' hell, I like that."

York was laughing now, too, for the first time since he

arrived in Chad. "Good idea, Jake. You think Frugenson will let us in the communications room?"

"Who said we were going to ask him." Jake smiled.

"Hell, yes, let's go. Top, you hold down the bar till we get back," said York.

Vickers's grin widened as he poured another drink and said, "Yes, sir, it's a shitty job but somebody has to do it."

The three officers laughed and headed to the side of the house and the communications room. The nomad cook finished cleaning the grill, and glancing unnoticed at Vickers, he nervously replaced the lid; then he stepped quietly toward the wall and slipped out one of the arched doorways, breaking into a dead run as he entered the street.

Mike Vickers was pouring another drink when Charles Murdock came down the steps. He walked up to the bar and extended his hand as he said, "Sergeant, I'm Charles Murdock. I don't believe we've met."

The fellow seemed friendly enough thought Vickers as he shook hands with the man. "Master Sergeant Mike Vickers, team sergeant of A-505. Nice to meet you, Mr. Murdock. Care for a drink?"

"Yes, please. Scotch will be fine. Thank you. Did you have a chance to eat anything, Sergeant?"

"Naw, we got here too late, I reckon, but that's all right. This ol' Jack will do just fine, sir," replied Vickers as he searched under the bar for the Scotch.

"Nonsense, I'm sure there's something left around here," said Murdock as he slid off the bar stool and walked to the grill. "Maybe the cook left a couple of steaks on the grill. Let's have a look."

Murdock's hand raised the lid a few inches. The courtyard shook from the explosion that rocked the enclosed structure. The sound of shattering glass and raining concrete carried out to the street. York, Hileran, and Jake came racing around the corner just as a piece of the grill crashed to the earth near the overturned, splintered bar. Frugenson and two of the Marine security force guards stepped gingerly through the remains of the double French doors that led to the patio. The glass crunched under their feet as they stared at the gray-white column of smoke that snaked its way skyward. As the smoke cleared, Mrs. Murdock, stunned, stood in shocked disbelief as she stared at what she knew was the lower torso of her husband. Only one blue pants leg remained on the shattered half body. One of the Marine guards caught her as she fainted. He carried her back into the house.

"Top! Where's Top?" yelled Hileran.

"Vick! Sergeant Vickers!" screamed York as he cleared the steps in one leap and raced to the overturned bar. Jake and Hileran were close behind.

"Ooow . . . ooow, what the . . . hell . . . happened?" came a slow moan from beneath the hardwood bar. The three officers grabbed the heavy structure and struggled as they lifted it off the team sergeant. Vickers lay on his back; a small pool of blood had formed next to his head.

"Oh, Christ," whispered Hileran.

Privett appeared at the doors.

"Privett, alert that Chambers woman we've got a head wound, and we'll be there in five minutes!" yelled Jake. Privett turned and ran into the house to make the call as Hileran and York gently picked up their team sergeant and carried him toward the side gate of the house. One of the marines had arrived from nowhere with a jeep and helped them get the wounded man inside. The marine jumped behind the wheel. Barely allowing Hileran and York time to leap in the back, he threw the jeep in gear and tore off down the street toward the clinic. Jake watched them round the corner on two wheels and disappear. General Gaafar appeared at his side. With sadness in his eyes he said, "It has already begun, Commander. This is a signal from my brother. He now knows the French are leaving. I am sorry the first casualties of this new aggression had to be visited upon two Americans."

"Yeah, that seems to be the 'in' thing all over the world lately, General. I think we had better get with the ambassador and get word of this off to the State Department right away."

"Yes, I am afraid Kueddei and his rebels will move quickly now to seize the moment. These next forty-eight hours will be crucial ones for my country, Commander. We must be prepared for anything."

Jake agreed with the military leader. Both men went back into the courtyard and joined Frugenson, who seemed a little pale from the ordeal. Gaafar informed him of his concerns. The men adjourned to the communications room to alert Washing-

ton of the events that had so suddenly and violently erupted in
the small nation. As Frugenson composed the message to be
sent, Privett took Jake aside and whispered, "Commander, if
this is a signal as Gaafar suggests, it is imperative that we rush
reinforcements to the air base at Abeche. Three fourths of the
country's air power is located there; it is sure to be a prime
target for Kueddei's forces."

"OK, Mr. Privett, as soon as Captain York returns, we will
get the team outfitted and take a company of Gaafar's troops
out there in the morning. What was the name of that place
again?"

"Abeche, it is about four hundred miles northeast of here."

"Do you know their troop strength?"

"I'm not sure. You'll have to ask General Gaafar, but I
believe there are about one hundred and fifty Chadian soldiers
and ten or twelve of the French pilots still there."

"Damn it," said Jake. "I wish Tanner and his boys were still
here. He'd know which units we could count on when the shit
hits the fan."

Privett cleared his throat before saying, "Well, there are
about a hundred legionnaires at Mangalme. I would think you
are well aware of their combat abilities."

Jake lowered his head and shook it slowly side to side.

"Boy, you policy guys are really something, Privett, you
know that? Hell, you don't even invite them to your party. You
turn your back on them and call them low-life shits because
they're leaving. Then have the gall to ask them to stay around
and get their ass shot off protecting you. You people are
unbelievable, un-fucking believable. Well, mister, you'd better
hope they have a warped sense of humor and a total disregard
for life; otherwise, you and that ambassador of yours are likely
to have your heads stuck on a spike at the front gate of this joint
by tomorrow night."

Privett knew the man was right. It was asking an awful lot.
The thought of him or Frugenson falling into the hands of
General Kueddei sent a chill up his spine. He had heard stories
of the man's cruelty. They were stories that went beyond
nightmares. "You will go to them and ask for their help, won't
you, Commander?"

"I don't see that we have any choice, Mr. Privett. Who

knows, they might just tell us to go to hell. Can't say I'd blame them, either."

Privett nodded his understanding and walked away. The worry lines reappeared across his tired-looking face.

Jake turned to a map on the wall. Pulling a pen from his pocket, he circled the name as he repeated it silently, "Abeche."

CHAPTER 4

The line of French Mirage F-5 fighters sat at a uniform angle along the flight line. The airport lights around the perimeter silhouetted the cockpit canopies of the first four. They had been raised and locked into position to facilitate rapid deployment of the four standby crews on alert duty for the night.

A government soldier on guard duty stepped from the shadows near the chain-link fence surrounding the airfield. He adjusted the sling of his rifle onto his shoulder slightly above the patch that identified him as a member of the regular Chad Army. As he walked from the shadows, his hands were busy fumbling at the buttons on the fly of his camouflage desert fatigues. Cursing silently at the difficulty of the task, he stepped into the faint glow of one of the lights, stopped, and looked down. He sensed the movement before he actually saw it. The dark blur came from his left and in the blinking of an eye was suddenly behind him. A hand covered his mouth, and a blinding pain shot through his chest as his body jerked twice. The powerful hand held him firmly in its grips, while the other drove the thin-bladed stiletto into his back for a third and final time. The dead man was quietly pulled back into the darkness and lowered to the ground. Wiping the blood from the blade onto the black coveralls of his Ninja battle dress, the shadowy figure merged once more with the darkness along the edge of the fence and moved with catlike motion to his next victim.

Across the runway, four figures dressed in similar black Ninja uniforms silently made their way up the steel stairway that led to the control tower. The lead figure crouched in the shadows beside the door, while the second man of the team crawled forward and pulled himself slowly up to the lower edge of the window in the door. Two soldiers sat on the floor and against the left wall, their rifles across their legs, their heads down; they were asleep. A Chad officer sat in a chair, his feet propped up on the tabletop that held the radar and radio equipment. A fourth soldier lay asleep on a cot next to the door, his rifle leaning against the wall. The figure in black lowered himself slowly into the shadows of the door, then held up four fingers to indicate the number of men inside. The leader of the group nodded, motioned the observer to move to the right of the door, and signaled the remaining two men to move to the top of the stairs. These masters of the darkness did not carry the normal armament of weapons, but rather the silent, equally deadly tools of the Ninja. The leader reached into the black sash around his waist and removed three shurikens, the metal throwing stars with seven points and razor-honed edges. He positioned one halfway under the sash so that it rested on his right hip. The others did the same. Satisfied that they were ready, the leader designated each man a specific target in the room. He reached for the doorknob and began to turn it ever so slowly until he felt the bolt free itself from the door frame.

In one swift, silent movement, the door swung outward, and the four men were in the center of the room. The officer in the chair turned his head toward the door. The Ninja leader threw the first shuriken by whipping the arm forward and snapping his wrist on the release. This provided deadly accuracy for the spinning star of death as it sailed across the room and struck the officer in the left temple, killing him instantly.

Simultaneously, his right hand retrieved the star resting against his hip as the leader pivoted; and with his left hand threw the second star overhand while the third was thrown underhanded and from the waist. Both stars were directed at the soldier sitting on the floor to the right. One star struck him in the forehead, the other in the solar plexus. Across the room the dead officer's body tumbled from the chair. The sound of the dead weight hitting the floor awakened the soldier on the cot. As he raised his head and opened his sleepy eyes, he was struck by a trio of pointed stars. He slumped lifeless on the canvas bed, bright red blood pumped wildly from the severed jugular vein in his neck. The final soldier, still sitting on the floor, opened his eyes and stared up in panic at the devils in black. Blood was everywhere on the floor. He attempted to raise his hands as a sign of surrender, but it did no good. A Tanto throwing knife sliced through the air and spilt the soldier's Adam's apple, impaling him against the wall. His eyes widened in shock as his mouth opened to speak. Only blood came out. The attacker stepped forward, planted his foot on the dying man's chest, and leaned forward to watch the soldier's eyes as he wrapped his black gloved hand around the handle of the knife and twisted it slowly in the man's throat. The soldier's body squirmed. His hands were slapped away as he tried to reach up to his throat. There was no scream, only the sickening gurgling of blood forming in the man's throat and mouth.

"Finish that business, for God's sake," said one of the men in black.

The remark brought a swift turn of his head as the knife twister stared back at the man who had spoken. Cold, calculating, steel-blue eyes cast their evil glare over at the speaker who lowered his head and turned away. Returning his attention to the soldier impaled on the wall, blue eyes gave the knife a final twist sideways, reached up with his left hand, grabbed a fistful of hair, jerked the dying man's head to the left, and at the same time forced the knife to the right in a slicing motion that nearly decapitated the soldier. What little blood was left in the man's body squirted from his severed neck like a bright red fountain.

Stepping back to admire his handiwork, he wiped the blade on his pants leg, reached up, and pulled the sweaty black ski mask from his face. His name was Hans Kruger, and he was a mercenary. His short-cropped blond hair, blue eyes, rugged square jaw, and broad shoulders left little doubt as to the man's nationality, German. He was the son of a former WW II SS commander and every bit as ruthless as his father had been under Hitler.

For Hans Kruger Hitler's reign over Europe had been lauded by his father's tales of great battles and of the power of the German Army during those glorious days. The stories had left the boy hanging on his father's every word. It seemed only natural that he, too, should follow the military ways of his heroic father. Along with the tales of glory had come the horror stories of torture and slaughter of those thousands who had been judged unworthy of life in a perfect Germany. He would always remember his father's eyes when he spoke of the interrogations and wholesale killing of the imperfect ones. His eyes would come alive as he detailed the ingenious methods he and his SS had employed to extract information and to rid the world of those worthless people; methods that were to become the trademark of the hated SS. It was those memories that remained with the young Hans Kruger as he grew into manhood and joined the West German Army of the early sixties. It was also those memories that caused his expulsion from that same army for his inhuman, cruel, and ruthless treatment of his own comrades. Hans Kruger soon realized he could not be the kind of military man he wanted to be in an army with such humane rules and controlled order. He soon discovered another field where only the ruthless survived and only the strongest ruled by unrelenting cruelty and iron-fisted command; Hans Kruger had entered the world of the mercenary.

His first test had come during the Congo uprising of the sixties. It was a time when mercenaries were actually being hailed as the saviors of countless whites who were trapped in a country gone mad with black cults and armies of machete-wielding fanatics. It was here that Kruger found his opportunity to put into practice the things he had only imagined as a boy while listening to his father's tales. He experienced the torture, slaughter, and murder of thousands, often emerging from battles with his arms covered with blood to the elbows.

In battle, he was like a madman. He was relentless in attack and merciless to those he defeated. He showed neither compassion nor hesitation in delivering the death blow to both armed and unarmed opponents. He reveled in the screams of the tortured. He was fascinated by the changing characteristics of his victim's eyes as they suffered through their prolonged hell, pleading for death as he would drive a nail through a man's testicle or peel the skin from a woman's breast to leave it hanging by the nipple before her crazed fluttering eyes. Their screams were like a heavenly choir to Kruger and served only to drive the sadist to new heights.

From the Congo to Angola to Central and South America, the name Hans Kruger began to spread among other mercenaries, as well as intelligence agencies throughout the world. Although many did not care for his tactics nor for his strange addiction to cruelty, there was one thing they had to admit: he got results. It was for that reason, he was now standing in the control tower of the Abeche airport in eastern Chad. Turning to one of his mercenaries, the tall German returned the knife to the sheath strapped to his leg as he said, "Ching, check with the others and see where they are. They should have taken out the perimeter guards by now and should be closing in on the troop quarters. Tell Kaufman I want one of the pilots alive."

The short, stocky Korean named Ching removed his mask; and without reply, he pulled a small radio from his side pocket and whispered into the mike. Kruger lit a cigarette and stepped out onto the metal platform at the top of the stairs. Inhaling deeply, he let the smoke fill his lungs for a moment, then he exhaled slowly as he looked out over the runway at the planes along the flight line. So far, everything was right on schedule, they would have full control of the airfield before dawn. Beyond the perimeter lights, the vast desert stretched its sand-blown emptiness to the horizon. By morning that emptiness would be filled with a flood of tanks, jeeps, trucks, and men, as an army descended on the town of Abeche, safe in the knowledge that any threat from the sky still sat idly on the runway below. Ching came out onto the platform.

"Kaufman said they are ready for the attack on the soldiers' quarters. He would like to know if you want a Chad prisoner or French?" asked Ching.

"I would prefer a Frog, but either one will do," replied Kruger.

Ching stood motionless with a look of momentary confusion on his face. Kruger smiled, showing perfect rows of large white teeth as he said, "A Frog is another name for a Frenchman, Ching."

Ching returned the smile, but Kruger could see the Korean was still trying to mentally make the connection between a Frog and a Frenchman.

"Of course, Colonel Kruger, I shall relay your message. Will there be anything else, sir?"

"No, Ching," said Kruger as he took another drag off the

smoke and turned back to stare out at the desert. He liked Ching even if he was a Korean. Ching was highly efficient and steadfastly loyal, a rare trait in a mercenary. Kruger turned his attention to the four long wooden barracks that sat across the runway and watched as Kaufman's men moved out of the shadows and along each wall. Some dropped off and took positions near the windows, while the others moved to the front and back of the buildings. Even in the semidarkness around the barracks and from this distance, Kruger could identify his fellow German and second in command by his hulking size. Adolf Kaufman stood six five and weighed close to three hundred pounds. Remarkably enough, this bear of a man possessed an uncanny sense of balance and coordination, a trait he was quick to attribute to his perfectly matched, pure-blood German parents.

One man moved into position in front of each of the doors. Within seconds, they stepped forward, kicked the flimsy portals in, and opened fire on the sleeping government soldiers. There was no longer a need for silence. The sounds of automatic weapons fire filled the night sky as half-dazed men raised up only to be slammed back in their beds or against wooden walls by a seemingly never-ending hail of bullets. In less time than it had taken Kruger to finish his cigarette, it was all over. There were only the occasional random pistol shots as the mercenaries made their way through each building administering a final shot to the head of the wounded. Kruger had neither time to deal with prisoners, nor the inclination to deal with the cumbersome problems presented by having to guard and feed a defeated enemy. His schedule did not allow for such nonsense. It was more economical and advantageous to simply kill them.

Kaufman moved into the light at the bottom of the stairs and looked up at his boyhood friend and commander as he said, "Hans, we have a Frenchman for you." The big man paused. A grin crossed his face as he laughed and continued, "You should have seen his face when I told him who was in charge of this operation. The poor fool almost fainted. I will have him brought to you right away. Do you wish anything else?"

"Were any of our men injured, Adolf?" asked Kruger.

Kaufman lowered his head and kicked at the sand beneath his feet as he said, "I'm afraid so, Hans. Two of Kueddei's men were killed by an overzealous member of Qaddafi's commando group when they entered the back of the pilot's quarters."

"Damn it," uttered Kruger. He knew those Libyan assholes were going to be a problem from the very beginning. The only reason they were here now was because of Colonel Qaddafi. After all, it was his money that was bankrolling this revolution. Kruger didn't care for the colonel, his country, nor its people. As far as he was concerned, the only thing worse than a Jew was a raghead—but then, five million dollars could make any man more tolerant—for a little while, anyway. He may have to run this operation with Qaddafi's men, but he was still the overall commander, damn it. He would not put up with inefficiency from the two hundred mercenaries he had hired, nor the stupid actions of this ragtag bunch of clowns who Qaddafi called "his elite forces."

"Adolf! Have that Frenchman brought up here, then find the man that killed Kueddei's two men. I want him standing at the bottom of these steps when I have finished with the Frenchman. Gather all of the Libyans for a formation in front of the tower."

Kaufman could hear the anger in Kruger's voice. It was a tone he had often heard from the man other mercenaries, as well as an ever-increasing number of people around the world, were now calling "Le homme de glace"—"The man of ice." It was that notoriety that had brought his name to the attention of Colonel Muammar Qaddafi. The Libyan leader was furious with the officers of his command following their disastrous defeat at the hands of the Chadian government forces during the attempted takeover of Chad in the spring of 1986. Counterattacks by Chadian forces had driven Qaddafi's army and the rebel coalition all the way back to a small section of the Aozou Strip, a hotly contested no-man's-land along the northern Chad-Libyan border. Qaddafi's embarrassment and rage at his defeat before the entire world brought a number of executions among the officers of his command, many of whom had deserted their men by fleeing during the critical moments of major confrontations. Their cowardice in that action had not gone unnoticed by the Chadian rebels under the command of Hissen Kueddei, leader of the Socialist Islamic Solidarity Party. He was a man who tolerated Qaddafi only because he needed the man's money and stockpiles of weapons to over-throw the present government. Kueddei had made promises he had no intentions of keeping. He would deal with that problem when it arose, for now they needed someone to lead their warriors; someone who would lead, not run; someone who could lead them to victory, not to the humiliation of defeat again. Qaddafi's answer to that problem was—"The Ice Man."

Hans Kruger was paid five million dollars to recruit a mercenary army of two hundred to train and to lead the SISP, with a contingent of Libyan forces, in another attempt at a military overthrow of the Republic of Chad. The recruiting, training, and planning had taken almost a year, culminating in the action at the airfield. There was little doubt in Kaufman's mind of the fate awaiting the unfortunate Libyan soldier who had accidentally lost control of his weapon and killed two men of the raiding party. The Libyan would not find sympathy in Kruger's cold, steel-blue eyes. He expected perfection from those under him; there were no excuses, no misunderstandings, and no second chances.

"Herr Kaufman, did you hear what I said?" asked Kruger from his perch at the top of the stairs.

"Yes, Colonel. It will be as you say," replied Kaufman as he snapped to attention, saluted smartly, then pivoted on his heels in the sand and moved toward one of the barracks, shouting orders for the Frenchman to be taken upstairs while the Libyans were to fall in at the base of the tower. Kruger watched the flurry of activity as three of his mercenaries dragged the Frenchman up the steps. His hands were tied behind his back. He slipped and fell on the steel steps three times, only to be jerked up painfully by his arms, pushed and shoved closer to the top of the stairs. Kruger studied the man's face as he came closer. The Frenchman was young, very young, perhaps no more than twenty-three or twenty-four years old. The insignia on his collar identified him as a lieutenant. The patch on his right shoulder was that of a fighter pilot. With each step the boy took he stared up at the looming figure in black waiting for him at the top of the stairs. Fear gripped his face as sheer panic appeared in his youthful eyes. He had heard the mercenaries talking as they dragged him across the compound. At hearing the mention of Kruger's name, his knees had buckled from under him, because he knew he was a dead man.

The Libyans had begun to form ranks in front of the tower as the boy was pushed up the last step to stand directly in front of Kruger. The Ice Man stood stone-still as he stared into the young pilot's eyes with a coldness that would have frozen hell itself. The boy's lower lip was bloody and quivering as he averted Kruger's stare only to see Ching come out the door of the tower with the body of a dead Chadian officer draped over his shoulder, blood leaking from the hole in the side of his head.

The Korean walked to the railing that surrounded the platform and nonchalantly tossed the body over the side, watching as it made the fifty-foot drop and slammed into the ground with a sickening thud. A wild cheer arose from the Libyans below. The boy's stomach churned and a bitter bile rose in his throat. He was going to be sick. Kruger nodded for them to take the pilot inside and strip him of all his clothes; he would be back in a moment. He had decided to deal with the Libyan first.

Kruger moved slowly down the steps, his eyes fixed on the formation at attention in front of the tower. He had only brought a force of one hundred to capture the airfield, twenty of his mercenaries, thirty of Kueddei's rebels, and fifty Libyan commandos. Kruger's men and the rebels now stood in a semicircle behind the fifty commandos, their weapons not pointing at the Libyans, but in position where they could be brought to bear on the group if it became necessary. Kaufman stood to one side of the formation holding the unarmed, frightened Libyan soldier tightly by the arm. Kruger stepped in front of the formation, spoke in perfect Arabic, and gave the men an "At ease" before he continued. "Gentlemen, as you can see, our plan for the attack on the air base has proven successful. Our months of training and preparation have reaped our just reward. Allah be praised. It was only through his divine guidance that such a plan could be formulated and executed with such precision."

There was a muttering of agreement among the Libyans as Kruger purposely paused for a moment to let them consider his well-chosen words. Kruger had learned early on that to motivate the Arab one needed only to invoke the name of Allah. He continued, "However, there are two of our number who lie dead, their blood providing drink for the sands of this place, and their spirits now sit in the banquet hall of Allah, who welcomes them with sadness in his heart. For they did not die at the hands of an enemy, but rather by the carelessness of a brother who now stands before us."

Kruger raised his hand and motioned for Kaufman to bring the soldier forward. The Libyan resisted for a moment, but had no chance against the strength of the powerful Kaufman, who now pulled him to the front, standing him next to Kruger. The man's head was bowed, his eyes fixed on the sand at his feet.

"My brothers, this is the man who has visited this sadness upon Allah, and shed the blood of fellow warriors through his neglect. I ask you my brothers, what shall be done with this man?"

The question left the group at a loss for words. There was perfect silence within the ranks. Each man knew that what had happened was an unfortunate accident; yet the manner in which Kruger had used such phrases as "A sadness within Allah," "the sand drinking the blood," and "fellow warriors" had stirred a feeling of resentment from them for their Libyan comrade. Kruger knew full well that he could not simply kill the man in front of these soldiers without first attempting to remove any feelings of sympathy they might have for him. After all, this was only the first step of the operation. No matter how he felt about the Libyans, he was going to need them for this job.

"Come, my brothers, tell me what justice I must deal to appease Allah and the spirits of our two dead comrades."

The Libyan commandos could not bring themselves to condemn one of their own. They remained silent. The accused soldier raised his head. A feeling of confidence was beginning to flow through him. His eyes showed signs of hope as they roamed across the faces of his fellow commandos, asking their forgiveness. Kruger glanced at Kaufman for a moment. He could see the big man was thinking the same thing. These cowards were no more efficient at making a decision than they were at warfare. Kruger was going to have to do something. He had no intention of letting the man live. Placing his hands behind his back, Kruger turned away from the commandos and took a couple of steps toward the tower. There, lying in the sand, was the answer to his problem, the dead Chadian officer Ching had tossed from the tower. Moving to the body, Kruger knelt down beside it. All eyes were on the mercenary leader's back as they watched him move the body around, pull at something around the man's waist, then stand up. When he turned back around, he held a .38-caliber revolver in his hand.

Kruger moved back in front of the group. The pistol was held high in his big hand so that all could see.

"My brothers, I sense that I have unjustly placed a heavy burden upon you, as well as upon myself. As it is Allah who has been offended by this man. Then it shall be Allah who will decide his fate." Lowering the pistol, Kruger snapped open the cylinder and ejected the six bullets that were in it. Holding them in his open hand he shook them loosely about; then, slowly, one at a time, he allowed five of them to drop to the sand at his feet. He held the last remaining bullet high in the air; then he brought it down and placed it in the cylinder. Ching appeared on the tower platform and yelled down to Kruger.

"Colonel, General Kueddei is on the radio. He wants to speak to you."

All eyes were on Ching as Kruger turned toward the tower and replied, "Tell him I will call him back in a few minutes."

"Yes, sir," said Ching, who turned to go back inside.

Kruger turned back to the group, the pistol still in his hand. The cylinder was still open out to the side. Taking his free hand, he spun the cylinder and flipped his wrist, locking the cylinder in place. Holding the weapon high once again, he said, "Allah shall judge this man."

The confidence of only moments ago faded quickly as Kruger extended the pistol to the now terrified soldier who took a step backward, away from the outstretched weapon. The ploy by the commando brought an uneasy muttering of dissatisfaction from the Libyans.

"Take the weapon, brother!" yelled one of the commandos.

"The colonel speaks the truth. It was you who offended Allah. It is Allah who should be your judge. Take the gun, brother," said another.

Others joined in now as Kaufman released the man's arm and stepped away. Kruger's arm remained extended, the pistol hanging loosely in his hand. His cold eyes fixed on those of the frightened man who now knew he had no choice but to leave his fate in the hands of Allah. Stepping forward, he reached up and took the weapon from Kruger's hand. He took two steps back and cocked the hammer of the pistol all the way back. Kruger and Kaufman both moved to the rear and behind the man who began to pray to his God as he slowly brought the barrel of the gun up and placed it at his right temple.

Out of the corner of his eye Kaufman caught a glimpse of a slight smile forming at the corner of Kruger's mouth. The roar of the pistol shot startled the big man, causing him to flinch as his eyes fixed on the man who had just blown his brains out. He lay on the ground. His feet and legs twitched three times as his blood pumped from the hole in the side of his head. There came one final violent jerking motion before he lay perfectly still. The Libyans uttered a series of whispered prayers as Kruger bent down, picked up the weapon, and held it high once more.

"Allah has judged, and so it shall be written. Return to your team leaders now. We will remain on full alert around the perimeter for the remainder of the night. This matter is closed. You are dismissed."

Kaufman moved next to Kruger as the Libyans headed off in the directions of their assigned positions. "You know that could have turned out very bad for us if that pistol had hit on an empty chamber. These men would have surely listened to a man who they thought had been personally blessed by Allah himself. It could have presented a problem, Hans. It is lucky for us all that the gun fired."

Kruger smiled. "I am surprised at you, Adolf. You are my oldest friend. You know that I do not believe in luck—luck is for fools and daydreamers. A smart man has no need for such absurdity."

Releasing the catch that held the cylinder in place on the .38, he let it fall open and removed the spent cartridge from the chamber; then he passed the weapon to Kaufman who stared with disbelief at the five remaining bullets that were still in the cylinder. "But . . . how? . . . I watched you drop five bullets in the sand in front of all of us. How . . . That poor bastard had no chance at all. That was why you were trying not to smile. You knew this gun was fully loaded."

"Of course," answered Kruger as he held up a small plastic disk with six holes and asked, "Do you know what this is, Adolf? But of course you do. It is a speed loader. Hardly anyone uses revolvers anymore. Automatics are the weapons of choice these days. When I knelt by the body, I found three of these in the officer's pocket. With an open cylinder, six rounds can be loaded in less than three seconds. When Ching came out and called to me, I turned my back to you all, ejected the one bullet, and speed-loaded all six. When I again faced you, I immediately spun the cylinder, then locked it in place and presented the challenge to the group. I thought it went rather well myself. A little more time-consuming perhaps, but it still achieved the desired results."

"But what if Ching had not appeared above at that exact moment. How were you going to use the speed loader?"

"Ah, Adolf, my dear friend, just as I do not believe in luck—I do not question fate. Now, come, we must see what information we can gather from our young Frenchman upstairs that may be of value to us."

"Are you planning to kill him afterward?" asked Kaufman as they moved to the steps.

"Having killed over one hundred men already tonight, I imagine I will have him shot, if he does not die from the questioning first. Why do you ask?"

"Some of the African boys were hoping you'd let them have him when you're through. They said he only had on a pair of bikini underwear when they captured him and he has very smooth skin. They asked that I remind you that there are no women out here. I see no need to say more," said Kaufman, his voice trailing off at the end.

"Do you find that revolting, Adolf, or are you simply jealous?" laughed Kruger as he made his way up the stairs.

"No, Hans, I still prefer women, but it may be entertaining to watch," replied Kaufman with a chuckle as he followed his leader to the top of the tower.

The young French aviator sat naked in a chair that had been positioned in the center of the room. He raised his head and turned toward the entrance as Kruger came through the door. A chill gripped the young man's heart as his body began to quiver—and well it should. The devil had just come through the door, and he was about to enter a hell beyond mortal man's meager imagination.

CHAPTER 5

General Raymond Sweet shifted restlessly in his chair as Charles Burrows, a member of the National Security Council, finished reading the report from the Thai Drug Enforcement Agency. He was reading it aloud for the benefit of Major General John Garland, Sweet's superior and the man who had recommended him for the job of keeping tabs on SOCOM.

"The government of Thailand hereby revokes any and all travel visas, passports, and agreements binding the two governments of the United States and Thailand in regard to one General Raymond Sweet, United States Army. These restrictions shall apply for a period of three years, effective this date." Burrows lowered the official document and stared across his desk at Sweet. "It's signed by the King of Thailand himself," he said dryly.

Sweet diverted his small beady eyes from Burrows and stared down at the carpet beneath his spit-shined shoes, all the while trying to force his five-foot-five, overweight frame deeper into the plush cushions of the oversize chair in anticipation of the verbal barrage he was positive would come from General Garland. Burrows flipped the report from his hand in disgust and leaned back in his chair to await the royal ass-chewing that was about to befall the inept little general who now sat in front of him.

Small beads of sweat formed along Sweet's forehead and upper lip. The room was silent as he raised a nervous hand that held a handkerchief to lightly dab at his forehead and lips. He pushed what few sprigs of black hair he had left over to one side in a futile effort to cover a shining bald spot.

"Gennnneral . . . Sweet!" said Garland in a long drawn-out tone. "Can you possibly, in some logical and sensible manner, explain to me how you came to the conclusion that you discredited General J. J. Johnson and SOCOM by getting yourself arrested"—Garland's voice began to raise—"by one of our strongest allies, for dealing in drugs, and getting yourself thrown out of the country for three . . . fucking . . . years!"

Sweet dropped the hand holding the handkerchief into his lap as the last three words seemed to echo around the room. Garland, his hands behind his back, strolled casually to the window behind Burrows and looked out over the Potomac River as he said, "Sweet, please explain that—if you can."

The handkerchief was in knots as he attempted to answer. "I—I . . ." Clearing his throat, he tried again. The voice was squeaky, almost irritating, but that was Sweet's natural tone. His nervousness only made it more irritating.

"Sir, I assure you, I had a solid plan when I arrived in Thailand. Why . . . I even discussed it with Mr. Burrows before I left."

Burrows was still leaning back in his chair. The fingertips of each of his hands were pressed together and resting against his lower lip. Feeling Garland's eyes on him from the rear, he nodded in agreement with Sweet's statement. Garland looked back out the window as he said, "Continue, General."

Sweet sensed that he might possibly still talk his way out of this mess.

"Well, sir, to put it plainly, I was set up and double-crossed at the same time by that goddamn Johnson and some asshole friend of his from the embassy. Hell, sir, I did the best I could, but it was a job for two people, not one. If there had been two people working on the plan, sir, it would have turned out differently; I assure you. My problem was I couldn't stick with Johnson and set up the drug deal at the same time."

"So, rather than finding the drugs in Major Mattson's and Commander Mortimer's luggage where you had planted them, they found the whole mess in your room after the operation was completed," said Garland.

"Yes, sir. I can't explain how that happened. I had Johnson

in my sight every minute after planting the stuff. I—I just don't know how they did it, sir. Sorry." Sweet sunk back even farther into the chair. Hell, that story didn't even sound good to himself. It was all immaterial now anyway. SOCOM had scored another coup with the President and had even gained a number of new followers in the Congress following their Burma rescue of a congressional party from a drug warlord. This had been Sweet's second attempt at discrediting the Special Operations unit, and he had failed as miserably this time as he had the first. Visions of commanding an iceberg in the far reaches of Antarctica staffed with an unlimited number of seals began to appear in his mind—and Burrows, the pompous ass sitting there with that shit-eating grin on his face. Hell, planting the damn drugs had been his idea in the first place—but he sure as hell wasn't taking any credit for it now.

General Garland turned away from the window. Here it comes, thought Sweet, assignment to the Twilight Zone.

"You know, John, he may have a valid point there." It was Burrows. Perhaps Sweet had judged him too quickly. Garland turned to the NSC man.

"What do you mean, Charles?" he asked.

Leaning forward on his desk, Burrows said, "I'm afraid General Sweet is right. It's impossible for one man to be in two places at the same time. Maybe that is where we have been making our mistake. We are relying on one man to do a job that actually requires two."

Sweet was sitting up straight now and on the edge of the chair nodding wholeheartedly in agreement with Burrows, his Peter Lorre face trying to hold back a sign of relief.

"It is clear now what General Johnson is doing. He puts in his best two operatives to evaluate and assist whatever force they request while he runs interference and shields their true activities back here."

"Yeah," chimed in an excited Sweet. "That is exactly what he's doing, sir—yes, sir."

"Calm down, Sweet," said Garland. "So what are you suggesting, Mr. Burrows?"

Burrows smiled. "I think we should give General Sweet the same advantage, sir. We should find us a man and devise an official purpose for putting him with Major Mattson and Commander Mortimer. Then we—"

"The M and M boys," interrupted Sweet.

"The what?" said Garland.

"The M and M boys, sir. That's what they have called Mattson and Mortimer ever since that Ecuadorian business earlier this year—stands for murder and mayhem—quite appropriate I might add. Those boys are damn effective at what they—"

Burrows slapped his desktop and leaned forward. "General Sweet, if you please, I am attempting to save your ass here! Glorifying the competition will hardly improve your case. Now, may I continue?"

"Ex—excuse me, Mr. Burrows, of course," whispered Sweet.

"As I was saying, sir, we put our man in the field with"—Burrows paused a moment—"with the M and M boys. He will be right on top of the situation and can report directly back to General Sweet, who in turn can run interference for any actions his man might need to take to sabotage the SOCOM mission. What do you think, sir?"

Garland walked back to the window, his hand pulling at his chin as he considered the idea. Without turning away from the window, he asked, "Mr. Burrows, you were rejected by the Special Forces school twice while you were in the service, were you not?"

The question brought Burrows straight up in his chair. Sweet smiled broadly as he leaned back and gloated at seeing Burrows now on the hot seat.

"Why . . . yes, I was, but I fail to see where that has anything to do with . . . I mean, I didn't really care whether I was accepted or not! They were against me from the very beginning—I was smarter than they were—"

Garland's back was still to Burrows as he raised his hand to halt any further discussion. "I am not interested in your personal vendettas, Mr. Burrows. They say misery has a long memory—I was just curious, and I sense that you 'cared' more than you knew. However, you are right, that has no bearing on this present situation. Do you have anyone in particular in mind for this assignment?"

Regaining his composure, Burrows answered, "There are a couple of people I had in mind, sir, but I'll have to have them checked out first. It could take a while." Pausing, Burrows made a point of looking directly at Sweet, "We want to make sure we get the right man—this time."

Unable to find cause to counter the cutting remark, Sweet again averted his eyes to the carpet. General Garland found the remark totally uncalled for—after all, as Sweet had said, he had discussed the drug business with Burrows before he left. If the plan had worked, Garland knew the NSC man would have been quick to take the credit for its success. He was about to remind Burrows of that when the phone rang. Burrows answered it. His mouth dropped open as he jumped to his feet, sending his chair backward with such force that the steel backing punched a hole in the wall. "What!" he yelled. "When?" There was a pause as the man listened with a look of total disbelief. "Holy shit! We'll be right there. Yes, General Garland is here with me right now. I'll tell him. We'll be there in five minutes."

Burrows hung up the phone and stared across at the two military officers, excitement dancing in his eyes. "That son of a bitch in Panama finally went too far. That was Secretary of Defense Bowers, Noriega's boys shot and killed a Marine officer at a checkpoint, and at the same time across town, the PDF arrested a Navy man and his wife. They beat the shit out of the guy and played a little grab ass with his old lady. The President's mad as hell. He wants the Chiefs of Staff and all military advisors at the White House ASAP. Bowers didn't come right out and say it, but the man is going to invade Panama."

Sweet fell back in his chair. This was the man the opposition had called a wimp.

"Well, come on, Burrows, let's get over there," said Garland. "Looks like we've finally got us a war."

"What about me?" asked Sweet.

Burrows was already going out the door as Garland said, "Raymond, you catch the first thing out of here and get back to MacDill, J. J. Johnson will be at this meeting. We'll try to stall him here in Washington while you handle things down there. Remember, General, I want main-line conventional forces conducting this operation. Give those Special Operations' Rambos only the shit missions and only when they are under the control of conventional commanders—you got that?"

Sweet snapped to attention as he replied, "Yes, sir! The longer you can keep Johnson out of my hair, the better, sir."

"We'll take care of it," said Garland as he headed through the doorway. He paused and looked back at Sweet. "Don't fuck this up, Raymond—three strikes and you're out."

Sweet watched his boss turn and walk down the hall. The man meant what he said; if he blew this, he was finished. The threat lingered for only a moment as it was quickly replaced by the realization that he would finally have a chance to command SOCOM without interference from Johnson and the M & M boys.

Whistling as he walked out of the office and headed for the elevator, the thought lifted his spirits. He would be in Florida within two hours—and he would be in command.

"Oh, Jonathan, you shouldn't have," said Helen Cantrell as the desk clerk handed her the bouquet of white roses.

"Just an old man's way of saying thank you for providing him with such wonderful company last night. I can't remember when I've enjoyed an evening more," smiled Johnson.

She returned the smile and took his hand in hers. "That goes double for me, Jonathan." Leaning forward she gave him a kiss on the cheek.

Johnson was tempted to take her in his arms right there and kiss her passionately to show her how he really felt. Their night out on the town had revitalized feelings and desires he had long since forgotten. Helen Cantrell had easily and totally stolen his heart. There was the expected hesitation at the door of her hotel room last night as he saw the uncertainty in her eyes. He knew she liked him; however, there was confusion mixed with desire registering in her eyes as she contemplated whether or not to take this man she had only know a short time into her bed.

All this had made him feel as if he were pressuring her. That was the last thing he wanted to do. He solved the dilemma for her with a simple kiss on the cheek and the promise to have breakfast with her this morning. It was a reluctant decision on his part, but one that he now realized had been correct.

The desk clerk suggested that she allow the bellboy to take the roses to her room while they had breakfast. Pausing to smell their aroma once more, she gave them to the boy and took Johnson's hand as they went into the dining room. Once seated, she smiled across at him and said, "Jonathan, I appreciate what you did last night. I won't lie to you, I was very vulnerable last night. If you had . . ."

"That's all right, Helen, you don't have to explain. Things were happening so fast. I just thought maybe it was best if we slowed it down a little bit. I didn't want you to feel you were obligated in any way."

Patting the back of his hand gently, she said tearfully, "Oh, dear Jonathan, always the perfect gentleman. They say there are no heroes left among us. You are a wonderful man, General J. J. Johnson."

They stared romantically at each other. She squeezed his strong hand in both of hers, releasing it only when the waiter arrived to take their order. All through breakfast they cast knowing glances at each other as they ate and talked about their jobs and where they were from. Helen was a senior bookkeeper for the logistics branch at Fort Benning, Georgia, and held the civilian rank of GS-14. She was presently on a two-week vacation.

"Helen, I want you to know that . . ." Johnson was interrupted by a series of soft tones omitted by the beeper inside his jacket. A waiter at a nearby table recognized the sound, brought a telephone to the table, and plugged it in for Johnson. The general nodded his appreciation as the waiter departed.

"Please excuse me, Helen, but modern technology calls."

She smiled as she stood. "That's fine, Jonathan. I have to run to the ladies' room anyway."

Only two people had his beeper number, Secretary Bowers and General Sweet. He called Bowers. The phone rang once.

"Secretary Bowers here."

"Charlie, J. J. Johnson, what's up?"

Johnson noticed the urgency in Bowers's voice. "Jonathan—thank God! Listen, you've got to get to the White House right away. The President has called an emergency meeting of his military advisors. This is hot, Jonathan. Get here as quickly as you can—good-bye."

Helen was returning to the table as Johnson lowered the receiver, stared at it a moment, then replaced it on the cradle. "Important?" she asked as she sat down.

"Yes, I'm afraid I'm going to have to go, Helen."

Helen had been married to a military man for over twenty years and recognized the secretive tone in his voice. He stood, walked around the table, and politely pulled her chair back for her. They left the restaurant and walked out into the lobby. Holding hands as if they were two high school kids on a first date, Johnson tried to mask the sadness he felt at having to leave her.

"Helen, I'm sorry about this. I had hoped we'd have the morning together. I'm not sure how long this business may take. Could I call you later? Maybe we could go to dinner again tonight."

Pressing his strong hand, she smiled at him as she said, "I'd be terribly disappointed if you didn't call, Jonathan."

Even before he realized it, Johnson leaned forward and kissed her. "You're wonderful," he said as he turned and walked for the front doors.

Helen stood watching him go across the lobby, her hand gently touching the spot where he had kissed her. Once again, the instincts born of a woman accustomed to military life and its uncertainty surfaced as she watched him go out the doors. Softly she whispered, "Please be careful, Jonathan."

A feeble scream made its way to the platform of the control tower where Kruger and Kaufman stood, each with his foot on the railing and a cigarette in his hand. It was early morning now, and they stared down at the row of bodies that had been removed from the troop barracks directly across from the tower. Twenty-six government soldiers had been killed in that one building alone. All told, the body count had been 131. Two tall black Simba mercenaries came out of the building laughing as they zipped up their pants. Another tortured scream came from inside. Kruger exhaled a slow steady stream of smoke from his lips as he watched the two men walk away.

"Just think, Adolf, there was a time when you and I were killing those black bastards by the hundreds in the Congo—now they work for us."

Kaufman looked off in the direction of the rising sun as if he had not heard Kruger's remark. Another pleading whimper came from the doorway across from them. A sudden sadness swept over the big man as he thought of the indignities being heaped upon the young Frenchman. The pilot had proved to be more of a man than either Kaufman or Kruger had first thought. The boy had endured the first hour of the torture remarkably well and had refused steadfastly to answer even the most insignificant questions about his name and age. This stubbornness had only delighted Kruger, who, although a sadistic bastard, admired courage in any man. At the end of the first hour, Kruger took a thirty-minute break from his work to go onto the platform and smoke while Ching revived the unconscious boy. The mercenary medic applied compresses to stop the bleeding from the open wounds from Kruger's razor-sharp knife.

It had proved a monumental task for the medicine man. There were four deep slashes in the chest area, two vertical and two horizontal, as if Kruger had planned to play tic-tac-toe on the man's chest. Another penetrating gash ran the length of the left arm from the shoulder to the back of the wrist. Through all of this, tears had streamed down the boy's face, but he had not muttered a sound. Undaunted by his silence, the Ice Man moved to the boy's right hand and turned the edge of his blade inward, placing it between the spread fingers of his thumb and index fingers. He then asked a question. There was no reply. The blade was pushed forward slightly and jerked upward at the same instant, serving the tendons. Then the knife was shifted to the next two fingers and the next and the next until, having run out of fingers Kruger went to the spaces between the toes. It was after cutting the last toe that the young Frenchman truly earned a measure of respect from the hard-ened men in the room. Kruger laughingly asked a question and the pilot spat in his face. Wiping the saliva and blood mixture from his face, Kruger, in a moment of frustration, placed the blade lengthwise across the toes of the boy's left foot and stomped on the back of the knife neatly severing all five toes from the flyer's foot.

It was at that point that Kruger realized he was losing control. The boy passed out. Ching was ordered to revive him while Kruger went out for a cigarette and a breath of fresh air. Kaufman was beginning to feel a sense of pity for the boy. Although the pilot had shown a resolve that was worthy of their respect, everyone in the room knew that in the end the Ice Man would win.

The second round of questioning began in earnest when Kruger walked back into the room. He went straight to the

revived pilot and cut off his right ear, dangling it in front of the
boy's startled eyes. There was a whimper—this first sign of
weakness brought a smile to Kruger's face and a crazed look to
his eyes. Had it not been for the tower radio coming to life with
a request for a radio check from the capital of N'Djamena, the
madness would have gone on for hours. Instead, Kruger found
it necessary to expedite the procedure. They found the code
books and the CEOI communications instructions; however,
they also knew that every code had a word or procedure
warning system built in to it to alert the different stations that
something was wrong or that they were sending their traffic
under duress. Kruger was certain the pilot knew what those
warning codes were.

While Kruger continued to work on the boy, one of the
mercenaries pulled the cables from a lamp, stripped back the
insulation, and quickly raised the cover of the radio. Pressing
the mike switch, he began repeating the call signs. At the same
time shorting the wire against the metal side of the radio caused
enough static so that the only thing audible was the capital's
call sign. He hoped that the base station at N'Djamena would
write it off to bad weather conditions or faulty radio equipment
problems. It worked, but Kruger knew the capital would be
calling again—playtime was over.

Forcing the boy's mouth open, Kruger jammed the point of
the blade into the gums of the top two teeth until he hit bone.
He then pried the teeth out while at the same time grinding his
boot heel on the foot with the severed toes. Suddenly the game
had ended. The pilot, his spirit and resistance flowing out of
him as freely as the blood from his wounds, gave them all the
information they wanted. As a reward, Kruger turned the boy
over to the Simbas. They laughingly dragged his bloodstained
body down the steel steps, through the sand, and into the
building. They threw him facedown onto the bed and lined up
to take their turns with him.

Kruger jokingly asked his old friend if he was still going
over to watch the action. Kaufman did not answer, but rather
walked out onto the railing and lit a cigarette, sorry that he had
made the earlier remark. Had the pilot been a sniveling,
whining coward, begging and pleading for his life, it would not
have bothered him; but that was not the case. He, Ching, and

the others from the room felt the boy had earned a quick death, or at least better than what was being done to him now.

Kruger glanced over at his friend who had his back to him. Letting the cigarette slip from his hand and watching it spiral its way to the sand below, he remarked, "Remember, Adolf, it was you who came to me with the Simbas' request."

"I was wrong," said Kaufman without turning around. "He was a brave man."

Still facing into the sun, Kaufman heard Kruger going down the stairs. The sound of his footsteps on the steel activated a silent time clock in Kaufman's mind. Ten seconds, twenty, thirty—the laughing and cheering of the Simbas had stopped. Forty, fifty—a single shot rang out. Kaufman exhaled deeply as the tension that had built within him faded with the echo of the sound that ended the young Frenchman's nightmare.

Ching came outside looking for Kruger. Seeing he was not there, he turned to Kaufman, "Major, General Kueddei has radioed that his helicopter is five minutes out and that the column is less than three miles away."

"I know," said Kaufman as he raised his hand and pointed to the huge dust cloud that extended nearly one mile in width and rose over a hundred feet in the air. "I'll inform the commander of the message. Have there been any problems with the communications checks with the capital?"

"No, Major—everything appears normal."

Kaufman turned and headed down the steps. "Notify us if there are any problems. We will be at the headquarters building with General Kueddei if you should need us."

"Yes, sir," answered Ching who started to salute but saw no need for the formality. Kaufman was already down the stairs waving to Kruger and pointing to the north. "Kueddei!" he yelled. Kruger nodded, and the two men headed for the office of the former Chadian commander who now lay sprawled in the morning sun, three bullet holes and a bloodstain adorning the left chest pocket of his fatigues.

"Remind me to find out who shot this man," said Kruger as he stared down at the neatly spaced shots. "I want him as our marksmanship instructor when this is over. Nice grouping."

The mercenaries in the immediate area cursed as Kueddei's helicopter blew stinging sand in all directions when it landed in the center of the compound. Allowing the dust to clear, the tall, husky general opened the door of the Bell chopper and stepped out into the heat that was already starting to climb into the eighties, and it was only nine in the morning. One of the mercenaries pointed out the headquarters building for the general who was joined now by his staff officers. Flanking their leader on each side, the group walked the short distance to the office and entered. Kruger was pouring a glass of cognac. "*Bonjour*, General. Would you like a drink?"

"*Merci beaucoup*," replied Kueddei as he acknowledged Kaufman, who sat in a far corner of the room, his 9mm Uzi submachine gun resting on an uplifted knee. Handing the drink to Kueddei, Kruger lifted his glass, "To success."

"To victory," answered the general as they clicked the glasses together and downed the cognac in one swallow.

General Hissen Kueddei was a big man, nearly six feet four, with a strong chest and wide shoulders. His eyes were coal black with a penetrating glare to them that often made others around him uncomfortable. His dark black face showed the effects of desert life, but what stood out more than anything else was a vivid white scar that ran from the corner of his right eye to almost the edge of his right ear. Judging from the width of the jagged line, it had been a deep and nasty wound. Kueddei did not offer to tell Kruger how he had received the scar, and Kruger didn't ask. Some had said it had been put there by his brother, General Gaafar, during the last attempted takeover by Kueddei and his rebels. It was a subject Kruger figured was better left alone.

"Were there any problems with the convoy?" asked Kruger.

"A few minor ones," said Kueddei as he sat down at a table. "Three of the Russian tanks and two of the half-tracks broke down but I do not feel that is a problem."

Kruger sat down across from the general. The staff officers remained standing behind Kueddei. One of them nervously eyed Kaufman in the corner. One could never tell about mercenaries; their loyalties could change as quickly as the wind, a thought that was obviously running through this officer's mind as he stared at the barrel of the Uzi.

"I take it, Colonel Kruger, that our plan has succeeded and the capital is not aware that we have occupied Abeche;

otherwise, my convoy would be under air attack even as we speak."

"So far, so good, General. I'd say we're right on schedule. I see no need to divert from our original plan. Herr Kaufman will keep one of the armored battalions and two of the mechanized infantry units along with one company of the Libyan commandos here to hold the airfield while you take two tank battalions and your guerrillas to knock out the French post at Mangalme. I contacted our Libyan friends before you arrived, and they had confirmed that the legionnaires at the post are the last remaining French military unit left in the country. You should have no trouble handling them. Last reports estimate they have less than one hundred men at the old fort."

Kueddei smiled as he sat back in his chair. "Yes, I am looking forward to grinding the bastards under the wheels of our Russian tanks. Had it not been for the cursed French, we would have succeeded in our last attempt four years ago, and all of this would not be necessary now."

"Nothing personal, General, but from what I researched from the reports of that last coup attempt, your brother, General Gaafar, and his troops proved to be a formidable opponent in that little contest."

Kueddei's hand went up to the scar on his cheek at the mention of his brother's name. "Yes, that is true, Colonel. Our failure was not in our fighting ability; but, rather, our lack of success at securing the main facilities of the government in N'Djamena—primarily the airport. But of course, we did not have you and your highly trained army of mercenaries to lead an airborne assault against that objective as you plan to do now. I feel confident that the results shall be quite different this time and it shall be my brother who runs this time."

There was a knock at the door and Ching entered. Knowing the general was in the room, the Korean followed the professional rules of conduct by taking three steps into the room, clicking his heels together sharply, and snapping up a rigid salute, saying, "Sir, we have been in contact with the transport flight leader. They are thirty miles out with an ETA of ten minutes."

"Thank you, Captain Ching," replied Kruger as he returned the salute. "Have the ground crews begin refueling as soon as the pilots have shut down. Get some of the men to unload the parachute gear and line it up alongside the runway. Then have our people start getting their gear together. Make sure they run weapons checks. We'll start rigging in four hours."

"Yes, sir." Another salute and Ching was gone.

Kruger devised the plan for an airborne assault after an intensive study of after-action reports from the failed takeover attempt three years ago. Kueddei had been right; their failure to secure the main airport had led to his defeat. With the installation still in government hands the French had managed to land thousands of troops, ammunition, and supplies, as well as using the runways as a launching pad for fighters and interceptors. The planes and reinforcements had made the difference in the battle for the capital. Kueddei had lost over half of his men trying to secure that airfield; even though they were outnumbered, the Chad Army, inspired by their leader, had held their ground against overwhelming odds. That inspiring leader was General Mohammed Gaafar.

"General Kueddei, are you sure four hours will be enough time for you and your men to reach Mangalme?" asked Kruger.

"Certainly, Colonel. We will begin our attack against the French at exactly the same time you and your airborne troops lift off for the assault on the capital. I estimate that it will take us no more than one hour to grind the legionnaires beneath the treads of our tanks; afterward, we will move with all haste in a straight line for the capital. You will drive the army out of the city to the east, and directly into our guns where we shall destroy them to the last man. You have devised a brilliant plan, Colonel Kruger." Kueddei paused a moment, leaning back in his chair as he continued, "There is one other thing, Colonel Kruger, Qaddafi has asked that no members of the Egyptian community in N'Djamena be harmed during the attack on the city. He hopes to cut a deal with them after the victory."

Kruger looked over at Kaufman, then back to Kueddei. "General, my boys don't have time to sort out the ethnic groups in this business. Egyptian, Chinese, American. We're going in hard and fast. As far as I and my men are concerned, anything that moves once we're on the ground and start clearing that city is considered a pop-up target and will be dealt with appropriately. We're going in there to overthrow a government, General, not to invite a select few to a fucking tea party! The Egyptians will have to take their chances like the rest of them. Is there anything else, General?"

Kueddei shrugged his shoulders. "I am but the messenger, Colonel."

The heavy drone of aircraft engines could be heard in the distance, signaling the approach of the C-130s that carried the men and equipment that would soon rain death from the sky onto the unsuspecting people of N'Djamena.

CHAPTER 6

For Jake, York, and the men of the A-Team, it had been a long night. Sharon Chambers and Sergeant Robert "Doc" Blancher, the team medic, had managed to keep Sergeant Vickers alive through the night. Chief Hileran returned to the airfield, told the team what had happened, then brought them and their equipment back to the small clinic where they took up security positions waiting throughout the long night to see if their team sergeant would survive. Now, standing in silence, they all watched as Master Sergeant Vickers was loaded aboard a U.S. medical transport plane that Privett had arranged through the embassy in Spain. The trauma team on board assured them that Vickers's condition was stable and that he would be at a U.S. hospital in Germany before nightfall. As they were watching the rear ramp close on the C130 transport, a Chad soldier stepped up to York, gave him a message, and left. It was from Privett. He and the ambassador needed them back at the embassy immediately. Privett sent an army truck so the entire team could ride back with them. Passing the note to Jake, he walked over to Hileran. "Chief, have the boys load up on the truck out front. We're going back to the embassy."

Jake read the note and took Sharon Chambers by the arm as he said, "You'd better come along with us, Sharon. I've got a feeling this town is about to become very unhealthy for Americans. You'll be safer with us."

The nurse didn't argue the point. Jake was right, there was something in the air. She could feel it. The team threw their gear into the back and climbed aboard the deuce-and-a-half, while Sharon rode up front with Jake and the Chadian soldier who had delivered the message. If the people of N'Djamena were as worried as the Americans, they weren't showing it. From all outward appearances, everything seemed normal as the truck made its way from the airport and along the busy crowded streets of the capital.

Ambassador Frugerson had doubled the guard at the entrance to the embassy. The marines were in full combat gear, including flak jackets, grenades, and automatic weapons. Two squads of government soldiers were busy replacing weather-torn sandbags with new, freshly filled ones. The front of the embassy was beginning to take on the appearance of a full-fledged combat fortress.

"My God, Jake, they're preparing for a war, aren't they?" said Sharon.

"I'm afraid so, kiddo," came the reply.

The truck was cleared through the gate and made its way around the building to the embassy motor pool. Off-loading the gear, York posted two of the team to watch over the equipment while the rest of them went inside. Privett was on the secure phone talking with someone at the State Department in Washington via SATCOM. General Gaafar and Frugerson were across the room going over a huge map of Chad that hung on the wall. Seeing them enter, Gaafar motioned for the officers to join him. Captain York turned to Doc Blancher. "Doc, you're the senior man on the team now. That makes you the team daddy. It looks like we may be here awhile. There's a little snack bar down in the basement. Why don't you take Miss Chambers and the boys down for some coffee. Don't forget Weathers and Peterson—somebody take them some coffee too, OK?"

"Yes, sir. Ms. Chambers, would you do us the honor of joining us for coffee?" Sharon smiled as she took Doc's arm in hers and said, "What girl in her right mind could say no to being surrounded by seven gorgeous hunks—lead the way, Doctor."

Fred Calhoun entered just as Privett was hanging up the phone.

"Fred, I'm glad you're here. It saves me the trouble of having to send someone for you. Come with me." Privett and

Calhoun joined the others at the map. General Gaafar was explaining the situation to the newly arrived officers.

"So you see, Captain York, it was not until after the third routine communications contact with Abeche that my signal officer began to suspect there was a problem at the air base. The first one that was missed at five this morning was attributed to static or faulty equipment. They thought little of it at the time. However, at the scheduled seven o'clock contact, Abeche sent us the incorrect authentication code, the one developed by your Captain Tanner and his communications NCO. When our operator asked for verification, they replied with the same incorrect code."

"And no one reported this to you, General?" asked Jake.

"No, Commander. I'm afraid my signal officer allowed his friendship with the communications officer at Abeche to override his logic. He had no desire to cause trouble for his friend and believed it to be a simple mistake by one of the younger operators."

"Makes sense to me, General," said York. "Our boys have been know to do the same thing on occasion."

"Thank you for your understanding, Captain. I suspect it is a problem in all armies. However, when the same thing occurred at nine o'clock, I should have been informed immediately, but unfortunately, the officer decided to wait until the eleven o'clock contact to be sure. Had it not been for one of the operators being overheard while talking about the matter, there is no telling how long it would have been before we found out."

"Shit!" cried Calhoun. "I'd have the bastard shot for that."

"I did," said Gaafar in a matter-of-fact tone. "Less than half an hour ago, regrettably, I might add, as he was my wife's only brother. I shall have to find a way to break the news to her. Perhaps I can say it was done on your recommendation, Mr. Calhoun."

Calhoun had not yet recovered from the shock of knowing that Gaafar had actually killed the man. God, he hadn't really meant what he had said. He had only wanted to impress York and the others. The man was sweating heavily as he raised his hands and nervously said, "No! No, General, that's quite all right. I have no desire to take credit for anything like that."

"I thought not," said Gaafar as he continued, "I am sure

there is no need to tell you that the eleven o'clock contact was also incorrect. Therefore, gentlemen, I believe we can assume that my brother, General Kueddei, has managed to secure the Abeche airfield and, along with it, over half of our air force."

"My god," sighed Frugerson. "Why didn't you tell us that earlier, General. Privett was just on the phone with the State Department. If we had known Abeche had been captured, we could have requested U.S. military support."

"I am sorry, Mr. Frugerson. What I have suggested is only an assumption on my part. I have no concrete information to support that conclusion. Therefore, I plan to order two of our reconnaissance planes to conduct a photo overflight of the base at Abeche. We shall then analyze the photos and go from there. If, as I suspect, they show my theory to be correct, you may then call your State Department and make your request."

"It wouldn't matter if you're right or wrong, General," said Privett.

Everyone in the room was facing the defense attaché now. "What are you talking about, Privett?" asked Frugerson.

"Something's up back at the White House, and I mean something big. I hinted to the State boys that we may need some U.S. backing before the week was out. They told me to hang it up—if anything goes wrong over here, we are on our own. There won't be any cavalry to the rescue."

"They bother to say why?" asked Jake.

"No, Commander, but I got the distinct impression from the man I was talking with that something along the lines of the Grenada affair was in the works."

"Well, brother, that rips it," said York. "If General Gaafar is right about Abeche and the rebels, they obviously know the French have pulled out of Chad."

"Yeah, and N'Djamena will be their next target," added Hileran.

Frugerson and Calhoun were looking a little pale as they contemplated the words of the military men around them. Privett was holding up better than the other two. He at least was attempting to contribute something of value to the situation. "What about the legionnaires at Mangalme? They are the last remaining French unit in the country. I believe they have nearly a hundred men at that old outpost. I am certain they will be needing us as much as we apparently are going to need them."

York found Mangalme on the map. "You have a good point there, Mr. Privett. General Gaafar, can you have your signal section contact the French at Mangalme and inform them of the situation? Perhaps they have additional information that can help us."

Gaafar glanced at Privett, who averted his eyes from the general. "I am sorry, Captain, but we cannot do that."

"Now, look, General, I realize that you and the French have been having a little pissing contest over the pullout, but I think it's time we drop this political snubbing of these boys simply because protocol dictates it," said Jake. "We're going to need those legionnaires, General."

"I'm afraid radio contact cannot be established with them, Commander." Gaafar paused as he stared at both Privett and Frugerson. "Not that I would hesitate to do so, were it within my power, but unfortunately we were advised to disregard any signal contact with the French at Mangalme. We changed our entire set of frequencies throughout the country. The legionnaires have no possible way of knowing what channels we are transmitting on. You see, Commander, the idea was to make them feel as if they had been totally abandoned, just as we were abandoned by them."

York glanced over at Jake who was now shaking his head slowly back and forth. "Excuse me, sir, but just whose fucking idea was that?" asked the Green Beret captain. Jake didn't have to wait for an answer. Turning to Privett and Frugerson, he said sarcastically, "Man, when you political boys want to snub somebody you go all out, don't you."

Frugerson started to say something in his defense. Judging from the looks he was getting from the officers around him, he realized he would find little sympathy from these men no matter what reasons he gave.

Chief Hileran stepped up to the map. "General, how did the French handle transportation from here to Mangalme and back?"

Everyone was staring at the map as Gaafar answered, "Normally, they flew from here to Abeche by C-130 transport and then by helicopter to Mangalme. The same procedure would then be reversed for trips to the capital."

"Well, if your theory is right, we can't very well fly into Abeche. Are there any other airstrips in the area that can handle a transport?"

"No, Mr. Hileran, I am afraid there are none."

"What are you getting at, Chief?" asked Jake.

"Well, Commander, even if we could talk to them on the radio, we'd still have to send somebody up there to talk to them face-to-face. Once we're in there and can explain the situation, I think they'll be more than happy to join us." Hileran tapped the location on the map marked Abeche. "Notice the distance between the air base and Mangalme. Now, ask yourself if you were a rebel leader about to attack a capital city and were planning to use this facility as your logical center and base of operations for launching that attack—would you, or, I should say, could you, ignore the fact that there are one hundred enemy troops less than a hundred miles away. Not just regular troops either, but French legionnaires, the best fighting force the French have."

"So, the French are right next to a time bomb and don't even know it," said York. "They won't find out until it's too late. Go ahead, Mr. Hileran, you apparently have a plan in mind."

"Yes, sir. General Gaafar, I noticed four CH-47 Chinooks and a couple of Blackhawk choppers at the end of the runway when we came in yesterday. Do you have any more?"

"Yes, but I'm afraid they are at Abeche. That was our main staging area for patrols throughout the region."

"OK, so we'll just have to make do with what we have," replied Hileran, who now took a grease pencil from the desk next to the mapboard and drew a circle around the name Bokoro. "Now, going by the scale on the legend of this map, I'd say that this small town of Bokoro is the halfway point between N'Djamena and Mangalme. I figure about one hundred and thirty miles. Is that correct?"

General Gaafar, as well as the others, were staring at the circle intently as the general nodded that the estimate was correct.

"Fine. Now, that still leaves us another one hundred and twenty or thirty miles to Mangalme. Obviously the CH-47s cannot cover the entire distance without refueling somewhere along the way. I propose that we load fifty-five-gallon drums of flight fuel on the Chinooks, fly to Bokoro, off-load the fuel, top off the tanks, and leave the remainder for the return trip from Mangalme. As for the communications problem, I would suggest that the general use one of the CM-170 Magister trainers that I saw parked near the helicopters to serve as a messenger boy. They could fly over the outpost and drop a streamer with a message and the frequencies for the helicopters, the general's base station, and the embassy communications room, that way everybody will know what's going on. That leaves only one final question, and being no more than a lowly Chief Warrant Officer, that question will have to be answered by you fellows with all the rank on your collars. Somebody is going to have to decide—do we fly troops into Mangalme or do we fly the French out?"

The room was silent for a moment as the men pondered the question. Calhoun was the first to speak, "Really, gentlemen, this whole melodramatic discussion is based on nothing more than a few letters in a code being misplaced by some communicator who obviously did not understand the system. Hell, he could have mistakenly grabbed the wrong set of codes this morning. No, I'm sorry. I fail to see where that adds up to a cry of Armageddon about to befall the capital. As for your actions concerning your signal officer, General Gaafar, I am afraid I have no choice but to advise my supervisors in Washington of the incident, and to follow whatever directives they may send in return. Now, if you will excuse me, I have more realistic matters to attend to in the village of Massaguet. Good day, gentlemen." With a smirk on his perspiring face, Calhoun wheeled about and left the room.

Frugerson moved next to the general, "General Gaafar, I will see if I can't persuade him to . . ."

Gaafar raised his hand, cutting the ambassador off. "No, Mr. Frugerson, the man is a fool! He does not recognize the situation for what it is."

"Hear, hear," nodded Jake as Doc Blancher, Sharon, and the rest of the team came back into the room.

The phone rang. Privett answered the call, then passed the receiver to General Gaafar. "It's for you, sir, your Com-Center."

York was explaining the possible situation to the team when Gaafar hung up the phone and asked for their attention.

Solemnly he asked, "Mr. Hileran, how many fuel drums will you require?"

It was as quiet as a graveyard in the room as Gaafar said, "That was my communications center. They have just received a message from a friend at the Egyptian Embassy. Less than one hour ago the crew of an Egyptian AWACS surveillance aircraft monitored a flight of ten C-130 aircraft from the Libyan base to the base at Abeche. They also reported heavy ground movement of armor and mechanized equipment around the same area. I believe there is little doubt now, gentlemen, that Abeche has fallen to the enemy. To answer your earlier question, Mr. Hileran, I am the ranking officer here and it is my desire that we initiate your plan and rescue as many of the French at Mangalme as possible. Mr. Ambassador, there are still three C-130 transports and two civilian airliners at the airport. I would advise that you gather all American personnel who you wish to evacuate and get them to the airport at once. I will have my staff alert the other embassies. Noncombatants, as well as the President and his cabinet, will be flown to Egypt immediately. I would suggest you hurry, sir, while the airport is still operational."

Frugerson seemed overwhelmed by the rapid change of events. He appeared confused and uncertain about what he should do next. Privett took him by the arm and led the man to the door where he paused and said, "We will have our people there in two hours, General."

Jake watched the men walk out, then he turned to York. "Randy, we have to get in contact with General Johnson. Maybe he can give us an idea of what's going on back there, and what, if any, help we might be able to get in here."

"I'm with you. We sure as hell are going to need help, ain't no doubt about that. Chief, I want you to plan this operation using the split-team concept. Jake and I will take half the boys with us on the choppers—you and the other half will stay back here to help General Gaafar with the defense of the capital. Doc, you'll be going with us. OK, Chief, get it cracking. We have to be in the air within the hour. General, if you could get that trainer with those frequencies on its way, it would really help us out. I want to be able to talk to those legionnaires before we get in there."

"I will take care of that now, Captain," said Gaafar as he left the room.

Hileran stopped York as he was going out the door. "Uh, Captain, what about Mr. Calhoun?"

"What about him?"

"Well, sir, I doubt if Privett will be able to reach him. He was going someplace called Massaguet when he left here. Should we send someone after him? If he misses that airlift out of here, he's stuck."

York smiled at Jake who knew what the man was thinking. "Tempting as hell isn't it?" he said with a laugh.

"Yeah, it would be a good chance to see just how big that arrogant little bastard's balls really are." York paused as if he was actually considering the idea. "Oh, hell, he wouldn't be anything but a royal pain in the ass if he stayed. Chief, you'd better send a couple of our guys after him. Since Murdock was blown all to hell yesterday, and since he threatened to report the general to Washington, he might be a little leery of going anywhere with a couple of Gaafar's boys. Make sure they know how to find the place. I don't want anybody wandering around lost out there."

"I know where it is, Captain," said Sharon. "I can ride along with them."

"Wait a minute," said Jake. "I don't think that's such a good idea, Sharon."

Flashing a smile, she stepped closer to Jake. "Did you happen to notice, Commander, that every time we are about to part company, the subject of 'balls' seems to come up."

"What?"

Stretching up on tiptoes, she gave him a kiss on the cheek. She laughed as she turned to the door and asked, "OK, boys, who's ready to take a drive in the desert?" There was a mad scramble for the door as seven Green Berets tried to follow the shapely woman through the doorway at the same time.

"Just two, gentlemen!" yelled Hileran. "Peterson—Roth, you're elected. The rest of you get back in here and put those hard-ons away. We've got work to do."

York and Mortimer walked in silence down the corridor that would take them to the ComCenter. Jake could sense the anxiety in the captain.

"Worried, Randy?"

"Yeah, I guess I am, Jake. We've got some gung ho kids on this team. They've got the heart and the determination, but that's no substitute for experience. Me, Vickers, and Doc were the only three combat vets on the team. Now Vic is already out of the game. Maybe for good, who knows?"

Mortimer tried to reassure him about Vickers. "Hell, Randy, they should be landing in Germany with Vickers anytime now. I'm sure he's doing fine. He's one tough son of a bitch, you know that. As for the kids on your team—they've got to start somewhere—we did."

York stopped, glanced at Jake, and leaned back against the wall. "You're right, Jake, but you heard what Privett said. Something big is going down back home, and you can bet your ass when it goes down there won't be anybody that gives a flying fuck about a team of Green Berets and a handful of legionnaires slugging it out in this oversize sandbox. I guess that's what's really bothering me. Dying is part of the business. I know that, Jake. It's just the thought of dying and no one taking the time to even notice that pisses me off—you know what I mean?"

Jake hadn't thought of it quite that way before, but Randy had a point. It would be real simple for them to be overlooked in an international crises. The idea left Jake with a bad taste in his mouth, but he hid it from York as he put his hand on the captain's shoulder and said, "Well, the rest of the fucking world can write us off but I know one guy who won't!"

York forced a smile at one corner of his mouth as he stepped away from the wall. "Q-Tip," he said quietly.

"You got it—let's make that call."

The Chiefs of Staff and their aides poured out of the presidential conference room like a herd of Wall Street brokers who'd just got a hot tip on the price of gold. The President's decision to invade Panama had been like sweet music to the ears of the military warlords. At last, they would have a chance to put into practice all the theories they had developed through humdrum years of training and evaluating. It would be a chance to test the true mettle of the men who had spent months and years preparing for just such an occasion. A live-fire exercise where real bullets, rather than beams of light and squealing boxes, would provide a true test of the soldier's ability. The color of blood would illuminate their mistakes. The President wanted a primary and alternate military plan ready for presentation in the next twenty-four hours. The invasion would begin immediately upon acceptance of the plan. Once put into action, it would not be halted until Noriega was captured and the entire country under U.S. control.

J. J. Johnson was apprehensive; images of Grenada flashed before his eyes at the beginning of the meeting making him feel as if he were watching a rerun of a bad movie. The President was only out of the room two minutes before the bickering began about who would do what and who would have the responsibility to provide this or that for the troops. It was a short-lived fiasco, however. It was cut short by Secretary Bowers who took complete control of the situation. He expressed the confidence of the President that there would not be another Grenada screwup and that joint cooperation would guarantee success. Anyone in the room who felt they could not fully support the joint cooperation theory would have an open appointment with the President immediately following the conclusion of the invasion. Although he never stated it as such, Bowers hinted that any officer in the room that cared to fill that appointment time had better be prepared to find another career.

J. J. Johnson was exiting the conference room with Sweet when Bowers's aide approached. "General Johnson, sir, the Secretary would like for you to join him in the President's office immediately."

"What about me?" asked Sweet.

"He requested General Johnson only, sir."

"Sweet, get in touch with Major Ericson at Tampa. Have him pull everything we have on Panama—reports, maps, the works. I want target analysis and acquisition photos. You got it?"

Sweet, unaccustomed to being utilized for anything of importance by Johnson, was taken by surprise at the order. "Uh, yes, General, I can do that."

"Tell Ericson we'll be on the first available flight to Tampa, and to cancel all passes and leaves. Everyone is restricted to the base. I'll meet you back at the hotel in one hour. Have our bags packed and ready to leave. That's all, General," said Johnson as he turned and walked away with the aide leaving Sweet with a bewildered look on his face.

General Garland and the NSC man, Burrows, joined Sweet near the door.

"What was all that about?" asked Burrows.

"The President wants to see him. I have no idea why."

"Why, Raymond, are you ready to take over SOCOM's part of this action?" asked Garland.

"Ha! you are joking of course, General. I was just given a list of orders that included packing that man's suitcase. That would hardly suggest to me that General Johnson is about to hand over his command."

Burrows was smiling that shit-eating grin again as he said, "Ah, but your commander now has two very serious problems on his hands, and even he isn't so talented that he can handle both at the same time. You should be smiling, Sweet, you've finally ended up in a no-lose situation. Either way it goes, you will come out smelling like a rose."

Sweet was totally lost. Looking to Garland he asked, "What the hell is he talking about, John?"

Garland was laughing as he placed his hand on Sweet's shoulder. They started down the hallway. "Let's just say that next Christmas you really should send Muammar Qaddafi a card."

J. J. Johnson stood and walked across the floor of the oval office. Bowers sat in the chair next to the President's desk as the top executive slowly turned a pencil aimlessly between his fingers and said, "General, I can understand your concern, but you must realize, in less than forty-eight hours the United States is going to invade a Central American country. I need not tell you of the complexities involved in such an undertaking. My God, Jonathan, you were at Grenada. You saw firsthand what can happen. I don't want that to happen this time. I am truly sorry, but there is no way I can divert another force to Chad at this time. My staff and I are going to have to spend hours on the phones explaining our actions to every Latin leader in Central and South America, as it is. Can you imagine the uproar if at the same time we invade Panama, I insert combat troops into a Moslem country? My god, the whole world would go crazy."

Johnson was standing at the corner of the President's desk.

"Yes, sir, maybe they would, but I don't think Captain York,

Commander Mortimer, the team, or any American who's going to be caught up in that bloodbath over there would really give a damn about public opinion—and that's what it will be, sir, a bloodbath. You've already got one diplomat dead and a soldier teetering on the brink. Egyptian and Israeli intelligence report heavy movement of aircraft and armor. It's going to be a full-fledged invasion, Mr. President, and our people are going to be caught in the middle. Without the French and African forces to slow them down, the rebels and Qaddafi will be in the capital in a matter of days. There has to be something we can do, sir? Hell, if nothing else, at least get them out of harm's way—send in evacuation aircraft and a squadron of fighters to cover them until they are out of there."

The President let the pencil fall free and stood, walking to the window that overlooked Pennsylvania Avenue. Without turning away from the window, he spoke quietly, "Jonathan . . . I . . . We can evacuate the civilians, but your—your people are going to have to stay."

Johnson looked quickly at Bowers who looked away. Crossing the room in three strides, the general now stood at the President's side as he said, "Excuse me, sir, but what did you just say?"

Resting his hands on the mantel in front of the window, the President leaned forward and lowered his head.

"I said your people cannot be evacuated, General. Since the French have pulled out of Chad, the responsibility has fallen upon us. The other countries in the region will be watching to see if we are as committed to that area of the world as the French once were. We cannot turn tail and run at the first sign of trouble. By leaving your people in there, we can demonstrate our resolve to stand by our allies. Now, Jonathan, I know . . ."

Johnson was struggling to control the anger that was building within him. "Excuse me, sir, you realize of course that without our support you are in effect condemning those men to certain death. Personally, sir, I think that sucks!"

Bowers jumped to his feet. "General Johnson! I will remind you that you are addressing the President of the United States, sir."

The President raised his hand, "No, no, Clinton, the general's selection of terminology is quite appropriate; it does suck! But I'm afraid there is little that can be done. I assure you, Jonathan, if there were any way possible, I would not hesitate to intervene in Chad, but Panama has to be our first priority. I'm sorry."

There was no mistaking the sincerity in the man's voice. Johnson knew that as he calmly replied, "I understand, sir. I don't envy you this job, Mr. President."

The room quieted when the phone rang. Bowers picked it up, then nodded to the President. "It's the communications section, sir. They have Commander Mortimer on the phone via satellite for General Johnson. Would you mind if he took the call here in your office?"

"No, by all means, please do, General. We can get an update on the situation firsthand. Put the call on the speaker, Mr. Bowers."

The three men gathered around the desk as Jake's voice came over the box, "General Johnson, I have Captain York with me, sir. We assume that you have been made aware of the incident that occurred at the ambassador's residence yesterday afternoon."

"Yes, I have been fully briefed on that, Commander. I am in the President's office right now. He and Secretary Bowers are with me and monitoring this conversation. Jake, have there been any new developments?"

"Yes, sir, I'm afraid so. All indications are that the rebels have captured Abeche and the air base there. This situation is changing almost hourly, sir. Mr. Privett, the defense attaché, has already started moving the embassy staff and American civilians out to the airport for immediate evacuation to Egypt. We're not sure how large the rebel force is, or what exactly we're up against; however, General Gaafar believes we could be facing an army of four or five thousand if this is an all-out offensive."

"Damn, Abeche is the second largest city in Chad," whispered Bowers.

"Jake, have there been any reports of enemy contact?" asked Johnson.

"Well, no, sir, not yet, but we've been receiving some pretty disturbing messages from Egyptian intelligence. There's no doubt something is going on, sir. If the rebels do control Abeche, then they also control over half of this country's air force. You can bet our boy Qaddafi has volunteered a few of his pilots to fly those planes in support of the rebels. Captain York and I believe that air attacks on the capital are inevitable. That's why we're trying to get all the civilians out of here as quickly as we can."

Bowers leaned forward and asked, "Commander, you say Mr. Privett is handling the evacuation. Where is the ambassador?"

"Sir, I'm afraid the shock of Mr. Murdock's rather sudden death combined with the rebel takeover of Abeche and the impending attack on the city proved too much for Mr. Frugerson. He had to be sedated. He will be going out on the first plane. Mr. Privett has assumed the primary duties at this time, sir."

"I—I see, thank you, Commander," said Bowers as he straightened and glanced worriedly at the President.

"General Johnson, we've kind of got the idea that something big is going on back there. Since we are on the scramble secure box, sir, do you think you might be able to let us in on it?"

Bowers frowned as Johnson looked to the President for approval.

"Go ahead, General, that's about the only damn thing I can do for them," said the President.

"Yes, Commander, we're going to invade Panama."

There was silence on the line. It seemed a full minute before Jake's voice came back over the box.

"B.J. always said that Pineapple Face was going to push it too far one of these days. I guess he knew what he was talking about. Well, guess that kind of leaves us swinging in the breeze, doesn't it, sir?"

Johnson's head sank lower as he stared at the desktop he was leaning on. "Jake, I . . ."

"Oh, hell, General, you don't have to explain anything. Be kind of hard for the President to justify two damn invasions at the same time. We know that. Don't you worry about us, sir. We're going to link up with some legionnaires down the road after we sign off. We figure between one A-Team and a hundred of those Legion boys, these rebels are in for a long day at the office."

Johnson bit his lower lip as he tried to think of something inspiring to say, but there wasn't anything left to say. It was apparent that both Jake and Captain York knew where they stood now. At no time had either man questioned the situation, nor asked for permission to pull the team out. They were U.S. officers; more than that, they were SOCOM officers. They knew why they were there and what was expected of them. They would not question that.

The President now spoke, "Commander Mortimer, Captain York, this is the President. I want you gentlemen to know that I will make every effort to secure some type of assistance for you and the Chadian people. You will not be forgotten, gentlemen. You have my personal word on that."

"Thank you, sir. We will hold out as long as possible. Rest assured, Mr. President, that Captain York and I both can appreciate your situation. Good luck in Panama, sir."

"Thank you, Commander. Please let your men know that they will be with me in my prayers."

"Roger that, sir. General Johnson, we'll keep Tampa advised of the situation. Negative further. This is Chad, out."

The steady hiss of the speaker box seemed to fill the room before Bowers reached over and switched off the box. He sat back down in his chair near the desk. The President returned to his place by the window, while Johnson remained standing and staring at the phone. He wasn't ready to write Mortimer and that team off, yet.

"Clinton, what about the United Nations? Couldn't we call for an emergency session and try to get them to run some U.N. troops in there?" asked Johnson.

The President wheeled around to await the Secretary's answer.

"You know, Jonathan, you may just have something there. Now, I'm not guaranteeing anything, so don't get your hopes up. It's going to seem a little strange for us to go in there and scream about Libya supporting an invasion in Chad while we're in the middle of an invasion of our own."

"But they're two totally different situations, Clinton," cried Johnson.

"Yes, from our point of view, Jonathan, but will a majority of the U.N. delegates see it that way, that is the question. An invasion by any other name is still an invasion, General."

The President was rubbing his chin as he crossed the room

and sat down behind his desk. Adjusting his glasses he looked up at Johnson.

"General Johnson, I am going to ask you a question, and I want you to seriously consider the consequences of your decision before you give me an answer. I am fully aware of the problem concerning General Sweet and his purpose for being placed in SOCOM to serve as your deputy. The question is, General Johnson, are you willing to turn over command of SOCOM to General Sweet and allow him to handle your end of the Panama invasion in exchange for a chance at saving your people in Chad?"

It was apparent that the President's question left both men stunned and surprised. Johnson's first instinct was to scream, "Hell no!" at the top of his lungs, but a sudden vision of Jake and the A-Team trying to fend off five thousand screaming rebels restrained the instinct.

"Sir, may I ask what you have in mind before I am committed to answering that question?"

"Fair enough, General. If you should agree to the proposal, I will dispatch you to Zaire, where, with a little political arm-twisting on my part and the use of your well-known talents of persuasion, we shall endeavor to convince the Organization of African Unity that a rebel victory in Chad will ultimately lead to a Qaddafi invasion of Nigeria, Cameroon, and Niger. The domino theory of Southeast Asia, only this one applied in Africa. When I was the director of the CIA, I seemed to remember that on a number of occasions Colonel Qaddafi tried to incite Moslem rebellion in Nigeria. He was hardly what they would consider a friend. I can provide you with the political and financial incentives, but it will still be up to you to convince the OAU that it is in their best interest to form a joint task force from Zaire and Nigeria to intervene in Chad. Needless to say, General, it is a gamble. There are no guarantees, but given our present situation, it may be the only chance your people have. In order to accomplish this, you will have to relinquish command of SOCOM for the Panama invasion. The decision now falls upon you, General Johnson."

Johnson cupped his hands behind his back and strolled to the window. His mind was reeling with all the possibilities while at the same time it was calculating the detrimental effects of

having General Sweet in charge of SOCOM during an operation as complex as the Panama invasion was sure to become.

Seconds of silence passed into minutes as the white-headed
commander wrestled with the problem that was sure to affect
the only thing he really cared about, the lives of his men. It was
a struggle inherent in men of command. After he had made his
decision, Johnson approached the President's desk.

"Mr. President, I accept these terms and request permission
to initiate your plan immediately."

"How many men will you need to go with you, General?"
asked the President.

"Only only, sir, Major B. J. Mattson. He is presently on
leave, but I am certain he will be more than willing to
accompany me on the trip." Johnson paused a moment,
glancing down at the right side of the desk, he asked, "Mr.
President, is the tape recorder running?"

Bowers sat forward with a shocked expression covering his
face as he cried, "Jonathan!"

The President only grinned. He had certainly chosen the
right man to run the Special Operations Command. Still
grinning, he said, "If you have something to say for the
'official record,' General, please do so."

"Sir, although I am turning over temporary command of
SOCOM to General Sweet, I wish to state, 'for the record,'
that I fully intend to instruct my officers that while under his
command they are to perform to their utmost abilities. However, they shall be free to utilize and initiate their own
judgment should they be given a mission or an order that they
feel is militarily unsound and detrimental to the lives of their
men. They shall do this without the threat of reprimand or
court-martial. I, and I alone, Mr. President, shall accept full
and complete responsibility for whatever action my officers
may deem necessary."

Secretary Bowers sat silently shaking his weary head from
side to side. The President removed his glasses and rubbed at
his tired, bloodshot eyes as he asked, "Do you feel that given
your advice, your officers will do that, General?"

"Yes, sir. Special Operations Command is made up of only
the highest caliber officers within the military structure. They
evaluate; they calculate; they think, sir. That's why we Special
Ops people are considered a threat by more than a few of the

idiots running loose up here, Mr. President—present company excluded, of course."

Laying his glasses on the desk and smiling, the President looked up at the old warrior and said, "Certainly don't sugar-coat your opinions, do you, General? Very well, so be it, you know your men better than I do. When can you leave?"

J. J. Johnson felt as if the weight of the world had been lifted from his shoulders. At no time had he forgotten where he was and to whom he was speaking. Feeling that he had secured a small but important victory for the men who would be left under Sweet's command, he anxiously replied, "Within the hour, sir."

"Good. Secretary Bowers and I will draft the letter for presentation to the OAU. Both countries have already made their yearly request for foreign aid. Full agreement to those requests will be included in the letter, as well as my personal guarantee that we will replace any and all equipment losses incurred should they decide to intervene on Chad's behalf. Of course, that will include additional financial aid as well." The President stood and extended his hand across the desk, "Jonathan, I pray that your mission is successful. If Commander Mortimer and Captain York are typical of the men under your command, you are a fortunate man. This country and I, likewise. Good luck, General."

Johnson snapped to attention, saluted, then stepped forward and shook the commander in chief's hand firmly before leaving the office with Bowers.

"I'll have the letter delivered to your hotel by special courier within the hour. What about flight arrangements, Jonathan?" asked Bowers as he struggled to keep up with the big man's long strides.

"I won't have time to be bothered with flight schedules and connections, Clinton. I'm going to need a release from you or the President for one of the CIA's Leer jets. I'll fly it myself. I need the flight time anyway. We'll need unlimited refueling authorization. I'll contact Major Mattson from the hotel and have him standing by at Tinker Air Force Base in Oklahoma City. A quick hop down there to pick him up and then on to MacDill and SOCOM Headquarters." Johnson suddenly stopped in the middle of the hallway and looked at his old college friend, "Clinton, I was serious about what I said about the men under Sweet's command. The responsibility for their actions will be mine and mine alone. Should anything happen to me, a signed and sealed letter formally stating that decision will be placed in the center drawer of my desk before I leave for Africa. If anything should go wrong, I want your guarantee that you will personally recover that document and use it. Will you do that, Clinton?"

The Secretary nodded that he would. He suddenly found himself unable to speak. Johnson's words had had a profound effect on him. During all the running about and talking to find solutions to these difficult problems, he had not even compre- hended the possibility that his old friend, J. J. Johnson, just might get himself killed before this was over.

Noting the gloomy look that besieged Bowers, Johnson slapped him on the back, "Jesus, Clinton, I only mentioned it as a precaution. You don't think I'm going to let those bastards put a graduate of Oklahoma University between a rock and a hard place? Not on your life."

Johnson's humorous attitude brought a sigh of relief and a smile to Bowers's face. Wanting to maintain that lighthearted feeling as long as possible, he waited until they started walking again, then asked, "You say they can't outmaneuver an OU man?"

"You got that right. Too fast for 'em."

"Yeah, but you're taking B. J. Mattson along, Jonathan," said Bowers.

"So what's wrong with that?"

"B. J.'s a Texas A and M boy, and you know how clumsy they are," laughed the Secretary.

"Damn, that's right, Clinton. Reckon I'll have to make sure they put him on a short camel. That way he won't fall so far."

The guards at the front doors of the White House figured something serious was going on by the number of VIPs who had been in and out all morning. But judging from the side-splitting laughter of the two men who just left, they must have been mistaken.

"Gosh, Dad, that's the biggest catfish I've ever caught out of Grandma's pond. He must be twenty inches long."

B.J. snapped the Polaroid, then laid the camera down. He carefully reached into the cat's big mouth and removed the barbed hook. The excitement and pride in his son's voice sent a warm feeling of closeness through him. He couldn't remember the last time they had spent this much time together doing the things that other fathers and sons took for granted. B. J. Mattson was loving every minute of it.

"Well, what do you think? Should we call *Sports Illustrated* and have them send out a photographer, or toss the old boy back and give him another chance?" asked B.J.

Jason's eyes studied the huge fish with the long whiskers as his father held it before him. Then he looked back across the large pond and its shimmering calm waters. The feeling of the battle that had happened only moments ago was still sending tingles through his hands. The old cat had fought him every inch of the way, and now he had to decide its fate. "Dad, how long do catfish live?" he asked.

Surprised by the question, B.J. smiled at his son as he answered, "Oh, I'm not sure, Jas—but I hear it's a pretty long time. Why?"

"Well, if I let him go, do you think he'll still be here when I get older and have a son?"

B.J. reached out and put his hand on Jason's shoulder. "It's possible, son. I hope you're not planning on having a son real soon," laughed B.J. "I mean, sixteen is a little young to be getting married. I don't think your mama's gonna go for that."

Jason laughed that special laugh that B.J. loved as he slid his arm around his father's waist. "Oh, Dad! No. What I mean is, catching this old-timer meant more because you were here with me when I did it. That—that kinda makes it special, Dad. Watching your face while I wrestled him back and forth and letting me do it all by myself made it all special. Oh, I don't know, I was hoping you would know what I meant. I guess what I'm trying to say is, I love you, Dad."

B.J. pulled his son tight to his side and looked away as water began to well up in his eyes. This was what Charlotte had been trying to tell him all these years. Time was slipping away for moments like this and once gone they could never be recaptured again. Wiping his eyes, he handed the fish to Jason, "I love you too, son. Now what do you think about old whiskers here?"

Taking the cat from his father, the boy stepped to the edge of the water and knelt down. The fish, sensing freedom near, jerked a couple times in a vain effort to break the grip that restrained him. Jason stroked him gently as he whispered, "Thank you, Mr. Cat." He slowly eased the fish into the water and let him swim away. He watched the turbulent water return to calm, then he stood and smiled at his dad. "I'm going to bring my son here one day and we'll catch him again."

"Not a doubt in my mind, tiger. You ready to go to the house? Mom and Grandma should have lunch ready by now."

"Sure, Dad, and I'm hungry, too. That old cat just about wore me out."

They talked about the fish all the way back to the house. As they pulled up to the front yard of the farm, the boy was bubbling over with excitement and could hardly wait to get into the house to tell everyone about the giant he had caught. With the dust of the driveway still swirling around the Ford Bronco, Jason hopped out, then paused at the door as he looked back at his father, "Thanks, Dad."

"For what, son?" asked B.J. as he shut off the ignition.

"Just for being the greatest dad in the world, I guess. Can we go fishing again in the morning?"

"Sure, sport, why not? We'll get up real early in the . . ." B.J. stopped talking as Charlotte came hurriedly out of the house and yelled, "B.J., General Johnson is on the phone from Washington. He says it's an emergency, Jake's in some kind of trouble."

Jason's boyish grin suddenly disappeared. He knew there would be no fishing in the morning. He watched as his father leaped from the truck and bounded the stairs three at a time passing his mother and running into the house. Slowly closing the door on the Bronco, Jason leaned his head on his folded arms. Charlotte felt as if her heart would break as she moved slowly down the steps and to her son. There was no sound, but she could tell he was fighting back the urge to beat his fist on the vehicle. Placing a hand on his back, she rubbed it in a gentle circle and tried to find the words to take away the pain. A pain she knew all too well. But there were no words. Turning away before she started to cry, she went back into the house.

B.J. was already off the phone and in the back bedroom throwing some clothes into a faded kit bag. He paused as she entered the room and looked up into her tormented face. "It never ends does it, B.J.? You know your son knows what this means. He's trying to hide it, but it's tearing him apart."

The words were like a red-hot poker piercing his heart. Easing himself down onto the edge of the bed, he sat with his hands interlocked as he stared at the floor. "Jake's in trouble, Charlotte."

Moving to the dresser, Charlotte leaned back against the polished cherry wood as she spoke. There was an edge of bitterness in her voice, "And B. J. Mattson is the only man who can save his ass, is that it?"

"You're closer to being right than you know, Charlotte."

"But of course you can't explain that, right? I mean it's some big classified secret, and you're leaving for someplace, you don't know how long it will take or when you'll be back. Damn it, B.J.! How long do you expect us to keep living this way? I thought . . . I thought you understood, these last two weeks have been so wonderful—or at least for us they have. We've actually been a family for once. Can't you just tell them no?"

B.J. never looked up. "Charlotte, this is Jake we're talking about—my partner, my friend. Don't you understand; I have to do this!"

Tears were flowing down her cheeks as Charlotte stepped away from the dresser. Raising her voice, she said, "And what about that boy out there? Isn't he your friend? Your partner? Or is he just a kid you drop by to take fishing once in a while?" Unable to contain herself, her voice cracking as she sobbed, "Damn you, B.J.! Damn you to hell! I wish that you had never come here." She was crying loudly as she stormed out of the room. B.J. sighed deeply. The words had cut deeper than any knife ever would. She just didn't understand. Maybe if he told her the whole story. No, it wouldn't matter. He would still have to leave. Looking up, he saw Jason standing in the doorway.

"Can I help you pack, Dad?"

Mattson forced back the urge to jump off the bed and clutch his son to him. It would only make things harder than they already were.

"No, that's OK, son, but thanks for the offer. I'm—I'm sorry about this, Jason."

"Don't be, Dad. If you were in trouble, Jake would do everything he could to help you. I know that. Mom'll be okay.

We'll talk after you're gone. I'll make her understand. You'll see." The boy suddenly seemed older than his years. He came over to his father and hugged his neck. "Dad, if you don't mind, I think I'll say bye now. Maybe I'll walk back down to the pond and sit for a while. I understand, Dad, really I do. It's just that seeing you leave would be . . . well . . ."

Jason was the first to pull away from the embrace. "Be careful, Dad," he said as he walked out of the room and onto the front porch where he turned and took one final look at his father. He broke into a run across the yard and out into the field that led to the pond. Tears streamed along the sides of each cheek.

Charlotte's dad came in and shook hands with B.J. Charlotte asked him to drive B.J. to Tinker Air Base. She could not bring herself to do it. B.J. told him he would be out in a few minutes. He removed the last of his shirts from the dresser. Turning to put them into the kit bag, he suddenly stopped. There, on top of the other clothes, was a Polaroid picture of a smiling boy and old Whiskers . . .

CHAPTER 7

Jake and Captain York leaned forward and stared down at the old adobe fortress that the legionnaires called home. It wasn't much. The south wall had collapsed and the ramparts to the east were practically buried by a mountain of sand. There were five buildings situated almost in the center, with two smaller ones near the north gate. York tapped Jake on the shoulder and pointed to the two mortar positions. From the air they looked like one heavy 4.2 and one 81mm. Jake nodded and in turn pointed out the two positions to Staff Sergeant Rivers, the team's weapons specialist. Small groups of French soldiers began to gather around the compound. Shading their eyes, they stared up at the four helicopters as they circled the fortress. Mortimer placed his hand over one side of his headset as he monitored the conversation between the pilot and the French commander below. He requested that the choppers land outside the compound near the front gates. They had been eating enough sand lately without having the rotor blades stirring up any more.

"Looks like the legionnaires got the message with the freqs dropped by that OV-10 you sent out earlier, Jake. Wonder if they've already contacted the embassy and know how terminal their situation could get out here?" asked York.

Jake cupped his hands in order to be heard above the heavy droning of the motor above their heads, "If they have, they're not taking it very seriously. Did you see that south wall?"

York nodded that he had and shrugged his shoulders as he

leaned back in his seat. The pilot was taking them down. Each chopper began to lengthen the distance between themselves as one after another they began their descent to the desert below. For Captain York the rising clouds of dust and swirling sand brought back nightmarish memories of another time when he had encountered these same elements. Only then, it had been Iranian sand and the mission was code-named Desert One. Sand and dust had played a major factor in the failure to rescue the American hostages held in Iran. The combination had proven unforgiving and deadly. Perhaps it was the vivid memories of that night that now made every muscle in his body tense. Randy York wanted only one thing, to be on the ground and as far away from this helicopter as possible before the others landed.

Legionnaires lined the top of the walls watching the air show as a small contingent of French officers went out the front gate to welcome their visitors. The blades of the first chopper were idling down as York and Mortimer, bending slightly forward, ran out from under the blades and made their way to the reception committee. Jake recognized the rank of colonel on the collar of the big man in the center of the group. Halting a few feet in front of the colonel, Jake and York saluted as Jake said, "Sir, Commander Jacob Mortimer and Captain Randy York, United States Special Operations Command."

The sand-blown ridges and weather-worn lines in the face of the elderly commander fashioned a smile as he returned the salute and replied, "*Bonjour*, Commander, *Capitaine*. Welcome to our little corner of the world. I am Colonel Jean Paul Claudel." Pointing to the shorter but huskily built officer to his left he continued, "This is Major Pierre Fenelon, my second in command." Fenelon saluted, and handshakes were exchanged.

"Colonel, have you been able to establish contact with the American Embassy?" asked Captain York.

"Yes we have, Captain. It would seem we have a very interesting set of events unfolding in our little desert kingdom. Your Mr. Privett did give me a generalized picture of the situation and informed me that you and Commander Mortimer would go into more detail upon your arrival. Shall we adjourn to my office, gentlemen. There is no air-conditioning, but the shade does help some."

"About my men, Colonel," said York.

Claudel raised his hand and waved to a sergeant, "Sergeant Le Fleur, see to it that the captain's men are made comfortable. I will advise you of what actions will be required after our discussion." The sergeant growled a compliance and headed out to meet the four Green Berets who had accompanied York and Mortimer. Both Americans could feel the eyes of the legionnaires on them as they made their way across the compound. Once inside, the colonel poured what was left of a bottle of cognac into four glasses and passed them around the table. "I am afraid that we are limited in our offerings, Commander. As you can see your timing is excellent. This is the last of our cognac. Santé, gentlemen." After the drinks were finished, Jake asked, "Just how much did Privett tell you, Colonel Claudel?"

The colonel undid one of the buttons at the front of his sweat-covered khaki uniform. Judging from the traces of gray along his hairline and the powerful lines around his eyes, Jake guessed the man to be in his mid-fifties, but with a body that had been maintained in great condition. Major Fenelon appeared younger, perhaps late thirties or early forties. His strong rippling muscles strained against the confines of the short-sleeved khaki shirt he wore. His dark blue eyes rested on Jake as Colonel Claudel answered, "Only that they had intelligence reports that verified an unusual amount of activity in the northern areas of Chad and that they had lost contact with the air base in Abeche. Of course, we were already aware of a problem there after we failed to receive our daily weather reports from the French pilots. Mr. Privett informed me that you gentlemen and General Gaafar believe that installation may have fallen into rebel hands, is that correct."

"Yes, sir, all indications are that General Hissen Kueddei and the rebels are attempting to mount a major offensive throughout the country. We also believe that Qaddafi has outfitted them with not only weapons but also a sizable force of Libyan volunteers. If our conclusions are correct, Colonel, then it will be only a matter of time before they realize they have to remove you and your command from this outpost in order to protect their supply line for the attack on the capital. How many men do you have, Colonel?" asked Jake.

"Eighty-two, Commander," said Claudel as he stood and moved to the map behind his chair. "Your theory of why the rebels have to attack us would seem quite valid, Commander. Kueddei cannot afford to ignore us here at Mangalme. Otherwise, what would stop us from attempting to retake the Abeche airfield. He has to attack."

"Exactly," said York. "The question is, Colonel, do you want to take them on here, or back in the capital? We brought some reinforcements with us. Should you decide to defend your position here, the choppers will return to the capital for more. If not, then we can pull you and your command out in two lifts. The choice is yours, sir."

Major Fenelon folded his hands on the table. Before the colonel could answer, he said, "Excuse me, gentlemen, but I am sure that you are aware of the fact that France has withdrawn from any and all obligations to the Chadian government. Our meager command here at Mangalme and the contingent of pilots at Abeche are the last remaining units in this country. We are scheduled to be picked up in a matter of days. I am certain that Kueddei and Qaddafi are equally aware of that; therefore, I see no reason for them to attack us. Why risk the lives of their men when they know we will be gone within days? I am afraid I do not appraise this situation with the same seriousness you obviously do."

Jake and Randy looked over to Colonel Claudel to see if he shared his major's opinion of the situation. It was apparent he was weighing the man's remarks carefully before he said, "Gentlemen, you will have to forgive my friend Pierre. He, as do many of my men, find it hard to forgive the rather shabby and insulting treatment that we have had to endure since the French pullout began. Treatment, I might add, that was condoned by your own government, Commander. However, I must be a realist. If this offensive has, as you say, started with the capture of Abeche; then I doubt seriously if Kueddei will find it in his black heart to forgive and forget that it was the French, the Legion, in particular, that led to his defeat three years ago. Rest assured, Major Fenelon, he would rather hang us from these very gates than let us walk away from here. He will come for us. Of that you can be certain."

Unable to contain a look of disappointment brought about by his commander's failure to agree with him, Major Fenelon slumped back into his chair and looked out the window, unconcerned with anything else the Americans might have to say. As far as he was concerned, Chad was their problem, now. Colonel Claudel returned to his seat and replied, "Commander, I would prefer that if we must face Kueddei and his rebels, that we do so in N'Djamena. At least there we would have the advantage of some artillery and air cover, as well as fortifications from which to conduct an urban battle. As I am sure you and the captain noticed flying in, our compound could not possibly sustain a major attack for any length of time. Can we arrange for my men to be moved by aircraft before this evening?"

York felt a sudden sigh of relief. He and Jake were counting heavily on the rugged, combat-experienced legionnaires to provide the edge that would make the difference in this situation. Major Fenelon's objections had worried both American officers. Without them, they felt they had no chance at all.

Jake assured Colonel Claudel that transportation would begin immediately. He explained how General Gaafar and they were planning to defend the capital. Captain York had split the team, leaving Chief Hileran and five SF sergeants in the capital to assist Gaafar, while he and Jake had brought the remaining four members of the team and two platoons of Chad Rangers to Mangalme. Having seen the condition of the old fort, both Americans were relieved that Claudel was willing to abandon the position.

"Well, Colonel Claudel," said Jake, "that's about it. If you will show me where your communications room is, I will contact Mr. Privett and inform him that we will be returning to the capital with you and your command."

"Certainly, Commander," said Claudel as he stood and walked to the door with Mortimer. "Major Fenelon, you will alert the command to begin preparations for departure. Have our demolition personnel wire all the structures, particularly the well. We will destroy everything before we leave. I wish to leave nothing of value for our friend Kueddei."

The major acknowledged the order and watched Jake and his commander leave the room. York could tell the major was still not happy about the turn of events. Standing near the door, he turned to Fenelon and said, "Major, I have a demo sergeant with me if your boys need some help. He knows his business and I'm sure he'd like to give them a hand."

Fenelon walked past York; pausing just outside the doorway,

he looked at the Green Beret captain and spoke in a bitter tone, "It is too bad you and your countrymen were not as willing to assist us in 1986, Captain York. But then, it was not in your interest then, was it? No, my people do not need your help, Captain."

York stood by himself in the doorway and watched the major walk across the compound. Major Pierre Fenelon was a bitter man. In a way, York could not blame him. Colonel Claudel and his men had been ostracized by the very people they had rescued in 1986. That rescue had not come cheaply. The legionnaires had lost 232 killed and another 600 wounded. The majority of those killed had come from Major Fenelon's command. As he went down the steps and headed for the commo room, York thought of what Captain Tanner had said before he had left, "Randy, you might not like some of their attitudes, but, brother, those Frogs are hell-on-wheels in a fight." Right now, attitudes were the last thing Randy York was worried about. He paused at the entrance to the radio room and looked up at the clear blue sky. There wasn't a cloud in sight, yet he could swear he heard the low rumbling of thunder. Turning on the front steps, he surveyed the sand dunes to the north and west. That was where the sound seemed to be coming from. Even the legionnaires were looking around, now. They, too, had heard the low, but distinctive rumbling as it seemed to echo, then grow louder as it spread across the sweltering sands.

Jake and Colonel Claudel came out the door and saw York staring off into the distance. He looked to the north. "What is it, Randy?" asked Jake.

York continued to stare and turn his head slightly as he replied, "I'm not sure, Jake, but I've got a feeling that whatever it is, it ain't good."

A huge column of dust began to rise beyond the dunes. "Shit!" said Jake as he watched the width of the dust cloud extend for what seemed like miles beyond the ridge line of the northern dunes. Major Fenelon walked calmly up to the group, his eyes were fixed on the same cloud of dust. He said, "Colonel, I believe the need for explosives to destroy this facility will no longer be required. Captain York, I would suggest that if you hope to get anyone out of here, you do so now while your helicopters can still get off the ground."

The rumbling thunder became louder now, as legionnaires were running to their positions along the wall. The mortar crews were scrambling for the pits and the protection of the ringed sandbags. No one had to tell the chopper pilots anything. They were already cranking the duel blades of the big CH-47s.

"How many people can you take out at once, Commander?" asked the colonel.

Jake looked to York. "What do you think, Randy?"

York quickly calculated the numbers in his mind, "We're looking at one hundred seventy-five to one hundred eighty men, Jake. Any way we work it, somebody is going to be left behind."

"How many, Captain?" asked Fenelon.

"I'd say about fifty, Major."

A haunting silence fell over the small group. They were waiting for the colonel to make his decision. It was clear by the pained look in his eyes as he watched the approaching cloud that it was a decision he had no desire to make. Beyond the gates the helicopters were reaching full RPMs and the Chadian pilots were now waving frantically for people to board. The sounds of the clanking tank treads and half-tracks were clearly distinct now. It was only a matter of minutes before they would crest the dunes.

"Colonel, we're out of time. You're going to have to call it," said Jake. Claudel looked sadly into Jake's eyes as he gave the order.

"Major Fenelon, you will take the scout platoon and the headquarters staff out with you. Commander, your Green Berets and the Chaidan Rangers can go out on the remaining helicopters. I will remain here with the second scout platoon. Now, gentlemen, I would suggest that we waste no more time. Major, give the order, they are to take nothing but their weapons and ammo."

Major Fenelon stepped in front of his commander and was about to protest the decision. "Colonel, I shall stay. You are needed with . . ."

"That was an order, Major! There is no time to debate on the matter. Now go! You risk the lives of your men each moment you waste."

Fenelon hesitated for only a second. A look of respect

passed between the two men, negating any need for words. Saluting smartly, the major turned and began yelling orders in French as he raced across the compound. Legionnaires from various parts of the compound began to run to the gates and out to the choppers. They were carrying only their weapons and combat gear. The legionnaires to be left behind moved to fill the positions left open by their comrades' departure. No one protested, nor bothered to look back at those who were leaving. They were legionnaires. If they were destined to die in this desert, so be it. They would fight to the last man.

York was screaming to his men to get the Chad Rangers on board. Jake and Colonel Claudel rushed back into the commo shack to request air support from N'Djamena. General Gaafar guaranteed that at least four F-5 Mirage fighters would be dispatched at once. York hit the door at a full run, "Come on, Jake, they're going to take off!"

Jake grabbed Claudel's hand, "Colonel, I wish things could have . . ."

The colonel squeezed his hand tightly. "*Au revoir*, Commander, perhaps we can buy you a little time. Good luck."

"Damn it, Jake, come on!" shouted York as he ran back across the compound.

Reluctantly, the Navy commander released the colonel's hand and followed York. Reaching the side door of the helicopter, Jake turned and took one last look at the colonel who was buttoning his shirt at the gate and staring calmly at the rebel scout car that had just crested the top of the northern dunes. A sickening feeling shot through Jake as he realized the air support would never arrive in time. Colonel Claudel had known that all along.

General Kueddei cussed under his breath as he watched the last of the four twin rotor helicopters gain altitude and head toward the west. If only they had arrived thirty minutes earlier. Raising his field glasses, he studied the fortified position below. He estimated no more than forty or fifty French were still there. It had hardly been worth his trouble to come to this isolated place, but now that he was here, there was no need to waste time. Steadying himself against the roll bar of the scout car, he raised his arm and waved for the tanks to come forward.

Colonel Claudel strolled calmly along the wall, smiling and

speaking to his men. "They think they have us, boys. But then they always do. Don't they? Hold steady and make every shot count. It may be a while before we are resupplied."

"Voilà," yelled one of the legionnaires as he pointed to the ridge.

Kueddei's army presented an awesome sight to the small outpost. No less than thirty Russian T-72 tanks leveled their 120mm cannons at the adobe walls. On the east ridge, over three hundred rebels stood posed for the attack. To the west, another five hundred waited to rush in after the initial bombardment to finish off any survivors. Glancing at his watch, Kueddei stared off to the north. Kruger and his mercenaries would be taking off right now, escorted by two flights of F-5s. Grinning to himself as he looked down onto the fort below, he knew they would roll over this place like it was no more than a pesky fly to be swatted out of existence. Then they would roll toward the capital. There he would find the true revenge that he sought. Kruger would drive his brother, Gaafar, and his army from the city and into his waiting guns. They would have them in the middle; he in front of them and Kruger behind them. This time they would eliminate all resistance once and for all. But first, he must swat the fly. Keying the mike he held in his hand, he yelled, "Fire!"

Hell rained down on Colonel Claudel and his brave men as round after round of cannon fire tore gaping holes in the walls and exploded buildings like matchboxes. The mortar pit crews were able to get off three rounds apiece before the tank zeroed in on them and blew them out of existence. Everywhere, men were dying or screaming as shell after shell exploded among them, ripping off legs and arms and tearing men apart. A white-hot piece of metal tore through Colonel Claudel's shoulder and slammed him to the ground. Two legionnaires grabbed the wounded leader and pulled him to one corner of a shattered wall. Ripping his shirt open, one of the men saw the jagged piece of steel protruding from the colonel's shoulder. Reaching up to pull it out, he jerked his hand back in pain as hot steel burned his fingers.

The firing stopped suddenly. A strange silence came over the smoky, dust-filled remains of the fort. Those still alive stumbled to their fallen comrades to see if there was anything they could do for them. Dead and mutilated bodies lay

everywhere. Colonel Claudel pushed the men attending him
back and rose to his feet. Blood covered his entire right side
from his shoulder to the top of his boots. He knew what the
silence meant and he would not die lying on the ground. It was
not the Legion way. "Legionnaires! To your weapons and rally
on me!"

From the tops of the dunes came the screams of the rebels,
eight hundred strong, as they charged down the sandy slopes
toward the shattered walls of the fortress. Inside, in a circle
formation, stood Colonel Claudel and the seventeen legionnaires who remained. The yelling hordes came over the rubble
of the walls like ants. The first wave brought down by a volley
from the legionnaires was replaced by a second wave, then a
third. One by one the French warriors fell, until finally none
remained.

General Kueddei stepped from his scout car into the body-
strewn courtyard. The effectiveness of the firepower of the
small group of legionnaires in their final desperate moments
was apparent by the number of rebel bodies that circled the
fallen Frenchmen. Kueddei did not bother to count his losses.
However, he estimated that swatting this fly had cost him close
to one hundred men.

Having inspected the area, Kueddei determined there was
little if any value in leaving troops behind to secure what
remained. Signaling for his column to move out in the direction
of the capital, he switched the radio in his scout car to the
frequency being used by the C-130s carrying Kruger and his
men. Once contact was established, he detailed the results of
the attack to the mercenary leader and mentioned the four
helicopters that had barely escaped them. Kruger seemed
disinterested in them. The parachute assault on N'Djamena
was less than thirty minutes away, and that occupied his every
thought for now. He would pass the information on to the
fighter planes flying escort for them. For the moment, the four
helicopters were no more than a target of opportunity. They
would have to take second place to the airborne assault.
Kueddei agreed and signed off. He waved his army forward. If
all went as planned within the next twelve hours, he and
Kruger would turn the desert into a killing field and a
graveyard for his brother and the army of Chad.

• • •

Mortimer and York stood next to the Chinook helicopter and listened as Major Fenelon, his voice straining with emotion, tried desperately to reestablish contact with Colonel Claudel's command. They had been monitoring the action as it was being passed along by the fort's radio operator. He had locked the handset to the open position; thereby freeing himself from the confines of the radio set. This enabled him to yell what was happening from across the room. They heard the sound of the exploding rounds as they impacted near the commo building. They listened as the radio man vividly described the havoc being rained down upon the defenders, and then as he reported that Colonel Claudel had gone down. The radio abruptly went dead after that, leaving nothing but a slow, steady hissing sound of empty airwaves coming through the headsets. Jake and Randy knew it was over. So did Major Fenelon. Having landed at Bokoro to refuel the choppers from the fifty-five-gallon drums they had placed there earlier, Fenelon held out one last hope that somehow the colonel might have escaped; with each unanswered call, the hope faded, until finally Major Fenelon gave it up.

Stepping out of the helicopter, he stared at York and Mortimer with resentment. He felt that if anyone should have remained behind, it should have been the Chadian Rangers under the command of the Americans. It was, after all, their damn country. "How much longer will we be here?" he asked, directing the question at no one in particular.

Jake stepped out from the shade of the chopper as the last two barrels of fuel were being rolled toward the fourth aircraft. "Another twenty minutes or so, Major. They've almost got the last one topped off." Jake took a couple of steps in Fenelon's direction as he said, "Major, we're sorry about Colonel Claudel. He was a fine man, and we . . ."

Fenelon spit in the sand. His eyes took on a hateful look. "Spare me your sentiments, Commander. You knew the man for what, an hour and a half, and now you wish to talk about him like he was a long-lost friend. You fucking Americans possess a remarkable amount of audacity. Do you know that, Commander? You paint yourselves as the saviors of the world; the righteous protectors of the weak and the oppressed; when in fact you are no better than the rest of us. You play politics with other people's lives. The amount of your righteousness depends solely upon what you have to gain from a commitment. As the old saying goes, Commander, 'No one does anything for nothing!' "

"Now, wait just a fucking minute," said York as he moved toward the major.

"Let it go, Randy!" yelled Mortimer as he stepped between the two men. "The major has a right to his opinion. I'd say it was one that you're not going to change in just twenty minutes standing in the middle of a desert. So just let it go."

York's face was crimson with rage. Jake was right. Beating the hell out of the man in the middle of this desert wasn't going to change his opinion of America or its soldiers. York turned and walked away, his hands clutched tightly into balled fists as he muttered something under his breath and slapped his fists against his legs.

"Your intervention was not necessary, Commander. I believe I could have handled the captain easily enough," said Fenelon with a smirk on his face.

Jake smiled slightly and turned to walk away as he said, "We may be audacious, Major, but if you believe that Captain York would be that easy, you're a dreamer. The world is full of audacious people, Major, but very few surviving dreamers."

After York climbed into the number one chopper, Jake joined him in the cockpit. The captain was on the radio talking with Chief Hileran. Sharon Chambers had found Calhoun. Through a little persuasion by Sergeants Roth and Peterson, Calhoun was convinced to return to the embassy with them. General Gaafar had mobilized every available piece of equipment and had called upon the people of the capital to join forces with him to provide protection for the city. So far the response had been good. Three companies of civilian militia had been armed and placed at strategic locations around the airfield. Gaafar was expecting the brunt of the attack to come from the desert in the form of an armored assault supported by the captured aircraft from the air base at Abeche. York, glancing up at Jake and noticing the worried look that appeared on his face, asked, "What's the matter, Jake?"

"I don't know, Randy. Gaafar seems to have the right idea. Hell, we've already seen some of the armor, and from the reports we have read, that's the way they did it the last time.

Came straight out of the desert and into the capital. Maybe that's what bothers me."

"What do you mean, Jake?"

"Why would you repeat a mistake?" he asked.

York thought about that for a moment, then keyed the mike, "Chief, how many military units are at the airfield with those civilian militia?"

There was a pause before Hileran answered, "Not a hell of a lot, Captain. Maybe a company or less. The general is convinced that he's going to need his regular troops on the outskirts of the city. Why? Is there something we ought to know."

York looked to Jake again, "Well?"

Jake straightened and rubbed the back of his neck as he tried to figure out what Kueddei was up to. Gaafar had said his brother was anything but an ignorant man. He had to have had a plan before he started this operation. Jake wasn't buying another armor attack from the desert theory. No, there had to be something else involved. Something they hadn't thought of yet. The airport seemed to be the key. "Randy, tell the chief he has to try to convince the general to reinforce the airport with more regular troops. Remind him that it was a terrorist dressed as a civilian who blew the hell out of the ambassador's patio. I don't know why, but I can't shake this feeling that the airport is going to catch hell this time around."

"Makes sense to me, Jake," said the captain as he once again keyed the mike and relayed the message to Hileran.

"OK, boss, but I don't think . . ." Suddenly Hileran went off the air. York repeated the call up, nothing. Adjusting the frequency knobs, he tried again, still nothing. Jake grabbed a headset from the copilot's seat and put them on. "Chief! Chief! Can you hear me? What's happening? Scotty, answer me!" Still no answer. Jake tried the call sign again, "Hilton Hotel X-Ray One Three, this is Hilton One Alpha, come in One Three!"

Hearing the excitement in Jake's voice, the other team members began to gather around the chopper. Major Fenelon climbed in and made his way to the cockpit just as a burst of static came over the radio, followed by the gasping, out-of-breath voice of Scotty Hileran. "One Alpha . . . We . . . we're under air attack. F-5s . . . they're all over the fucking sky . . . the embassy has taken two direct hits, casualties are heavy. Antiaircraft positions have been knocked out along with the power station. We're on auxiliary power right now. Don't know how long we'll be able to stay on the air. They came out of nowhere, Randy. I don't think the air force got one plane off the ground. I'm at the top-floor window of Privett's office. There are pillars of black smoke coming from all over the airfield."

"Scotty, has Gaafar reported any ground action outside the city?" asked York.

"No, nothing out there. Gaafar is trying to move troops toward the airport right now to assess the damage and do what he can to get anything that'll fly into the air. I think they . . . Wait a minute! Those aren't fighter planes coming in from the east . . . they're . . . they're C-130s! Oh, shit! Randy, they're dropping paratroopers over the airport. Jesus, there must be hundreds of them. Randy, there's no way those civilians can take on a combat airborne unit. They'll be overrun in a matter of minutes. Damn it. We never planned for this! Hold on, Gaafar is on the other radio."

The three officers in the cockpit stared silently at the knobs of the radio. Hileran was back. "Randy, the general said we can write the airport off. He and his men were just fired on by a group of the civilian militia guarding the main gate to the airstrip. Looks like Jake was right. Gaafar said there were a lot of civilian bodies out in the road. The terrorists in the group cut them down before those loyal to the government could react. We don't have any idea how many were in the other two groups. Guess it doesn't really matter now, does it? Any suggestions, boss?"

"Stand by, Scotty. I need to find a map," said York as he passed the mike to Jake and went back to the rear of the chopper to search for his map case. Fenelon slid into the seat across from Jake as he said, "It would seem I am not the only one who will lose friends today, Commander."

Jake's jaw tightened as he stared at the Frenchmen. "Don't start with me right now, Fenelon. I'm not in the mood. If you can't suggest anything helpful; then get the hell out of here!"

The major almost smiled as he leaned back in the pilot's seat. "No, I think I would prefer to sit right here and watch how America's finest work under pressure."

Jake fought back the urge to reach across and knock the man's teeth down his throat. Pressing the mike, he said, "Scotty, you still with us?"

"Sure enough, Jake. Ain't a hell of a lot of places to go. That's the problem! Your friend Calhoun just came through here. He's screaming for Privett to get everybody but the damn Oakland Raiders in here to help us. Course, we can't talk to anybody outside the country. Half the damn roof is gone off this building and with it the antennas and the satellite equipment. Oh, yeah, Jake, in case you were wondering, Sharon Chambers is here with us at the embassy. She's OK. Did you get the legionnaires out of there? Boy, we sure could use them at that airport. Those guys are a class act all by themselves. If I had about two hundred of them here right now, I could hold this city until hell freezes over. They're some of the best troops in the world, you know that, Jake?"

Mortimer glanced over at Fenelon, his earlier cockiness was gone now as he stared at the radio and thought of Colonel Claudel and the others back at the fortress. It was just such heroics that had gained the Legion its fame and this warranted praise from the man called Hileran. A man whom Fenelon had never met.

"Yeah, I know that, Scotty," replied Jake as he looked away from the major. York came back to the front of the chopper and spread the map out. Jake passed him the mike. "Scotty, listen. You and the others are going to have to hold out until dark. Then, try to work your way across the Chari River into Cameroon. There's not a hell of a lot six guys can do against an airborne assault. So as soon as it's dark you guys get your asses out of there. You got it? Let General Gaafar know we're not running out on him. We just need a place to get reorganized."

"But what about you guys, Randy? You sure as hell can't fly into the airport, and you didn't take enough fuel out to Bokoro to go on a sight-seeing tour. How are you going to get back?"

"You don't worry about that, OK! We'll get out and link up with you in Cameroon. The first chance you have, get hold of MacDill and let them know what's happened. I mean it, Scotty. Get our people out of there! You roger that?"

"OK, you're the boss," said Hileran reluctantly. "I'll get 'em out. Anything further?"

"Negative! Hilton One Alpha, out."

York hung the mike back in the slot next to the radio. "Come on, Jake, let's brief the people on what's happened. Then let's get the hell out of here."

The refueling was completed as the men gathered around their leaders who told them the depressing news. They would not be flying back to N'Djamena, but rather to the northwest and Lake Chad. The pilots were not sure if they had enough fuel to make it that far. However, they would get them close enough so that it would only be a short walk, and they wouldn't have to worry about running into the rebels. The briefing complete, York ordered the pilots to start up the choppers and the mixed expeditionary force to begin loading for departure.

The first three birds were about to reach lift-off RPMs when Major Fenelon suddenly sat upright in his seat and tilted his head slightly as if straining to hear something beyond the deafening whine of the twin turbos overhead. Undoing his seat belt, he jumped to his feet, ran to the side window of the CH-47, and looked skyward. Jake and Randy unfastened their belts and were about to join him when he abruptly pulled his head back inside and yelled, "Get them off! Get everybody off, quickly!" Then he repeated the same thing in French.

The legionnaires jerked their belts free and ran for the side exit door, leaping into the sand and scrambling away from the helicopter.

"Fenelon, what is it? What's wrong?" yelled Jake.

The major was bent over helping one of the Chadian Rangers who had twisted his seat belt in the panic. He couldn't get free. York bent down next to him, pulled a knife from the side pocket of his fatigues, and cut the nylon belt releasing the frightened soldier. "Damn it, Fenelon, what's going on?" asked York.

"F-5s! The F-5s that attacked the capital! It has to be—they've spotted the choppers. They'll be making a gun run on us any minute. We've got to get everyone away from these helicopters! Don't you understand, Captain? You just topped them off with fuel. Now come on!" Fenelon ran for the door and jumped into the sand. York and Mortimer were right behind him.

Mortimer hit and rolled, performing the best parachute landing fall of his life. Wiping the sand from his mouth and eyes, his gaze was drawn skyward by the high-pitched sounds of the F-5 French Mirages as they peeled off and dove straight for the CH-47s. Two of the flight crews had already abandoned their helicopters leaving the huge twin rotors still turning. The crew of the third were dragging their personal equipment off the rear ramp while York was screaming at them to leave it and get out of there. Realizing he was going to have to find cover, Jake jumped to his feet and quickly surveyed the area. That was the problem with deserts, there just weren't a whole hell of a lot of places to hide. Spying a slight depression beyond a sand dune, he broke for it at a dead run. Clearing the small rise, he leaped into the shallow area and practically landed on Doc Blancher.

"Jesus H. Christ! I expected to get blown to hell, Commander, not kicked to death!" shrieked the team medic.

"Sorry, Doc."

Blancher looked up and over the small pile of sand in front of him. "I don't fuckin' believe this! Look at that stupid bastard out there. He thinks he's going to get that damn chopper out of here before those fighters tear him a new asshole. He'll never make it."

Jake stared unbelievingly at the crew of the fourth bird as they attempted to reach maximum RPMs for lift-off. The crew must have thought that if they could get the cumbersome helicopter in the air they might be able to outmaneuver the planes and make good their escape. It was a bad idea; yet amazingly enough, the F-5s ignored the rising behemoth and concentrated on their primary targets, the choppers still idling on the ground.

The first fighter peeled off from the group and moved at such incredible speed that Jake first thought the pilot had lost control and was going to drive the sleek silver plane straight into the ground. At the last possible second, the high-pitched scream erupted into a roar as the pilot pulled out of the dive and streaked headlong for the first chopper near a pile of empty fifty-five-gallon barrels. The rhythmic thud of 40mm cannon fire seemed to echo on the wind as a string of exploding geysers of sand appeared directly in front of the CH-47 continuing the deadly walking pattern until the objective was reached. The snub-nosed front of the chopper was first to go, then the forward rotor, until finally one of the rounds found the gas tanks.

The explosion rocked the desert as Jake and Doc pressed themselves hard into the sand. The pilot pulled the F-5 straight up into the air. Jake swore he could feel the heat from the fighter's afterburners blow against his face as the man climbed for the sky directly above them. The high-pitched whine of the second fighter was already in the air when both men heard someone scream, "Medic!" From instinct, Doc raised his head and tried to locate the person calling for help. Jake grabbed him and pointed to the second F-5, about to pull out of its dive and begin its gun run. "Better wait until this asshole has his fun, Doc."

Blancher grinned a broad Arkansas grin as he said, "Don't got to tell this ol' country boy twice, Commander. A dead medic ain't no good to anybody."

Both men watched the pilot level off and come straight in. The lift-off chopper was twenty to thirty feet off the ground now.

"They'll nail his ass, now," said Doc. But again, the airborne chopper was totally ignored as the second pilot concentrated his cannon fire on the second and third choppers sitting almost in a straight line. Jake had no idea who was flying these planes, it could be Libyans, Russians, or Cubans, but whoever it was, they had gotten their money's worth of flight school. This pilot's firing time was half that of the first plane and twice as effective. Jake and Doc buried their heads in the sand again as both choppers exploded sending gigantic twin fireballs rolling into the clear sky. Jake felt a momentary breeze on the back of his sweat-soaked shirt. Tilting his head sideways, he looked up in time to see a blade from one of the rotors pass less than three feet over his head, still twirling.

The desperate cry for a medic rose again. This time Doc had a fix on the location. It was coming from another depression in the ground about twenty-five yards to his left. Doc could feel the heat from the burning choppers on his cheeks. Sweat made little rivers down his face and neck as he looked at the third fighter that was about to go into his dive. Jake could tell the middle-aged medic was having second thoughts, and who could blame him. It was one thing having a guy shooting at you with a gun, but having someone come at you at Mach one with a chorus line of 40mm cannons made it a whole new ball game. Doc planted his push-off foot and glanced nervously up at the plane once more. The pilot was almost at the pullout point. In a matter of seconds he would be coming right at them.

Someone yelled, "Medic! Medic! Doc, this guy's bleedin' to death over here!"

Blancher's heartrate jumped fifty points on the scale. "Oh, fuck it!" he yelled as he pushed forward to his feet and began a wild scramble across the open ground, his boots sinking ankle deep into the sand. The pilot leveled off and immediately triggered the duel cannons, 40mm rounds began their walking pattern toward the struggling man. The muscles in Doc's legs were on fire and his feet felt as if they were metal weights, each step sinking him farther into the shifting sands. Looking back over his shoulder, he saw the fountains of sand being tossed into the air behind him. "We ain't gonna make it, son," he whispered to himself as the sound of the exploding rounds became louder. "Well, screw this, shit! We ain't runnin' no more."

Doc stopped dead in his tracks and turned to face the oncoming plane. Dropping his med bag, he calmly raised his hand and, making a fist, extended his middle finger and raised the arm high into the air as the 40mms formed a corridor of explosions going left, right, left, right, and headed straight for Blancher.

Jake closed his eyes, not wanting to witness the effect the shell would have when it made contact with the man. Hearing the jet pull out of the run and bolt skyward, Jake peered over the sand in front of him and had to rub his eyes twice to make sure he was seeing right. Doc was still standing and dusting himself off. As he bent down to retrieve his med bag, Jake could see the man was talking to himself. Swatting the sand from the canvas bag, he walked over to the wounded men who were in need of his services.

Jake searched the skies for the three fighters. They were regrouping off to the right and above the Chinook helicopter that had somehow escaped the fate of the others. York jogged across to Mortimer's position and occupied the spot formally held by Doc.

"Did you see what Doc did out there?" asked a still-unbelieving Jake.

"Yeah, he's always been a big George C. Scott fan. Must have watched *Patton* a hundred times. Wanta guess his favorite part of the movie?"

"Unreal," said Jake, shaking his head.

"What do you think these fly-boys have in store for us next?" asked York.

Jake stared in the direction of the fighters as they banked around, spreading out into a three-stacked formation, and headed downward.

"Well, right now, I'd say they were going after our boy who thought he was free and clear."

No sooner had the words left Jake's lips than a muffled explosion echoed in the distance, followed by a column of black twisting smoke rising from beyond the dunes to the west. Both men lowered their heads as Jake commented, "Too bad—I was hoping the poor bastards would make it."

"So what now, Jake?" said York as he flipped at the sand with his finger and stared out at the smoldering remains of the CH-47s that had been their passport home. Jake wiped a trickle of sweat from his eyebrow and rolled onto his back. Staring up at the bright yellow sun, he began to formulate a plan. A smile suddenly appeared, and he began to laugh.

"Something funny?" asked York. "Hope you'll tell me. I could use a good laugh right about now."

"Oh, I just got this picture in my mind of how ironic this whole thing is. I mean, here you've got a Navy SEAL, lying on the sand in the middle of a fucking desert trying to come up with a plan, and his biggest problem is going to be—water. Ironic, don't you think?"

York was laughing now. "Guess you got a point there."

After a few minutes, Jake's smile disappeared. "Randy, you know those guys could have pulverized us if they had been carrying a full load. All we got were the leftovers from the attack on N'Djamena."

"You're right, Jake. You and I both know they'll be coming back as soon as they can get refitted. They know we're sure as hell not going to fly anywhere."

"Yeah, them or that damn armor column that hit Mangalme this morning. Ten to one they called in our position to those boys, and they're rolling those treads toward us right now."

A shadow fell over the two men as Doc walked up. "Either one of you two guys hit? Uh, I mean hit, sirs."

"Naw, we're OK. How'd we come out, Doc?" asked Jake.

Blancher sat down, crossed his legs, and dropped the med bag in his lap as he said, "Not too bad I guess. Our guys came out all right. Rivers got a few splinters in the shoulder, but it was minor. He ain't gonna die from it. Nine of the Rangers were killed and three wounded, none serious. Three of the legionnaires bought the farm and two more were hit. One's pretty bad, caught a piece of metal in the gut. If we have to spend the night out here, I'm afraid the kid will go terminal by morning." Doc paused as he stared at the sand for a moment before saying, "Captain, I don't mean for this to sound cold or anything, but considering that we had over a hundred guys in the open when this shit started, all in all, I think we came out pretty good."

Jake rolled over into a sitting position and brushed the sand from his arms. "You're right, Doc, but that was just round one." Nodding toward the burnt-out choppers, Jake continued, "And round two's going to get pretty nasty before it's over."

Major Fenelon came over and knelt next to Blancher. "Doctor, could I trouble you to take another look at Corporal Du Bellay. He is in much pain."

"Sure, Major, I've got just the thing for that right here in my wonder bag," said Doc as he stood and walked away.

"We owe you one, Major," said York. "If you hadn't heard those F-5s they would have blown us out of the sky like a bunch of lame dick ducks."

"It was lucky for all of us, Captain. I have what they call super-sensitive hearing. Colonel Claudel said that . . ." Fenelon paused and rephrased the statement, "Colonel Claudel used to say it was a gift provided by God and intended for use by the Legion. Perhaps he was right. It has served me well over my years with the legionnaires—especially in Southeast Asia and the jungles of South America."

"How long you been with the Legion, Major?" asked York.

"Twenty-five years, Captain."

"Excuse me, sir, but you don't look that old. You must have joined when you were still a kid," remarked Jake.

"I was fifteen, Commander."

"Fifteen! Jesus, I was still trying to figure out how to put on a rubber at fifteen," laughed York.

"We were a poor family. There were thirteen children. When my father died, it fell to the eldests to feed the family any way they could. I was caught stealing from an American tourist. That was considered a major crime in those days. The magistrate gave me a choice, the island prison or the Legion. As you can see the choice was not a difficult one. I did not receive one franc of payment from the Legion until my thirty-first birthday. All of my pay went to care for the others until they were able to go out on their own. The Legion is my life and Colonel Claudel was like a father to me."

Jake glanced over at Randy. They both knew they were thinking the same thing, this guy Fenelon wasn't such a bad type after all. York pulled the map from his pocket and spread it out in front of them.

"Major, Jake and I were just discussing our rather delicate situation here. Needless to say, you are the most experienced officer here. Do you have any suggestions?"

Major Pierre Fenelon smiled for the first time since he had met these men. Perhaps he, too, had been too quick in his judgment of the American officers. He had said things he had not meant, more out of pain over the loss of Colonel Claudel than anything else, and now even after his slanderous remarks, these two Americans demonstrated the true meaning of the words "officers and gentlemen," a fact that Colonel Claudel had recognized at once.

"Please, call me Pierre."

York grinned and reached out his hand while Jake slapped him on the shoulder and smilingly said, "OK, Pierre, show us how we're going to get out of here."

CHAPTER 8

The two slugs from a 7.62 that tore through the corrugated tin, only inches above Kruger's head, went unnoticed by the mercenary leader as he keyed his hand-held radio and shouted instructions to Ching and his platoon that were storming the control tower.

"The machine gun on the left, Ching! Get the machine gun—use the M-72 LAW on the bastards!"

Ching acknowledged and waved the man with the light antitank weapon forward. It was a lethal weapon used primarily against tanks, but it was equally devastating against personnel in bunkers and fortified positions. Ching pointed out the target as the man knelt and placed the weapon on his shoulder. After a few seconds for sight adjustment, he fired. The rocket hit dead center of the machine-gun position sending both the gun and the soldiers behind it flying into the air. The shredded leg of one of the men from the bunker somersaulted through the air and landed a few feet in front of Kruger who leaped to his feet and yelled, "Yeah!" as if he were cheering at a ball game.

"Black Raven one, Black Raven two, over." It was Kaufman. He and his people had engaged a platoon of Chad regulars along the east perimeter. It hadn't been much of a battle. The soldiers had put up a good fight in the beginning, but that had been mainly due to the threatening orders of a young Chad officer who had stood behind them and said he would shoot the first man who tried to run. A mercenary with a sniper rifle climbed on top of a hangar and placed a perfect bull's-eye shot dead center of the officer's nose. With their captain dead, the soldiers quickly lost all resolve for a full-fledged engagement with the white mercenaries. The smart ones threw down their guns and ran. The dumb ones dropped their guns and raised their hands to surrender. They were cut down where they stood as the mercenaries rushed by them in pursuit of the fleeing soldiers. Kruger's rule of no prisoners was obeyed.

"Raven two, Raven one, go," said Kruger.

Kaufman brought the radio up to his mouth and replied, "East sector secure. Enemy has been routed—we are in pursuit. Where do you need us next? Over."

"Raven two, stand by. Break-break, Ravens three and four, do you require assistance in your sectors? Over."

"Raven one, this is three. Negative, all secure."

"One, this is four. We have encountered numerous personnel in civilian dress, some with weapons. Cannot tell which are supposed to be friendlies and which are loyalists. We have received small-arms fire from some of the houses. Request instructions. Over."

Kruger stared at the radio for a moment. If he had the man who was talking in front of him right now he would slap the hell out of him. Pressing the switch in frustration, he growled into the radio, "You shoot them all, you dumb son of a bitch, we'll sort out who's friendly when the shit's over, you got that?"

"Yes . . . yes, sir, four, out!"

Kruger remembered that Kaufman was still waiting for instructions.

"Raven two, this is one. Establish security in your area and return to the tower. I will meet you there. Raven one, out."

Leaving the hangar, Kruger walked casually across the runway, stepping over a body here and there. Some were his men. Others were civilians or Chad regulars. Gunfire still resounded in isolated parts of the airport as die-hard holdouts fought to the bitter end, preferring to die the hero's death rather than surrender. Kruger wanted nothing more than to break out from the airfield and begin the pillage of the residential areas that spread outward from the airport. One could never tell what he would find, even in a country that seemed as poor as Chad:

gold, diamonds, money, even some cocaine on occasion. But most of all, that was where they find the women. The thought was tempting, but Kruger was a military man and his military logic overruled his desire.

The first point of logic was simple. To attempt a sweep through the city with only the force that had parachuted on the runway would be courting certain disaster. In order to search the town he would have to split his forces, one to search and one to secure the airfield. Two halves are always easier to defeat than one whole. No, he would be patient. The reinforcements would begin landing by transport at any moment now. The reinforcements would secure the airport for the transport planes that would begin flying in the supplies and ammo later in the day. Secondly, there was the matter of General Gaafar and his army. They were out there in those streets somewhere, and there were a lot of them. Kruger had kept a running tally of the number of regulars who had been encountered during the assault and estimated that at best they had engaged no more than a company or a company and a platoon. That was hardly the four thousand that had been reported in his intelligence reports. It was apparent to Kruger that the airborne assault had caught the Chad military totally by surprise, but then that had been his intention.

Kaufman and his men rounded the corner of the tower just as Kruger arrived. The two exchanged hearty handshakes and smiles for a job well done. Tellling his men to rest, Kruger accompanied Kaufman upstairs into the tower. The first of the C-130s carrying Qaddafi's volunteers and over five hundred of General Kueddei's rebels was already circling for a landing. Seven more were in trail and began an orbital pattern to await their turn.

"Have we had any word from General Kueddei?" asked Kaufman.

Kruger was changing the frequencies on one of the tower radios as he answered, "No, nothing since his report on the destruction of the legionnaires' fortress at Mangalme. He did mention something about some helicopters leaving before he could attack, but I was too involved with the airborne operation to pay it much mind. I'll try to raise him now."

Watching the first transport touch down and taxi past them,

Kruger pressed the key on the mike, "Leopard one, Black Raven one, over."

Kueddei's voice came over the radio loud and clear. "Raven one, this is Leopard one. I've been waiting for your call. Was the operation successful? Over."

"Roger, we have secured the airport and are receiving incoming transports and reinforcements at this time. What is your present location? Over."

"Allah be praised! We are proceeding as planned. Our coordinates are Foxtrot Tango six-one-four, eight-two-two, over."

Kaufman lay his map on the table in front of him and marked the location. Kueddei was making good time. He was sixty miles due west of Mangalme.

"Excellent, Leopard one. We are right on schedule. What about the helicopters you reported earlier?"

"They apparently had a refueling site at Bokoro. All four were destroyed. Our returning fighters caught them on the ground. They reported nearly one hundred men in the area. I intend to alter my course slightly so that I may track down those who escaped me at Mangalme."

Kruger glanced up at Kaufman who shook his head as he shrugged his shoulders. He knew Kruger didn't like that idea. It was not in the plan. The German firmly believed that alterations in an operation this large could lead to not only unnecessary delays but also unexpected problems. Keying the mike again, he tried to convince the rebel leader to leave the stragglers to the desert or at least to the fighters. Any delay in the arrival of the armor column could leave escape routes open for General Gaafar and his forces. Kueddei was persistent and refused to accept Kruger's suggestions. The general wanted all the legionnaires, not just half. Seeing there was no way to change the man's mind, Kruger asked that he keep him informed of his progress and signed off. Throwing the mike on the table he stomped out of the tower. Leaning against the railing, he lit a cigarette. Kaufman came out and stood next to him.

"Adolf, if that man screws this operation up, I will strip the skin from his body with my bare hands," said Kruger as he inhaled deeply from the cigarette in an effort to calm his nerves. Then he said, "It will be dark soon. I will have to halt the arrival of the planes. We may control the airfield, but we do not yet control the city. There are too many guns still out there. Have the Libyan and rebel commanders report to me in two hours. I want to move our people out along the Chari River just in case our friend General Gaafar has any ideas about sneaking across the border into Cameroon. Besides, I did not bring two hundred mercenaries here to pull guard duty on an airfield. I brought them to fight."

Kaufman placed his big hand on his friend's back, "As you say, Hans. In the meantime, why don't you try to get some rest, you have been going for days with hardly any sleep. I worry about you."

Kruger flipped the cigarette away and gripped Kaufman's arm as he laughed and said, "There is plenty of time for sleep when one is dead, my friend. Now go. It will be dark soon, and I must work out a plan to stop anyone who might attempt to cross the river tonight."

Fredrick Calhoun sat at a desk in the far corner of Privett's office, sulking. The man's continued raving had finally driven Privett up the wall. He had found it necessary to tell the man to either shut the hell up or he'd have the embassy marines throw him out on the street. For the moment the threat was working. Calhoun hadn't said a word for over an hour. He was content to sit quietly and write down the names, times, and the insulting threatening remarks made toward him during this ordeal. He was convinced, in his own mind at least, that he had powerful friends in Washington who would make them pay for their treatment toward him. General Raymond Sweet was one of those important friends and these Green Berets were going to catch hell.

Chief Hileran entered the room with Sharon Chambers and three members of the A-Team who were wearing combat gear, their faces covered in camouflage. Privett joined the group at a large map of the capital that hung on the wall. Hileran had sent the three out to recon the situation at the airfield. Their report did little to raise the spirits of those in the room. The civilian militia had all but disintegrated into nothing more than an armed mob. They were now taking advantage of the confusion and using the weapons they had been given to rob and loot the stores in the city.

"What about the airfield?" asked Hileran.

Staff Sergeant Mike Roth, the team weapons man and leader of the patrol, stepped forward and pointed to four locations around the airport. "They've buttoned it up pretty tight, Chief, here, here, here, and here. We had a healthy exchange of small-arms fire with about ten to twelve guys in cammo fatigues along this western sector. They weren't Libyans, and they were too light to be Chadian rebels. Whoever they were, they knew their business. I mean they weren't some ragtag outfit. These guys moved like they had been around awhile. They were all Caucasian and big fellows, and they could shoot pretty damn good, too. They killed three of the Chad Rangers and one of the marines I had with me."

Privett raised his eyebrows and looked at Hileran. "We had reports that Qaddafi had hired himself a force of mercenaries. Seems the reports were correct."

Roth nodded in agreement. "Did you see any of General Gaafar's men out there, Mike?" asked the chief. "For some damn reason we haven't been able to make contact with him on the radio."

"Yes, sir. As a matter of fact, they opened up on us before we could identify ourselves. Damn near killed Peterson. They weren't carrying a radio with them, and I wasn't about to go out there and wave at 'em. So we split. It's real crazy out there, Chief; lots of jumpy people with guns and practically no communications or coordination going on. It's damn sure not a place for an afternoon walk."

"What about activity on the airfield?"

"Heavy, sir. We counted seven C-130s landing and another five or six in a holding pattern waiting to come in. Lots of troops, ammo, and supplies were being off-loaded. At the rate they're bringing the stuff in, I'd say we only have a few hours before they make their push into the city. Maybe less."

"So they haven't started making sweeps beyond the boundaries of the airport, yet. Is that right?"

"Yes, sir. As far as we could tell they are staying on the inside."

"What about a place to cross the Chari River? Did you find anything that looked promising?"

"Yes, sir. That area just south of the European Hospital where the ferry used to dock looks promising. They sunk the ferry, but the cable's still intact. It's lying a couple of inches below the water. If we use it to hold on to, the current shouldn't be any problem."

"Good job, Mike. You and the boys get some rest while you can. Since you've already been out there, you'll be the ones to lead us out when we go after dark."

"Yes, sir. Thank you, sir," said Roth as he gathered his team and departed for the kitchen and coffee.

Hileran turned to Privett and asked, "I know we got most of the people out on the planes to Egypt, but how many do we still have here?"

Privett thought for a moment, adding up the numbers in his head, four of his staff, Calhoun, Ms. Chambers, five Marine guards—no, make that four, one had been killed on Roth's patrol. "Counting your men, sixteen," replied Privett.

Hileran stared up at the map and the river that separated them from Cameroon. It didn't seem far, less than half a mile, but they were going to have to walk that half a mile. The air strike had destroyed the motor pool. Even worse, they had sunk the ferry that linked Cameroon and Chad. Once at the river, they would have to swim across. Like Roth had said, there were a lot of crazy people running around out there. He felt Sharon Chambers's eyes on him. He turned and smiled at her, "You really should have gone out on the plane, you know. Things could get out of hand before long, and Jake would never forgive me if you got hurt."

She was scared, but she wasn't about to add to Hileran's problems. Placing her arm around his waist, she smiled as she said, "We'll talk about that in Cameroon, okay?"

"You got a deal," said Hileran as he gave her a kiss on the cheek and turned to Privett. "Have your people ready, Mr. Privett. We leave in two hours." Taking Sharon's hand the chief pulled her toward the door. "Come on, I'll buy you a cup of coffee and tell you all the reasons you shouldn't associate with Navy guys."

Privett watched them leave, then looked at the map again. A half a mile, that wasn't that far. What could happen in a half a mile?

"Kaufman, are we ready?" yelled Kruger as he stood leaning against the 50 caliber machine gun that was mounted on his lead jeep. He stared back at the long column of heavily armed jeeps and half-tracks. Kaufman waved as he had his jeep driver pull up alongside Kruger. "We are ready, Herr Colonel."

"Very well. Remember, I want only to seal off any escape route across the river. In the morning, we will deal with the police headquarters and the federal buildings as well as the town hall."

"Where do you intend to spend the night, Hans?" asked Kaufman.

"Somewhere south of the hospital. I will radio you once I am in position. Good luck, old friend. I shall see you in the morning." Kruger tapped his driver on the shoulder. They began driving out the gates of the airfield and onto the highway that led to the city, his legion of mercenaries and their vehicles of destruction following close behind. In the west, the sun was already beginning to set as Kruger placed his foot on the dash and looked at his map. He still had to decide where he would spend the night. His eyes came to rest on a building designated hospital. That meant nurses. Seemed as good a place as any to find a few women, but they would have to wait until morning. It was possible Gaafar had stationed soldiers there. That presented no problem. They would find a position nearby to spend the night.

After drawing a circle on the map, Kruger laid the map in the seat. Within the circle, there were the words "Chad Ferry."

B. J. Mattson stared across the table at the three black Zairian generals as they listened to J. J. Johnson's briefing of the current situation in Chad. At the head of the table sat President Mobutu, the leader of the central government. All four men were listening politely to the American general. B.J. got the impression that the leaders of Zaire were not that concerned with the problems in Chad. He and Johnson had arrived in the country twelve hours ago, going immediately to the presidential palace. They had requested to see Mobutu. After expressing the urgency of their mission in Zaire, they soon discovered that the first thing this famed nineteenth-century colonialist country had adopted from the twentieth century was the world's love of bureaucratic red tape and protocol. One could not just fly into a country and ask to see the President. There were embassies, ambassadors, and formal ways of doing such things. They were politely but abruptly sent away and told to use the proper channels if they wished an appointment. B.J. and Johnson reluctantly departed for the embassy in frustration. Eleven hours later, they finally managed to get the powers that ran the place together in one room so they could present their case. Jason Hobart, the American attaché to the U.S. Embassy in Zaire, sat in one corner of the room. He had arranged the meeting.

B.J. leaned back as he rested his chin on his folded hands. All their time wasted because the bastards weren't buying it. Johnson stepped away from the map as he concluded his briefing with, "President Mobutu, as you can see, intervention on your part and that of the other OAU members would not only be conducive to both our interests, but highly profitable for those who should choose to intervene on our behalf. The decision is now in your hands, gentlemen. Since time is a crucial factor, I would ask for your decision as soon as possible. Hours and minutes will make the difference in the number of lives that could be lost in Chad. Thank you, gentlemen."

Johnson returned to his chair next to B.J., giving him a questioning look as he sat down. The lives of Jake and the others now rested in the hands of Mobutu and the three generals at the table. The President stood suddenly, causing a flurry of movement from the others in the room as they too rose to their feet.

"General Johnson, you present an admirable case on the behalf of the Chadian people. The letter from your President appears promising; however, I shall have to take this matter under advisement with my staff and the other member nations of the Organization of African Unity. I am certain you can understand the complexities involved in such a venture. Rest assure, General Johnson, I shall waste no time in pressing for a decision in this matter. Now, if you will excuse me, gentlemen. I have a previous engagement that demands my immediate attention. Please excuse me. We will be in contact with you, General. Good day."

Johnson nodded as he watched the President and his generals leave the room. Jason Hobart came around the table.

"Well, what do you think, Mr. Hobart?" asked Major Mattson.

The look on Hobart's face was anything but promising. "I'm sorry, gentlemen. I wish I could say you'd get the answer you are hoping for, but in all honesty, I'm afraid you have made a long trip for nothing."

Johnson stepped quickly in front of Hobart, staring straight into the man's eyes. "Would you care to explain that statement, sir?"

"Whoa there, General, I'm on your side, remember. Like the President said, you presented a very good case on behalf of the Chad government. I'm just afraid that Mobutu does not share your commitment."

"Now wait a minute, Hobart. These are the same guys that went in with the French and kicked the hell out of Qaddafi's army in 1986 when he tried this same crap in Chad. So why is this any different?" asked B.J.

"Oh, there is a very marked difference, Major. Zaire was obligated to the French government then. That is no longer the case now that the French have deserted Chad. You see, Major, they have no obligation to the United States; therefore, they see no reason to become involved in the matter. I'm afraid that without a commitment from Zaire, the other member countries in the OAU will decline your proposition as well. I'm sorry, gentlemen. I really am."

Johnson stood silently considering all that Hobart had said. As much as he hated to admit it, the man had a point. Mattson, however, refused to accept the theory. "But couldn't you be wrong, Hobart? I mean, what you're saying now is nothing but pure conjecture. Isn't that right? What makes you so sure that Mobutu isn't even considering the idea?"

Jason Hobart looked at both men knowing that neither one would want to hear what he was about to say. However, B.J. had left him little choice. "You know that pressing engagement that required the President's immediate attention before he could begin action on your proposal?"

"Yes, what about it?" said General Johnson.

"It is for the dedication of a botanical garden at his new residence. The ambassador received an invitation yesterday. Sorry, Major, but like I said, there is no obligation involved. Can I give you a ride back to the embassy?"

Johnson felt both rage and resentment welling up within himself; yet there was nothing he could do, and he realized that. B.J. on the other hand started for the door, his voice filled with emotion, "I'll wring that motherfucker's neck!"

Hobart leaped in front of the door, panic showing on his face. "Are you crazy, Major? You touch that man and they'll shoot all three of us dead where we stand! General, please, talk to this man!"

"He's right B.J.—there's nothing more we can do here. I know how you feel, son, but no matter what you do, it won't help Jake. Come on, now, let's go back to the embassy with Mr. Hobart and see if we can find another way." Johnson stepped forward and took B.J.'s arm. He could feel the major's arm trembling; pure anger was flowing through every muscle of the man's body. "Come on, B.J., you know I'm right, don't you?"

Mattson breathed deeply and let it out slowly. Gradually the rage began to subside, "OK, General, we'll go, but whether we find someone who will help us or not, I'm going to Chad, even if I have to go in there by myself."

Johnson placed his hand on the major's shoulder, "If we can't find help, B.J., you won't be by yourself; I'll be with you." Mattson could tell by the look in the general's eyes he meant what he said. The two officers walked out of the room and headed for the front doors. Jason Hobart followed them outside, wiping his brow with a handkerchief. My God, these Special Operations people are crazy, he thought to himself as he climbed into the front seat and directed the driver back to the embassy. Watching the sun disappear on the horizon, Hobart was hopeful that there would be some good news awaiting them when they arrived. The two men in the backseat definitely could use some good news right about now.

Mike Roth moved quietly along the edge of the stucco building, his eyes fixed on the street at the end of the alley. Peterson was on the other side of the alley moving with the same catlike ease. Twenty feet behind both men, Hileran and the others knelt in silence against one wall waiting for the signal to advance. They had been out of the embassy and on the streets for fifteen minutes now. So far their only encounter had been with an old wino who had stumbled out of one of the side doors. Roth tapped the man on the side of the head with the butt of his twelve-gauge shotgun and pulled him back inside the building. The four marines from the embassy were providing the rear security. Sharon and Privett were directly behind Hileran, while Talbot, Henderson, and Weathers, the other three team members of A-505 had placed Calhoun and the four staff people in the middle of the group. Calhoun was against the move at first, until he was left with the option of coming along with the group or remaining in the embassy by himself. He quickly reconsidered and decided to follow the group.

Reaching the end of the alley, Roth and Peterson knelt down as they slowly peered around the buildings and across the street. Three bodies lay near a streetlight at the corner. They were the same three that had been seen during the recon. Either the people were afraid to touch them or they just didn't give a damn. Roth was willing to bet it was the latter. Raising his arm, he waved the group forward. Hileran stressed the importance of moving as quietly as possible. Renewing the warning, he motioned for them to follow as he made his way to Roth's position. Roth looked back as the line of figures moved along the wall. Chief Hileran came up and knelt beside him, "How much farther, Mike?"

Roth pointed across the street at a small park plaza dotted with palm trees and benches. In the center was a single fountain approximately ten feet high that was surrounded by marble blocks. "The other side of that park, Chief. The dock is maybe fifty, seventy-five feet beyond the street. That white-looking building you can see through the trees there is the blockhouse for the engine they used to pull the ferry back and forth. The docks run about fifty yards to the left and right; the cable's lying on the dock directly in front of the blockhouse. It's pretty open out there, sir. We're going to have to play it real careful and real, real quiet. Anybody spots us out there, and they'll eat our lunch, that's for damn sure. I'd like to take Weathers, Talbot, and Pete with me, sir. That'll give me a wider pattern of search."

Hileran could feel the adrenaline pumping through his veins. Sweat was forming on his forehead. Nervousness gripped his stomach. He knew if he didn't have all these civilians with him, there wouldn't be the knots in his gut, but he did have them, and it was up to him to get them out of here in one piece. "Go ahead, Mike, take them with you. We won't move out of this alley until we get the all-clear from you."

Roth swung the mouthpiece portion of the Walkman-style headset in front of his lips and whispered into the voice-activated transmitter, "Pete, you got me?" Peterson gave the thumbs-up signal from the other side of the alley.

"Roger, I got you, too," said Hileran. Roth nodded, then slowly stood, pointing to Weathers and Talbot. He was motioning for them to join him. Sending Weathers to join Peterson, he and Talbot moved across the street into the park. Taking up positions behind the first set of palm trees, they peered into the darkness around them. Minutes seemed like hours as Peterson and Weathers knelt next to the wall waiting for the signal to cross. This was something they had practiced a hundred times back at Fort Bragg. But this time a mistake could get them killed.

There was the signal. As they moved quickly and quietly across the street, Roth and Talbot were on their feet running for the fountain. Once there, he whispered, "Chief, the park's clean, but I wouldn't move anybody until we have a look on the other side."

"I agree, Mike, we'll hold here till you check it out," answered Hileran.

Peterson and Weathers joined Roth at the fountain. Sharon Chambers had moved up behind Hileran. He could feel her rapid breath on the back of his neck. He knew she was scared, but then, so was he. They watched as the two teams split up and moved through the shadows to the right and left of the manmade waterfall until finally they faded into the darkness of the far side of the park. Hileran could hear the breathing of one of his men; his mike open. It was the breathing of excitement mixed with fear.

"What the hell are we waiting for?" The words sounded like a cannon going off, startling everyone in the group. Hileran twirled and made his way back down the line. Henderson was trying to put his hand over Calhoun's mouth.

"Get your hands off me!" said Calhoun, his raised voice echoing even louder in the confines of the alley.

Hileran dropped down next to the man and whispered, "Shut up, you idiot! You want to get us all killed! Henderson, go to the front and keep an eye on our people." Sergeant Henderson nodded and moved off.

"Listen." Hileran reached out and grabbed the man by the

collar. "You open that fucking big mouth of yours again and I'll personally strangle the shit out of you right here. Do you understand me? You want to talk, you whisper, you don't yell. Now what the hell is your problem, Calhoun?" asked Hileran as he released the man's collar and smoothed it down with the palm of his hand.

Calhoun's eyes were as big as silver dollars as he whispered, "I—I was just wanting to know what was taking so long, that's all."

"We're trying to make sure we get you out of here with your ass still intact. We don't have any idea who's out there, Calhoun. You understand. Now, please, keep it down. It won't be much longer, believe me, you're not the only one that wants out of here, OK?"

Calhoun nodded and Hileran went back to the front. Roth was on the radio again, "Chief, you're clear to move to the park."

"Roger, sending them across two at a time, out." Hileran pointed to two of the marines to bring them forward. Checking the street, he tapped them to move across, taking cover in the trees and pointing their weapons down both ends of the street. Next went Sharon and Privett. The move across the street took less than five minutes. Within ten minutes, they had moved past the fountain to the tree line across from the docks. Chief Warrant Officer Scotty Hileran had his people one step closer to home.

Roth and the others fanned out making a sweep of the docks, working from the far ends toward the center and the blockhouse. Peterson was the first one to spot them. "Hold it!" he whispered into his radio. Roth and the others froze where they were as Peterson whispered excitedly, "I've got some people on the left side of the dock. Five, maybe six—they're armed. Can't make out if they are Chad regulars or the bad guys . . . wait a minute . . . there's four more. They're big guys, could be the same ones we tangled with this afternoon. Looks like they're spending the night on the docks. There are a couple asleep on some crates near the water. I'm pulling back."

"Roger, Pete, drop back. Go around and join me on the left side. Maybe we can find another spot to cross. Did you monitor, Chief?" asked Roth.

"Roger, Mike. I'm moving the people to the left now, out."

"Mike, this is Weathers. I've got a bunch of vehicles parked down here on the right, machine gun-mounted jeeps and half-tracks—bad news, the tracks are Russian." Roth rogered and told Weathers to join him.

Roth now had the other three men with him near some old building just beyond the docks. They watched as the two men in front of them smoked and whispered back and forth. From what they could tell, the two were the only ones on this end of the dock. One of them laughed as he flipped his cigarette into the water. He turned and came toward the building. Roth reached down and pulled his combat knife from his boot, signaling the others to do the same. Peterson nodded toward the man still on the dock, then drew his finger across his neck. Roth agreed and pointed to Weathers to go with him. Both men faded into the shadows toward the dock.

Roth could hear the dirt crunching under the man's boots as he neared the building. Gripping the knife tightly in his fist he timed his move perfectly, allowing the man a half step past the corner of the building. He reached out, clamped one hand over the man's mouth, and drove the blade of the knife straight up under the back of the skull twisting it twice. The man's body jerked once, then went limp. Lowering the body to the ground, Roth knelt as he watched Peterson and Weathers close in on their man. Suddenly Peterson stepped out onto the dock a few feet behind the unsuspecting man. Quietly he said, "Excuse me." The man turned, surprised to see anyone there. Weathers took three quick steps, grabbing the man, placing his hand over his mouth as Peterson drove the blade into the man's heart killing him instantly. Weathers lowered the body over the edge of the dock and into the water. Then both men raced back to Roth who was now on the radio, "Chief, you got a fix on us?"

"Roger, Mike."

"This looks like it's as good a place as any to take them across. It's not as wide as the cable area, and there won't be anything to hold on to when the current hits them."

"Got you, Mike, we can't be choosy. We'll have to take what we can get. I'll have them there in two minutes, out."

Roth positioned his men. As he was waiting, two groups of men appeared on the dock. They were coming from both directions. Somewhere down the street, they heard a half-track and a jeep crank their engines. Everything seemed to be

happening at once. Hileran, hearing the vehicles' engines,
waved the group back to the trees. Calhoun, in a moment of
panic, slipped and fell in the middle of the street. He yelled in
pain as his knees slammed onto the concrete. His loud cry was
heard by the driver of the half-track who switched on his
headlights to bathe the whining man in a flood of light. In the
same instant, the two groups of men on the docks swung their
weapons into the ready position and began running for the
street. Knowing he could not let them get behind him, Roth
yelled, "Take 'em!"

The four Green Berets opened fire on the two groups of men,
taking down five in the initial burst. The others spread out and
dropped to the prone position to return the fire. Calhoun was on
his feet now, his hands raised high in the air as he yelled,
"Don't shoot! We surrender! We surrender!"

"We!" exclaimed the half-track driver. "There's more than
one, Kirk," he yelled to the jeep driver who had switched on
the spotlight on his jeep swinging it toward the park.

"God damn you, Calhoun!" screamed Hileran as he and the
marines who were caught in the light opened fire on the jeep.

Fredrick Calhoun stood with his hands out to his side,
confused and dazed. What had he done? Why was Hileran
cussing him? It was a question for which he would never
receive an answer. The track driver thumbed the safety off the
50-caliber machine gun and depressed the twin triggers. His
first two rounds cut Calhoun in half.

Sharon screamed as she watched the man literally being torn
apart. Hileran shoved her to the ground as the man swung the
big gun toward them. One of the marines took out the jeep
driver, but before he could fire on the man behind the
60-caliber machine gun mounted on the jeep, a line of bullets
crawled up his legs and blew his chest wide open. "Oh, Jesus!"
cried Hileran as twenty to thirty more men came running down
the street, flanking them. Two of the staff people tried to run
back toward the alley. They were ripped apart by a hail of
bullets from the mercenaries who now surrounded the fountain.
Two more marines went down. Hileran felt something hot hit
him in the side, then his leg and a final pain in his chest. The
impact threw him to the ground. Sharon was screaming again.
Privett cried out as two bullets slammed into his back and
drove him face first to the ground only a few feet from Hileran.

Raising his head, blood flowing from his nose and streaming from his mouth, he painfully looked over at Hileran and muttered, "Only half a mile . . ." His head dropped and Wayne Privett was dead. Henderson took out three of the men at the fountain and changed magazines in his rifle as he ran to help Hileran. The 50-caliber caught him in the open; one round decapitated him, while another took off his leg at the hip.

Sharon crawled to Hileran's side and cradled his head in her lap. Tears were running down her face. Scotty could hear the firing still coming from the buildings near the docks. Roth and the boys were giving them their money's worth. Hileran found some consolation in that as he smiled up into the soft eyes of Sharon Chambers. Even with her mascara streaking down her face, she was beautiful. "Remember . . . what I told . . . you about those . . . Navy guys, beautif . . ." Hileran coughed once, sending a spray of warm blood onto her arms, then sighed deeply and closed his eyes, drifting into a never-ending sleep. She was still cradling him to her when they came up and surrounded her. Looking up at them, she saw the lust in their eyes and knew the fate that awaited her. Lowering her head back down, she leaned forward and kissed Hileran gently on the forehead. Her hand came out from under his body so quickly that none of the mercenaries around her had time to react. The gun was already cocked. It was only a matter of putting it to her head and pulling the trigger.

Mike Roth shoved the final three rounds into his shotgun. Weathers lay dead, half his face blown off. Peterson was down, but still firing. Talbot was hit but was holding a good position trying to keep them off Peterson. Two men broke around the corner of the shed. Roth twirled and leveled the shotgun with its double-aught buck and pumped twice, catching one man in the chest and the other in the face. Peterson yelled. Roth jacked the last round into the chamber and turned. He was too late. The mercenary emptied an entire clip from the MP-5 into Peterson as he lay helpless on the ground.

Roth, enraged beyond human endurance, screamed at the top of his lungs and ran at the startled killer who was trying to reload. Body blocking the man into the side of the wall, Roth stepped back, held out the shotgun with one hand, placed the barrel against the man's head, and fired. Letting the shotgun fall free he jerked his 9mm Beretta from his shoulder holster.

Still screaming, he charged out onto the docks, firing at anything that moved, and yelled for Talbot to come on.

Talbot pushed a crate out of the way, reloaded another magazine in his CAR-15, and dragged his wounded leg as he hobbled out beside Roth. Standing back to back, the two Green Berets took on all comers as they tried to make their way to the edge of the dock and the water. Roth heard Talbot groan once, then felt the man's blood run down the back of his neck. The bullet had hit Talbot in the side of the head. He dropped like a rock. The bodies of the dead were everywhere as two more mercs ran out onto the dock. Roth blew two holes in the first one and wounded the second. Then the Beretta clicked—he was out of bullets, and there were no more magazines. The wounded man was trying to raise his weapon. Roth threw the Beretta, catching the man in the head. Then he charged forward tackling him, sending them both off the docks and into the water. They were struggling and thrashing about as more mercenaries ran to the edge of the dock and pointed their weapons waiting for a shot at the Green Beret. Suddenly Kruger appeared and looked down at the two men in the water. "What are you waiting for?" he yelled.

"But, sir, that is Captain Ching!" said one of the men.

"So! Kill them both!" shouted Kruger as he turned and walked toward the park. They leveled their guns and were about to fire when a hail of automatic weapons fire ripped through three of the men on the dock and pitched them into the water. The sole surviving marine from the battle in the park stumbled from the corner of one of the buildings. His M-16 was spitting thirty rounds of certain death into the group on the dock. They scurried for cover.

Kruger, hearing the screams of his men, walked back around the building. Seeing the marine, he calmly stepped up behind him and blew the top of his head off. By his actions, the marine had given Roth the time he needed. The Oriental he had been battling in the water passed out. Keeping his grip on the man, he managed to reach the halfway point of the river. The current carried them out of the sight of those on the docks who were still firing into the water. They fired more out of fear of Kruger than anything else. They would report to the German that they had killed the two men.

The mental and physical ordeal of the past twelve hours had

taken its toll on the young sergeant. Pure determination and the physical endurance born of rugged training were the only things sustaining Roth as he reached out and grabbed hand after hand of water, pulling himself ever closer to the banks of Cameroon. On more than one occasion he had been tempted to let go of the Oriental and allow him to drown. Yet Roth knew this man was their only true source of hard intelligence. They were going to need him to find out who they were up against, how many, and what, if anything, the man knew of the overall plan. No, Mike Roth wasn't going to let this man go. Too many good people had already died to let this all slip away in the currents of the Chari River.

Feeling the sandy bottom of the bank come up under his feet, Roth gasped for air as he clawed his way onto the shore, pulling his prize possession alongside of him. Suddenly the sky lit up as a thundering roar of artillery rounds exploded on the other side of the river. Huge fireballs rolled and blossomed their way skyward, turning night into day as round after round hit the airport. Although he was tired, Mike Roth felt a renewed surge of energy streak through his body. General Gaafar and the Chad Army hadn't given up yet.

Major Fenelon waited as Jake and Captain York counted the number of canteens they had within the group. The good news was that the sun was going down. The bad news was that most of the men had taken off their web gear when they were on the choppers. In the mad scramble to get away from the highly flammable targets, many of the men had left their gear on board. What the explosions didn't get, the fires that followed had. Counting the dead and wounded, they were down to ninety-six men. The count presented a problem at first. The numbers just didn't add up right. They had left Mangalme with 118 people, not counting the crews. Subtract the KIAs and the WIAs, and there were still twelve men missing, all of them Chad Rangers. In the end they had concluded that the men must have stayed aboard the fleeing chopper in hopes that the pilots could escape the fury of the F-5 fighters.

Jake and York returned and sat down in the sand next to Fenelon. Jake pulled a pen from his shirt and began doing some quick Harvard math on a piece of paper. When he finished, he looked over at Fenelon and asked, "Pierre, what were those figures again? You know, how much water to go how far and all that."

"*Oui, monsieur*. In a desert such as this, it will require a minimum of one gallon per day per man. If we move only in the evening hours and throughout the night, we can control the amount of perspiration, allowing us to cover as much as twenty miles with each move. Keep in mind, my friends, man can go for days without food, but out here the importance of water can not be overemphasized. Without it we are dead men."

Jake did some figuring, then tossed the paper in the sand. "How'd we come out, Jake?" asked Randy.

"Counting every canteen we've got and assuming they are all full, we have about one hundred and eighty gallons of water. Using Pierre's calculations of the minimum requirements, we're about seven gallons short. We can go forty miles before we're running on empty. I figure another twenty on pure guts and determination, but, brother, that last twenty-five miles to Lake Chad might as well be two thousand. There are just some things that guts and a good attitude can't change and the body's need for water is one of them."

"Well, we've ruled out going any other direction. Lake Chad's the only way we can go without running into the bad guys, and that's a maybe, at best. I know one thing, we're going to have to do something. We just can't sit here and wait for those tanks to roll over us. What do you think, Pierre?"

"But of course, *mon ami*. My legionnaires and I have no desire to take on tanks with only small arms. That is why we must move to the northwest. The armor unit is obviously meant to play a major role in the capture of the capital. The farther we move northwest the less likely he is to divert from his primary mission. Besides, who is to say that we will not find water during our journey? There are nomad tribes who have wandered these deserts for hundreds of years. I have never yet, in all my years with the Legion, found a nomad who has died from thirst—Legion bullets perhaps, but never from lack of water."

Jake glanced over at York. "He makes it sound almost easy, doesn't he?"

York smiled at Pierre as he answered, "Hell, Jake, I don't even care if he's lying, at least he makes it sound possible. Let's do it."

Jake looked over at Fenelon who was smiling along with York as he said, "That is unless you've got something else to do, Jake."

Jake sat up and began brushing the sand off his arms. Fenelon reached over and stopped him. "First lesson," he said, "don't remove the sand, it will provide protection from the sun during the day."

Jake turned to York who suddenly stopped brushing himself off. "Oh, hell, I knew that," he said.

"Right!" laughed Jake as he stood up and called for Doc and the others to form a circle around them.

"Gentlemen, we have decided that our only way out of here is to make for Lake Chad. That's eighty-five miles to the northwest. Now, I don't have to tell you how important water is going to be on this little hike. Some of you Rangers were born in this desert, and most of you legionnaires have fought in them for years. All I can say is use that experience as a guide. We have no idea what the situation is in the capital at this time, but we do know there is an armored column roaming around somewhere behind us. How far away they are is anybody's guess. We don't plan to wait for them to catch up. We'll move in the evening and throughout the night, then find what cover we can and rest during the day. The way we figure it, we should reach Lake Chad on the morning of the fifth day and cross over into Cameroon. Do I have any questions?" There were none. "OK, we move in fifteen minutes. That's all."

Fenelon called out to Blancher, "Doctor, a moment please." Doc stopped and came back over to the major. "Yes, sir."

"My corporal, how is he?"

Randy and Jake paused in putting on their gear, waiting for Doc's answer. Blancher looked off to the horizon, the first stars of the night seemed to be coming up out of the sand like magic. "He's pretty bad, sir. The morphine doesn't seem to help anymore. I'm afraid they blew half his guts out his side. He's in a lot of pain, Major, a lot of pain."

Fenelon's voice was heavy with sadness as he lowered his head and said, "I see, thank you, Doctor." Blancher glanced at Jake with a look of helplessness. He had done all he could under the circumstances. Sadly he turned and walked away.

York fastened his web belt and slung his rifle over his

shoulder as he said, "Pierre, I'll get some of my men to help carry him."

The legionnaire reached down and opened his pack. "That will not be necessary, Captain, but thank you." Bringing the silencer up in the fading light, he removed his pistol from his shoulder holster and locked the silencer in place. He walked slowly toward the wreckage of the first chopper where his corporal lay moaning in agony. The legionnaires, seeing him approach, gave their friend a final glance and walked away.

Jake stood next to York and asked, "Could you do that?"

Randy York didn't answer as he turned away and stared across the vastness of the never-ending sand. It seemed to be encompassed in a strange, haunting darkness from which a million tiny lights were suspended to create the perfect stage for the stillness. So still, that the *whiffff* of the silencer seemed like a roar. The sound sent a chill through York. Jake's question remained unanswered. Randy York hoped it never would be.

Returning to his pack, Fenelon dropped the silencer back into his bag, tightened down the straps, and swing it onto his back. Without speaking, he and three of his Legion took the point and began the long journey for Lake Chad. A somber mood fell over the group as they adjusted their equipment and fell in behind the leaders to begin the first leg of the march. They had all known the young corporal was going to die. The wound had been too serious for him not to. Yet as they trudged through the sand passing the still body of the boy who awaited the final touch of the gravediggers who were preparing a place for him, they could not help but wonder what fate had in store for each of them in the long walk ahead.

CHAPTER 9

Jason Hobart poured three cups of coffee and took them into the operations room. B.J. and the general were watching the teletype as the reports of the Panama invasion were being sent to every American Embassy in the world. It started at midnight. Fighting was going on all over the country. Noriega's men were putting up stiff resistance in some areas of Panama City. For both men it was a frustrating time. The embassy in Cameroon reported gunfire in the city of N'Djamena and an artillery attack on the airport. To add to the frustration, no one had been able to talk with anyone at the Chad Embassy since the air attacks on the city. Civilians from the villages on the Cameroon side of the Chari River had told of huge planes dropping men from the sky. They reported hearing heavy fighting around the airport. The few radio communications that had been intercepted coming out of Chad made no mention of the fate of the embassy personnel nor the A-Team. From what they could tell, General Gaafar was attempting to reorganize his troops. The airborne assault on the airport had caught them totally by surprise.

Passing out the coffee, Hobart asked, "How are we doing in Panama?"

"It's hot and heavy at the moment. They still haven't found Noriega," replied B.J. who in turn asked, "What about Mobutu? Has he even begun discussions with anyone?"

"No, he was exhausted from his busy schedule and has

retired for the night. He'll start on our request first thing in the morning."

Johnson stared up at the clock on the wall. It was four in the morning. He couldn't remember the last time he had slept, but who could sleep anyway. He had troops committed to combat in two countries at the same time. One group was involved in a full-scale invasion and under the command of a man with a General Patton ego and Roger Rabbit capabilities. The fate of the other group hung on the balance of a decision that would have to come from a man who wore himself out cutting a ribbon in honor of a damn bunch of flowers. Johnson tossed the Styrofoam cup of coffee into the trash as he said, "God damn it, Hobart, there has to be something we can do! Something we can use to convince Mobutu that he'll be up shit creek without a paddle if he doesn't help us on this thing."

Hobart was about to say something when one of the operators tore a hard copy of a message from his teletype, crossed the room, and handed it to Hobart. "Sir, you'd better have a look at this," he said.

Hobart read the message quickly, then looked at Johnson as he said, "OK, General, you want to do something besides just stand around here; then I would suggest that you and the major fly to Cameroon immediately. One of your people, a Sergeant Roth, has made his way out of Chad. He was found wandering around the jungle by some villagers near the river. Our embassy people are on their way to pick him up right now. They say he's worn out, but OK. He brought a prisoner out of there with him, an Oriental according to the report. You may want to talk to him yourself. He should be able to tell us what has happened over there and where the rest of your people are." Passing the message to Johnson, he said, "And don't worry, General. The minute Mobutu makes his decision; I'll let you know."

For the first time since the meeting with Mobutu, Hobart saw an easing of the tension in the general's face; at last they had received some good news.

"Thank you, sir. We'll leave immediately. Let's go, B.J."

Jason Hobart watched as the two officers departed. Sipping on his coffee he glanced down and read another report coming across the teletype. It was a classified report from Egyptian intelligence. Photo reconnaissance verified the total destruction of the fortress at Mangalme and the visible count of forty-four bodies on the ground, all legionnaires. The attacking force had consisted of an armor column that included thirty tanks. The column was last reported less than ten miles from a place called Bokoro.

At the first sign of the approaching sun, Fenelon, taking advantage of the natural terrain, led the unit into a dried riverbed that ran north and south. They could use the four-foot-high wadi banks to shade them from the sun during the morning. Then they could switch over to the other side in the afternoon as the sun passed over and to the west. Doc moved along the line of tired men checking each one for any sign of heat cramps or heat exhaustion. So far they all appeared to be in good shape. They were more tired than anything else. Some had already drifted off to sleep.

Jake and Randy lowered their weary bodies down against the hard-packed walls. Jake never realized how exhausting walking in sand could be. Fenelon joined them. "How many miles you figure we covered last night, Pierre?" asked York.

Fenelon stretched out his long legs and leaned back, closing his eyes before he answered, "Twelve, maybe fifteen miles, perhaps. It is often hard to tell in the desert. We will do better tonight with an early start."

"Damn, I wish we had a radio. I'd sure like to talk to Scotty and find out how they're doing in the city," said York.

"Yeah, makes you feel kind of isolated from the world out here, doesn't it. Wonder how the boys are doing in Panama?" said Jake.

"Wish you hadn't mentioned that," groaned York. "They are probably getting rained on right now. It's the monsoon season there you know. Hey, Fenelon, you ever been to Panama?" Receiving no answer, York glanced over at the legionnaire. Pierre was already asleep. Looking back at Jake, he saw the Navy man had done likewise. Shifting into a more comfortable position, Randy York saw the first traces of sunlight cast a narrow line along the bank across from him. It was just past six in the morning and the temperature was already 90 degrees and rising. Closing his eyes, the Green Beret captain thought of his home in Colorado with its picturesque mountains of snow.

• • •

"Halt!" yelled Kueddei as his track crested the dunes overlooking the burnt-out choppers below. Raising his field glasses, he made a sweep of the area. His quarry was gone. Pressing the switch on his headset he barked, "Move out, but keep your eyes open. We have no idea where they may be."

The high-pitched roar of the armored column resounded across the open space of the desert as tanks and half-tracks rumbled down the side of the dunes and toward the wreckage. Ordering a halt at the lead chopper, Kueddei dismounted and went forward to examine the exceptional work that had been performed by his F-5 pilots. Others dismounted their vehicles and began a search of the area. One of the rebels called to Kueddei and pointed to the right track of his tank. A piece of khaki cloth was caught up in the treads. Kueddei approached the tank and stared curiously at the rag while calling to the tank driver to back up. Revving the motor the man slowly began to ease the heavy tank backward. The treads caught another piece of cloth this time, pulling something out of the ground with it. Slowly the men around the rebel leader began realizing what it was that was being unearthed by the tank. It was the body of a young legionnaire. Kueddei raised his hand, and the driver stopped. Those around the gruesome sight reached for hand-kerchiefs or raised the corners of their shirts to cover their noses, warding off the smell that had been hastened by the heat of the midmorning sun. Kueddei knelt down next to the body as if immune to the distasteful odor. He felt the face, the arms, and finally the legs of the body. Looking at his watch he rose and walked back to his track. The man had not been dead long, perhaps twelve hours or less. Climbing topside, he again swept the area with his glasses, searching for any sign that might indicate to him which way the enemy had gone. Had he arrived sooner, there might have been a trail left by such a large body of men, but the morning winds were too strong, and now all signs of the departure had been erased by the shifting sands.

Pulling the earphones from his head, Kueddei's driver held the headsets up to his leader. "It is Colonel Kruger, sir. He wants to talk to you." Taking the headset, he placed it on his head and pressed the talk switch, "Ah, Colonel Kruger, how are you this morning? You slept well, I hope."

There was no immediate reply. When Kruger finally did

speak, there was a noticeable surliness in his voice. "For your information, General, I did not sleep well. We spent half the night attempting to contain your bastard brother and his army within this city. It has cost me a number of my best men, I might add. Where in the hell are you, General?"

Kueddei grinned, he really enjoyed upsetting this soldier of fortune who fought for mere money. So he had lost some men. That was what they were paid for. Why complain to him. "I am at Bokoro for the moment, Colonel. I have found the wreckage of the helicopters that escaped me at Mangalme. I have been debating the idea of perhaps pursuing the survivors."

"General, I will remind you that at first light this morning we launched an all-out offensive on the city. Your brother and his so-called ragtag army have given us nothing but hell from the very start. We are having to take this place one street at a time and it is becoming very costly. I need those tanks here, and I need them now, General. We can go after your damn legionnaires after we have eliminated your brother and all the opposition. Can't you see that? I'm losing men who are fighting an army while you run around with your dick in your hand chasing a few stragglers who couldn't possibly have an effect on the outcome. So let's knock off the bullshit, and you get your ass in here, now!"

The driver who monitored the conversation on his headset smiled up at Kueddei as he remarked, "I think you have managed to piss him off, General."

"Yes, it would seem that our Ice Man is not so cool at the moment," laughed Kueddei. Perhaps Kruger was right. Pressing the mike once again, Kueddei was about to tell Kruger that when the men in the scout car along the ridge shouted down to him that they had found the route taken by the legionnaires. Kueddei paused, releasing the mike button. The legionnaires were on foot. They had buried the boy less than twelve hours ago. Even walking all night, they could not have possibly covered more than fifteen or twenty miles. They would need to rest during the day. He could surely overtake them by early afternoon, wipe them out, and return at full speed to N'Djamena just in time to deliver the coup de grace to his brother and what was left of his army. It was the perfect plan. Keying the mike, he said, "Colonel Kruger, you are absolutely correct. We will start for the capital immediately."

"Roger, General. That's more like it. I will see you when you arrive. Out." Kruger dropped his handset in the seat and stared over at Kaufman. "That son of a bitch is going after those Frenchmen before he brings those tanks here."

"But, Hans, he said . . ."

"I know what he said, Adolf. He told me exactly what I wanted to hear. That's why I know he's lying. He didn't come back with any smart-ass remarks. Let's get back to the airport. If I can't get the tanks here, maybe we can blast Gaafar out of here with the F-5s—won't be much left after they're finished, but if that asshole Kueddei doesn't care, then neither do I. The bastard can rule from the top of the rubble that's left. Let's go."

Kueddei sent his scout cars far out in front with instructions to radio in as soon as they had visual sighting of the objective. Swinging his track around, the driver ran over the body they had unearthed. Kueddei stared back at what remained as he said, "Fear not, Frenchman, you shall soon have the company of your friends."

The two legionnaires on guard duty scrambled over the side of the riverbank and excitedly shook Fenelon awake. *"Commandant! Commandant Fenelon! Beaucoup de véhicules blindé!"*

Fenelon awoke instantly, jumping to his feet. Jake Mortimer opened his eyes and used his hand to shield the brightness of the sun. He looked up at the Legion officer, "What is it, Major?"

"Armored vehicles. Many of them coming from the east."

"Shit!" said Jake as he turned to shake the still sleeping Captain York awake. Fenelon was already climbing out of the riverbed behind his two guards as Jake pulled York to his feet, crying, "Come on, Randy. We've got company." York, his eyes still not adjusted to the brightness of the noonday sun, followed Jake and the others toward the dunes that lay only a few yards away. Fenelon already had his field glasses out and was peering over the top at the huge dust cloud that rose from the sand flats below.

"How many?" asked Jake.

Fenelon passed him the glasses and stared back at the anxious faces of the men now lining the top of the wadibank. The distant roar of the diesel engines became clearer with each advancing yard of the clanking treads. "Too many, my friend," replied Fenelon.

"Jesus!" sighed Jake as he swept the line of half-tracks and tanks through the binoculars. York crawled up next to Jake. He didn't need the field glasses now. His eyes were fixed on the two scout cars that were far out in front of the armored unit that was heading straight for them.

"I don't suppose we have anything big enough to take these boys on, do we?" asked York.

"I am afraid not, Captain. We have perhaps two or three M-72 LAWs. Other than that, we are limited to grenades and small arms. Hardly the materials one uses to attack an armored column," answered Fenelon.

Raising the glasses again, Jake asked, "What about a couple of 106s and a 50-caliber machine gun? Think we could keep their attention with something like that?"

"*Oui*, Commander, but where will we find these things?" asked Fenelon.

"We won't have to, Major. They'll find us." Lowering the glasses, Jake pointed at the two scout cars that were less than three miles from them now. "Those two scouts out front each have a mounted 106mm and that one on the right has added a 50-caliber on the right side. The way they're tracking, they'll be sitting right on this very spot in about ten minutes. What do you say we take their weapons away from them to even things up a bit?"

Fenelon was smiling. "Ah, Jake, you have the heart of a legionnaire."

"Yeah," exclaimed York, "and one hell of an imagination. This is kind of like David and Goliath, and we're not exactly the ones carrying the big stick you know. You really think a couple of 106s are going to make that much difference?"

"Why sure, Randy," grinned Jake. "Just like little David, we'll knock out one of those tanks. Then I'm going to tell the rest of them that we have them surrounded and they have one minute to surrender or we'll destroy their asses in place." He winked at Fenelon as he finished saying, "Just don't know what the hell we'll do with that many prisoners. Come on, let's set up a little surprise party for our guests." York was still staring at the two laughing officers as they made their way back to the riverbed. "Jesus, they're both crazy," he whispered to himself as he slipped back from the slope and followed them.

The dark-faced Chadian rebel squinted his eyes against the sun as he searched the riverbed. He ignored the heat in anticipation of doing battle. They roared up the dune fully expecting to find the legionnaires fleeing in panic, stumbling their way through the sand somewhere in front of them. The signs they had been following left little doubt in his mind that they were closing in on their quarry. But now, there was nothing. Nothing but endless miles of sand. Kueddei was not going to be happy. Leaning forward on the windshield, he asked his driver to hand him the handset of the radio. Wiping his sweat-drenched face with the dirty cravat around his neck, the driver reached for the mike. Suddenly he stopped. Slapping his commander on the leg, he pointed to a khaki shirt that lay only a few feet away in the sand. The three men in the other scout car spotted another shirt lying off to the right and down the slope. "Delwata! What does that mean?"

The commander of the first car raised his hands questioningly. "How should I know. There is one lying over here, too." The men climbed out of the scout cars. Stretching aching muscles, they moved toward the objects at each location. One rebel paused to relieve himself a few feet from the scout car as the others stood around the shirts and stared out across the desert. Midway through the function, the man looked down at the ground and noticed a small black piece of metal protruding slightly above the sand. Finished, he zipped up his pants, leaned forward placing his fingers on the metal object, and pulled. The legionnaire buried under the sand sat straight up. The handkerchief that had been covering his face fell away and he smiled in delight at the shocked look in the rebel's eyes as he drove his knife into the man's throat.

The commander of the first scout car caught the movement out of the corner of his eye. Twirling around, he reached for his pistol. It was too late. Fenelon's silenced pistol whispered its death call. The bullet caught the man behind his left ear and exited his right eye. As the commander fell forward, the others broke for the cars. Legionnaires began raising up as if from the dead and tripping the fleeing, frightened men. The resurrected legionnaires fell on the men, driving their knives through their hearts or cutting their throats. It was all over in less than a minute. Two legionnaires were already in the cars and turning them around to face the oncoming onslaught of the armored column.

Fenelon came running forward excitedly, "Just as you planned, Jake. It was brilliant. I would never have thought of such a thing."

"Thanks, Pierre, but I can't take the credit for it. I saw it done in an old western movie a long time ago, only the Indians used reeds to breathe through while they were under the sand. Your boys may be spitting gun oil from these pistol barrels for a while," laughed Jake.

Randy York was checking the 106 on the first car. The gun was already loaded. There were ten more shells in the ammo compartment. A check of the second car found the same thing. Jake called to Sergeant Rivers and his Rangers to remove the 50-caliber and ammo from the track to set it up 300 yards to the left of the scout cars. One platoon of the Chadian Rangers assisted Rivers. Fenelon and Jake stayed with the 106s to do the firing. York took Sergeants O'Riley and McNeil, the team's demolition specialist, and forty of the men out to the far right. They would have the three M-72 LAWS, their rifles, and grenades to stop any flanking movement from that direction. They were all in position. Now all they had to do was wait. All eyes were on the Goliath that was roaring unknowingly closer and closer to the little David who readied his slingshots in preparation for the fight of his life.

Kueddei peered through his binoculars as he scanned the ridge of the sand dunes that lay ahead. He had neither seen the scout cars since they had paused on the ridge and disappeared over the hill, nor had he been able to establish radio contact with them. His driver attributed this to the heat and the fact that the dune was so large that it was blocking out their signal. That sounded reasonable to Kueddei. If the scouts had run into trouble, he would have heard gunfire by now, but there was nothing. Only dry, dusty, blowing sand and the infernal heat of the sun that now hung directly above them. Glancing at his watch, he thought of Kruger and how the mercenary leader must be cursing him now. Perhaps he should call him? No, he would wait until they topped the ridge that lay only a short distance ahead.

The sudden explosion of the 106 firing was followed immediately by a second explosion as the round hit the lead tank, blowing a large chunk of the turret away and causing the barrel to drop to the side and drag in the sand. Kueddei brought his glasses up in time to see the smoke rise from the second 106 as it fired. Another of his tanks was hit in the right track, the metal tread crawling off the wheels like a snake. The men inside scurried out the turret only to be cut down by Rivers and the 50-caliber machine gun. Confusion rained as the tracks cut hard to the left to avoid the 106s. The tanks cut left to do the same thing. Some collided with the scout cars that had been caught in the middle.

The 106s were firing round after round with deadly accuracy, taking out another tank and two of the half-tracks. Dazed, confused men leaped from the burning vehicles only to be caught in a crossfire from the machine gun on the right and the small-arms fire on the left. Remarkably, during this whole time, Kueddei's force had not fired one round in answer to the attack. Panic and confusion reigned supreme. Finally Kueddei began screaming orders over the radio, giving locations of targets and yelling for his men to open fire.

The tanks were the first to respond. Two tankers swung the barrels of the 120mm cannons toward the 106 position in the center of the ridge and fired. Both rounds fell short and blew huge piles of sand into the air. Sand rained down on Jake and Fenelon as they loaded another round in their 106s and swung them at the two tanks. Both men fired at the same time. A wild cheer came from the legionnaires as the two tanks exploded into twin balls of rolling fire and smoke. Kueddei was incensed with rage as he screamed at his men to correct their fire.

The cheering along the ridge suddenly stopped as three tanks came on line and fired in unison. Each round struck perfectly along the top right of the ridge. The 50-caliber machine gun disappeared in a cloud of sand, dust, and flying bodies. Over half of the Rangers around the big gun had been killed. Rivers was gone, his body vaporized by the direct hit. Doc Blancher was already running in that direction to see what, if anything, he could do for the wounded.

Kueddei regained control of the situation. He ordered the

infantry troops from the half-tracks to form up and assault the men on the left flank while the others drove straight for the middle. York and his men were holding their own for the moment, but the sheer weight of numbers was against them. Of the forty legionnaires and Rangers he had with him, thirteen were already dead and ten were wounded. It was only a matter of time, now. Sergeant O'Riley yelled a warning to York, then stood and fired over the captain's head. The front of the rebel's shirt jumped outward three times as the bullets impacted in a neat row across the man's chest. The rebel fell forward and on top of York. Before O'Riley could drop back to the prone, a bullet shattered his right knee. He pitched sideways and over the front of the dunes. The rebels went crazy. This was the first clear shot they had had at one of the enemy. A hail of bullets hit all around O'Riley as he withered in pain from the shattered kneecap.

"Hold on, Irish. I'm coming," screamed Sergeant McNeil as he locked in a fresh thirty-round magazine. His partner took another hit in the shoulder. Jumping to his feet and yelling for cover fire, he charged over the dune firing full automatic at the four rebels who were less than twenty yards away. Two grabbed their chest and fell dead. A third had his legs shot out from under him, and the fourth was killed by Captain York who was screaming for the Rangers to increase their fire. Tiny puffs of sand popped and jumped in the air around McNeil as he slid down next to O'Riley. He bent forward to hook his hands under the man's arms. York heard the sickening impact above the rattle of gunfire as a bullet hit McNeil in the center of the head and exploded it like an overripe melon. O'Riley let out a cry and wiped the brains and blood from his face. He tried to crawl, only to be ripped apart by a hail of bullets from a machine gun. York started to stand, but one of the legionnaires grabbed him. Pulling him back down, he said, "You can do nothing for them now, Captain."

Jake and Fenelon loaded the last rounds in each of the 106s and fired. The legionnaire's round took out a half-track that was directing a heavy volume of machine-gun fire at York's position. Jake caught a tank broadside. It exploded with enough force to engulf the scout car to its left. Screaming men, their clothes aflame, ran blindly around on the desert floor until they finally fell to the sand; their bodies consumed by the fire.

The tanks began to find the range of the 106s. Round after round of cannon fire tore the tops off the ridge causing Jake and Fenelon to abandon the now-useless cars. Doc dived to the prone position as a tank round exploded to his left. Leaping to his feet, he scrambled to the edge of the riverbed where he joined Jake. Nearly out of breath, sweat pouring down the sides of his face, he gasped, "Commander, we've . . . we've lost twenty-three out of thirty-five Rangers on . . . on the right. Another four won't last an hour. Rivers is gone. You've only got eight men left on that side who can still put up a fight . . . I haven't even checked on Captain York, yet, but they have been taking a beating over there."

"Okay, Doc, take a breather while the major and I try to figure a way out of this damn mess. Come on, Pierre, let's go see what it looks like." Both officers made their way back to the top of what was left of the ridge and took in the sight below. Kueddei had them on the ropes, and he knew it. The firing from the 106s had stopped. He knew they were out of ammunition so he swung the main portion of his forces toward Captain York and his men. Nine tanks, five half-tracks, and three scout cars were burning. The bodies of more than two hundred dead men lay sprawled in the sand. The eight Rangers on the right were being overrun as Kueddei's rebels attacked in waves. Once the right flank fell, it would be all over. They would no longer be able to hold the line. "Well, Major Fenelon, we gave it our best shot. Looks like David's out of rocks, and Goliath will win this one. At least we extracted a little payback for what they did at Mangalme."

Fenelon yelled to one of his men to work his way over to Captain York and tell him to withdraw to the riverbed. Yelling to another legionnaire, he told him to do the same on the right. He stopped when he saw the eight Rangers stand. They were out of bullets and were taking on the rebels hand to hand with rifle butts and knives. It was a valiant effort, but the odds were too great. One by one, they went down until all eight were dead. The rebels slashed and stabbed at the bodies after they fell. Finally they raised their rifles in a victory cheer as they began their charge toward the center of the riverbed. Kueddei's tanks were on line again and moving straight for them. Fenelon turned to Jake, "Commander, gather all the men at the west end of the riverbed. Have them remove their belts and hook them through the back loop of their trousers. Quickly, Commander."

Jake stared at the man in total bewilderment. "What are we doing, Pierre? It would take a miracle for us to walk away from this."

Fenelon raised his arm and pointed to the east. "There comes your miracle, Commander."

Jake turned and looked to the east. "My God, what is that?"

Behind Kueddei's men a wall of dark, rolling clouds rose upward from the desert floor. Stretching nearly a thousand feet into the air, it wasn't clouds, but swirling dust and blowing sand and it was over a mile wide.

"It is what we call a harmattan," yelled Fenelon as he tried to be heard over the already increasing scream of the winds that were driving this giant sandstorm toward them. "In a few minutes no one will be able to see their hand in front of their face. You may wish you had let the rebels kill you before we come out of the harmattan. It is our only chance. Now, hurry, Jake. Get the men tied together. When the main storm hits us, we will try to slip away."

Jake was still in awe of the sight that rolled steadily toward them. It reminded him of a scene out of the movie *The Ten Commandments*. Fenelon slapped him on the back and yelled for him to go. Fenelon raced for the scout cars and began pulling the robes from the dead rebels. Jake hurried down the slope. The experience of the legionnaires served them well. They already had their belts off and were helping Doc and the others. Randy York ran up to Jake. "God, have you ever seen anything like that?" he asked.

Fumbling with the back loop of his pants he replied, "No, and I don't think I'll ever want to again."

Fenelon gathered them all in a group at the end of the riverbed. Running along the line, he dropped the robes at every fifth man and yelled, "Jake! Randy! Tear a piece off and wrap it around your neck and face. Leave only a small slit for the eyes." Both men did as they were told.

Losses had been heavy. There were only forty-four men still alive. Pierre yelled for them to kneel. The winds became stronger and seemed to scream over the dunes. The towering black cloud loomed high in the sky. The rebels who had broken through on the right appeared suddenly along the ridge.

Ignoring the storm, they raised their weapons and prepared to fire into the group of men who knelt together like a flock of sheep. Before the first shot could be fired, the full force of the harmattan swept over the ridge engulfing rebels and legionnaires alike. The wind blew Jake and the others over. Stinging sand pelleted the men who struggled to regain their balance. Each man held tightly to the end of the belt of the man in front of him.

Major Fenelon worked his way to the head of the line. Making sure the first man behind him had a tight hold on his belt, he began to crawl north away from the riverbed. Neither Jake nor Captain York could see a thing. Their only guide was the pulling forward of the belts in front of them. The wind screamed around them like a thousand banshees. The driven sand felt as if it were shredding the skin from their hands one layer at a time. Jake had overheard one of the legionnaires telling York that a storm such as this could last an hour, or it might last for days. Fenelon was right. To die on the dunes would have been better than this.

General Johnson reached for the pitcher, poured Sergeant Roth a glass of water, then handed it to the young soldier. "Here you go, son."

"Thank you, sir." Roth's exhaustion was clearly noticeable. The doctors had found three minor grazing wounds, one along his side and two on his right leg. What Roth suffered from most was sheer exhaustion. He had not slept since Master Sergeant Vickers had been evacuated.

"We've read your initial report, Mike. I'm sorry about Chief Hileran and the others," said Johnson.

Roth stared down at the glass of water and slowly turned it in his hand as he whispered, "So am I, sir. They put up one hell of a fight at the end. You know, I—I could have sworn that Ms. Chambers shot herself in the head. I mean, I only looked back a couple of times, but for some reason, that keeps sticking in my mind. She just . . ." His voice trailed off.

B.J. put his hand on the sergeant's arm, "You did good, Mike. You got out with a prisoner and not just any prisoner. This guy Ching is a high-ranking officer in Hans Kruger's mercenary army."

Roth looked up at Mattson. "Kruger, Hans Kruger, I've

heard or read that name somewhere, one of our classes on Africa or someplace like that. They have a nickname for him . . . the . . . the something man."

"The Ice Man," said Johnson.

"Yeah, that's it, sir. Jesus, you mean it was his guys we took on at the docks? No wonder we had such a hard time. He's supposed to have the most elite force of mercenaries in the world working for him."

"That's a fact, Mike," said B.J., smiling, "but we had a Special Ops man who was better."

"Thank you, Major Mattson," replied Roth with a hint of pride in his voice. "There were a couple of guys who said they were DOD, but I think they were really CIA. They were going to question Ching. Did he tell them anything?"

"Not at first. The guy's a pretty damn tough little Korean. He held out through two straight hours of intense physical persuasion without so much as a whimper. Probably would have died without saying a word, but General Johnson offered him a deal, a one-way ticket home in exchange for Kruger's plan of operation. He had to think about it for a while."

Roth sat up in his hospital bed and shook his head. "I don't know why? While we were struggling in the water I heard somebody on the dock above us tell the men to shoot both of us. I'd bet that was Kruger."

Johnson nodded. "You'd win that bet, son. That was the key in Ching's decision. He realized he didn't owe Kruger anything. He told us the entire layout from day one, when they arrived in Libya, how long they trained, all about the raid on Abeche, everything. Now, if we can just get Zaire to play along, we can tear that bastard a new asshole."

"What about Captain York and Commander Mortimer, sir? Any word on them or the other guys from the team?" asked Roth.

B.J.'s face showed the concern he had for the others as he said, "No, Mike, afraid not. No radio contact since they left N'Djamena. They're a sharp bunch of guys, I'm sure they're still alive and kicking out there somewhere."

Roth leaned back on his pillow as a sudden sadness came over him. "Then Top Vickers and I could be the only two guys left of A-505. Jesus, sir, this was supposed to be just another MTT mission. What happened? Peterson, the chief, Weathers,

Talbot, all those people . . . gone." Roth's hand came up to cover his misty eyes.

The commander of SOCOM felt the same pain during the roll call of the dead. Reaching out, he placed his hand on the young sergeant's shoulder gently, "You get some rest now, Mike. They've scheduled you for a medical flight out of here. In a few hours you'll be back at MacDill. Major Erikson will be there to meet you. He's already got you a room at the base hospital. I want you to take a few days to rest up. This will all be over in a few days, and I'll be coming to see you."

"Sir, I'd rather stay with you and Major Mattson," said Roth, his hand still covering his eyes.

"No, son. You've already done more than your share. We'll take it from here. You just get better, okay. We've got to go now, Mike. See you back at MacDill. Good job, Green Beret."

Johnson and Mattson were going out the door as a nurse was coming into the room. She held a needle in her hand. She paused to let the men pass, and whispered, "It'll help him sleep."

Mattson glanced over at Johnson. Both veterans of this deadly game knew the shot would help today, but that from now on there would be a lot of sleepless nights in young Mike Roth's life. The faces would always be there.

Jason Hobart was waiting at the airport for Johnson and Mattson when they arrived in Zaire. Mobutu and his council had reached their decision on the Chad affair and wanted the three men at the presidential palace at three that afternoon. Hobart said it didn't sound good and they should be ready to consider other options. He informed them of the latest intelligence reports they had received regarding the Panama invasion.

Scattered fighting continued, and Noriega was still at large. U.S. casualties numbered eighteen killed and twenty-five wounded. Hobart did not know if any of those casualties had been Special Ops people.

The three men arrived at precisely three o'clock and were shown to the main conference room where President Mobutu and his staff were waiting for them. They could feel the eyes of the generals on them as they walked to the end of the table and sat down.

"Ah, General Johnson, I appreciate your dedication to punctuality. It is a true sign of both a diplomat and a military leader," smiled Mobutu.

Johnson could smell the bullshit clear across the room, but he bowed his head slightly as he politely replied, "Thank you, Mr. President. We are most grateful to you and your advisors for the expediency you have shown in considering our request. It shall be noted by our President when I return to Washington."

The generals shifted their eyes to Mobutu who leaned forward, folding his hands in front of him, trying to maintain his earlier toothy smile as he said, "General, after much deliberation and soul-searching by my officers and myself, I am afraid that given our present situation here in Zaire, the commitment of our troops to you would pose a serious threat to our international relationships with certain other countries with which we are required to conduct business. Therefore, I have decided that, regrettable as the situation in Chad may be, we cannot afford to interfere in the internal matters of another country. I am sorry, gentlemen, but that is my decision."

The disappointment registered clearly on the faces of the two American officers. Hobart's expression never changed, but he had expected the answer they had just received. "But, Mr. President, there comes a time when a country must take action to protect their future interest, regardless of the risk," said Mattson.

"Much the same as you are doing in Panama at this very moment. Isn't that right, Major Mattson?" said one of the generals sitting across from them. "But you see, Major, we are neither a national power, nor do we have a canal that is of interest to us. We have only Zaire. We have no need to go searching for trouble, Major. We have quite enough as it is."

Johnson realized that they would not change the decision and saw no need to waste more time. Standing, he reached out his hand to President Mobutu. "Mr. President, I wish to thank you for your time and consideration in this matter. We can fully understand your situation. I know that you have reached this conclusion out of consideration for the welfare of your people. We must be going now, sir."

Mobutu stood and looked into the older man's eyes. It was normally difficult for one bullshiter to fool another, but if

Johnson held any resentment toward him, it did not show in the man's steel-gray eyes.

"I wish you luck in finding a solution to this matter, General Johnson."

Mobutu and his officers began to file out of the room as B.J. turned to Hobart and said, "Well, I guess Kruger and his mercenaries are going to pull it off for Qaddafi." Mobutu and his men stopped abruptly in the doorway. The President pushed his way past one of his generals, walking straight up to Mattson. Mobutu's eyes were wild-looking as he slowly said, "Did you say Kruger? Hans Kruger?"

The other generals flocked around the table awaiting B.J.'s answer.

"Why, yes, sir, Mr. President. Hans Kruger. They call him the . . ."

"You don't have to tell us what they call him, Major Mattson. All in my country know that name. Just as you use your Bogeyman, my people use the name of the Ice Man to frighten their children into obeying them. Hans Kruger is the man responsible for more death in my country than all the diseases we have experienced in twenty years. I would give up my presidency in exchange for having that man in my prison interrogation room for one hour." The generals around the table all mumbled in agreement.

"Where is this bastard of the devil himself, Major?"

Mattson glanced over at Hobart and Johnson as he replied, "In Chad, sir. He and his men are attempting to drive General Gaafar and his army out of the capital and into the desert where they can slaughter them. I don't have to tell you what he will do to the civilians of N'Djamena."

Silence prevailed for a moment as Mobutu turned to face his officers. Staring into their eyes, he saw the same hate and desire for revenge that he knew was in his own. So be it. Pointing to one of his generals, he said, "Have the garrison alerted for immediate departure. I want us to be in the capital city of Chad by the time the sun rises in the morning. Coordinate with our brothers in Nigeria for additional aircraft to transport our troops. Now, go, all of you. There is much to be done and little time."

The excitement in the room reached a fever pitch as the officers saluted and ran yelling from the room. Mobutu looked to Johnson, "If we had known that Kruger was involved, we would not have hesitated to help you, General."

"We just found out this morning, sir," said Johnson. "You must want this man very badly."

"More than you can imagine, General. There is not one of my officers or soldiers who has not had a family member tortured and killed by that sadistic madman. He has escaped us on two occasions, once during the Congo rebellion and again in the last coup attempt against me. This time we will have him. General, if you gentlemen will join me, we will go to my office and plan our strategy for the liberation of Chad and hopefully the rescue of your men."

B.J. was the last one to leave the room. Turning to shut the doors, he glanced at the map of Africa that hung on the wall and whispered, "Hang in there, Jake; we're coming."

CHAPTER 10

Jake slowly opened his sand-burned eyes and felt the layers of sand sliding from his clothes as he moved to sit up. The backs of his hands were nearly raw from the windblown sand that had tore at them like rough-edged sandpaper. York and Fenelon lay next to him, still sleeping. The men had formed a circle around them. They had kept their backs to the gale force wind and had huddled with their knees drawn up and their heads lowered in an attempt to ward off the winds and biting sand that had whipped at them all through the long night. Jake had no idea where they were. As he focused his eyes and looked at the terrain around him, he saw only the sand dunes and the rising sun. Reaching for his canteen, he removed the lid and raised it to his cracked, dry lips. The water was warm, but it felt good as it cleared the choking dust from his throat. He was about to tip the canteen back again when he froze.

The sight that appeared directly in front of him almost caused him to drop the precious container of liquid gold. There, on the dune straight across from him, stood ten men wrapped in white sheets. Black turbans with black scarves covered all but their eyes. All of them had rifles. They were staring down at the sleeping party of men and Jake. Slowly lowering the canteen, he saw ten more men riding camels coming from the right. He didn't have to turn around to see if there were others behind him. He could feel their eyes on his back.

Slowly holding his hands out to the side to show he had no

intentions of reaching for a weapon, Jake set the canteen down and tapped Fenelon on the shoulder. The legionnaire moaned in his sleep and shifted slightly, then went back to sleep. Jake pushed on him harder this time. "Pierre! Pierre! I think you had better wake up. We've got company."

Fenelon raised his head. "Wh—what is it, Jake? Why did you wake . . ." The Legion officer stopped talking when he saw the men on the camels approaching. More of the men were waking up now. Jake reached over and punched York awake. One of the Chadian Rangers made a sudden move for his weapon. A rattle of metal bolts pushing forward and safeties being flipped off resounded across the stillness of the desert. Fenelon stood quickly and raised his hands, yelling, "Wait!" Turning to Blancher, he said, "Doctor, please be so kind as to take that weapon away from that fool before he gets us all killed." Doc reached over slowly and pushed the Ranger's gun barrel down toward the sand. He shook his head as if he were a father scolding his child. The Arabs on the ridge relaxed their stance but kept their rifles in the ready position. "Who are they, Pierre?" asked York.

"Nomads—they are the true people of the desert. They are more curious than anything else. It isn't often they see men without vehicles or animals roaming around in the middle of the desert."

"Will they help us?" asked Jake.

"I doubt it. They do not care to become involved in other people's troubles, not that they are afraid to fight. These white Muslims are perhaps the most deadly force in all of Africa. They only do battle when it pleases them. Let's hope that this is not one of those times. Come on, we'll see what they want. Keep your hands high and do not make any sudden moves. One shot could lead to a massacre."

Fenelon and Jake walked toward the men on the ridge, keeping their hands held high. "If it comes to a shoot-out, we might have a chance. There's only twenty of them," said Jake.

A grin broke at the corner of Pierre's wind-burned mouth as they continued to walk. He whispered, "Another lesson, my friend, for every ten you see, there are fifty you don't."

They stopped at the base of the dune as two of the Arabs broke from the line and made their way cautiously down the side of the hill to meet them. Stopping a few feet in front of them, the Arabs studied the burned, windblown faces of the two officers for a moment. The bigger of the two reached up and undid the scarf from his face. Tossing it loosely over his shoulder, he asked Fenelon in perfect French what business they had in his desert, and where were their machines or their camels?

Fenelon quickly explained the situation as Jake cursed himself for not staying up with his French classes. He was only able to catch a phrase every now and then as Pierre paused to point back in the direction of yesterday's battle. The Arab listened intently, showing little expression one way or the other. Fenelon finished his explanation. The tall man asked him if they had a doctor with them. Pierre replied that they did. This brought a look of relief to the man's face as he hurriedly spoke to the man next to him in Arabic. The man ran back up the hill. "Pierre, what's going on?" asked Jake.

"They wanted to know if we had a doctor with us. I told him we did. This one has sent a messenger back to inform the tribal leader. We are to wait for his instructions. Whatever problem they have, it must be pretty bad. These people hardly ever want a doctor for anything."

The messenger came scurrying back over the dune yelling to the man with them. "He says they are to bring us to their camp," said Fenelon with a worried look on his face.

"What else, Pierre?" asked Jake.

"They want us to give up our weapons."

"Damn it, Fenelon, I don't think our boys are going to go for that."

"They no longer have a choice, Commander," said Pierre as he nodded toward the ridges around them. As Jake looked up, he saw over a hundred Arabs mounted on camels and horses, their rifles held against their hips and pointing skyward. Fenelon had a point.

Their weapons handed over, the men of Fenelon's command swung up behind the mounted horsemen and proceeded to the camp of Habelu-Hesin, the leader of the Kurtiwa nomads of the northern desert. The man's son was near death and all the prayers to Allah had done little to ease the tortured pain that tore at the boy's stomach. Doc Blancher was going to have an opportunity to show what he had learned from one year of Special Forces medical school and two years of emergency

room residency work. From the symptoms described by
Cishim, the tall Arab who had spoken with Fenelon, Doc
guessed his diagnosis would be appendicitis in the advanced
stages.

Jake and the others were already sweating heavily from the
effects of the early morning sun as the tents of Habelu-Hesin
came into sight. The tents were nestled in a circle around an
oasis. A towering group of palm trees rose toward the sky
providing some shade for most of the tents. No one in the
group was sweating as much as Doc Blancher. He had done a
lot of things as a medic, but an appendectomy wasn't one of
them.

General Kueddei cursed his men, cursed the gods, and he
especially cursed the desert storm that had snatched a victory
from him just as he had it in his grasp. They had searched the
desert throughout the night for the elusive survivors of yesterday's battle, but the harmattan had erased all traces of the men.
It was as if the sands had risen up and swallowed them. Now,
the heat and senseless wandering about in circles was beginning to draw complaints from his men who wanted to abandon
the search and drive on toward N'Djamena. It would be a
chance to get out of this burning inferno. Adding to the man's
frustrations were the outright threats he had received from
Kruger over the radio less than half an hour ago.

The mercenaries along with the Libyan troops and the rest of
Kueddei's rebel army had driven his brother Gaafar and what
was left of the Chadian army into the eastern sector of the
capital, but they had not been able to push him out into the
desert. Gaafar grouped his artillery around him in a final
desperate effort to hold back the rolling tide. So far it was
working. The continuous air strikes Kruger had called in on
Gaafar had done little more than turn buildings into rubble that
provided additional cover for the artillery pieces. Kruger
needed the tanks to counter the artillery. His losses had already
exceeded over four hundred dead and double that number
wounded. Fortunately for Kruger, practically all of those
casualties had been Libyans and rebels. If this operation failed
because of Kueddei, Kruger vowed he would hunt the man
down. He would delight in skinning him alive. The mercenary

had given Kueddei four hours to reach N'Djamena or else he could consider himself a dead man.

The threat enraged the rebel leader so that he broke radio contact with the capital. Who did Kruger think he was? He was nothing more than a hired gun. How dare he threaten the next President of Chad. Kueddei would have the sadistic bastard hung from the palace balcony when this was over. Four hours indeed! He would go to the capital when he was ready, and that would not be until he had captured and eliminated those damn legionnaires.

The nomads of the Kurtiwa tribe were gathered around the tent in which Doc Blancher was working diligently on the son of Chief Habelu-Hesin. Their prayer rugs were cast upon the sands. They faced the sun, chanting to Allah for his generous mercy. Jake, Fenelon, and Hesin's second in command, Cishim, stood beside another tent away from the crowd. Since the junior medic, Sergeant Weathers, had remained in the capital, Doc asked Captain York to assist him. Randy had reluctantly consented. Jake was surprised to find that the tall, deeply tanned Arab with the dark brown eyes spoke English, as he asked, "Your medical man is one of those who wears the green hat, is he not?"

"Yes. He and Captain York are both Green Berets. I am a Navy commander," replied Jake.

Cishim gave him a strange look and asked, "You are a Navy man? Why should a man of the water be here among the sands of the desert?"

Jake managed to laugh. "Believe me, I have asked myself that question at least fifty times in the last twenty-four hours."

As Blancher and York came out of the tent, the one hundred or so nomads rose to their feet. Jake and the others walked through the parting waves of men as Cishim led the way. Both Doc and Randy were covered with sweat. "How'd it go, Doc?" asked Jake.

Pulling the surgical gloves from his tired hands he answered, "It's a good thing we happened along when we did. Another couple of hours and the damn thing would have ruptured. He was pretty weak and was burning up with fever, Commander. I don't know; we'll just have to wait and see. He's still out right now. We should know something in about four or five hours.

I did the best I could for him, Commander. I hope they know that."

Cishim stepped forward and took Doc's hand. "We know you did, my friend. You men of the green hat are well known for doing no less, and we thank you. The soul of the boy now rests in the hands of Allah—his will be done." Cishim clapped his hands in the air twice and two of the Kurtiwa suddenly appeared at his side. "You are both tired. My men will show you where you may rest. Should the boy awaken, I will send someone for you."

Blancher released his hold on the man's hand and only nodded in agreement. He was too tired to talk. York waved to Jake, telling him to wake him in a couple of hours. Habelu-Hesin came out of the tent and walked up to the group. Following Cishim's lead, the American and the Frenchman bowed slightly at the waist. Habelu-Hesin was a huge man, perhaps 260 or 280 pounds with a slightly protruding stomach and large arms. His face showed the signs of a long and rugged life in the desert. In a heavy voice, he said, "Cishim, I see no reason to keep the weapons of our newfound friends. Have them returned to them. Your doctor appears to be an accomplished man at his work. I could see the caring and concern he had for my boy in his eyes. I feel that Allah will surely reward his kindness with the recovery of my son. Please, gentlemen, honor me with your presence in my tent. I have some very good wine. Cishim has told me a little of your problems with some rebels. I would like to hear more about that."

Cishim relayed the order to return the weapons as he followed the three men into Hesin's tent. Underneath a triple group of palm trees, Doc and Captain York were already sound asleep. It was 10:00 A.M.

B.J. pulled the handle on the side door of the C-123 and slid it upward out of the way. Pushing the AK-50 with the folding stock to one side, he turned to stare down the aisle at the black faces of the Zaire commandos. No one was carrying rucksacks on this jump, only web gear, a full load of magazines, grenades, and weapons. Five more C-123s were flying in trail behind them, all carrying commandos. The commando leader tapped B.J. on the arm and held up six fingers. They were six minutes from the N'Djamena airfield. B.J. leaned out the door.

Squinting his eyes against the blowing wind and prop blast, he saw the Zairian fighter planes going in for the first bomb run. Three more followed in rapid succession.

Pulling himself back inside, he turned to the group and held up five fingers. If these boys were scared, they weren't letting it show as they calmly checked their gear while continuing to watch Mattson for the hand signals. B.J. looked at his watch, it was 10:15 A.M. General Johnson and his group should be over Abeche right about now. Looking back out the side door, he saw smoke rising from a line of F-5s burning and exploding on the runway.

B.J. raised three fingers and screamed, "Three minutes," then pointed to the first man and then to the door. The commando was on his feet without hesitation and in the door as the others in the stick lined up behind him. Across the aisle, the Zaire commander had his men lined up in the other door.

Mattson's heart was pounding like a sledgehammer as he leaned out past the man in the door to see the end of the runway coming up fast beneath the plane. Counting to ten under his breath, he slapped the lead man on the butt, and out he went, followed by the entire line. As the last man went out, B.J. threw his own static line back on the cable and leaped out the door. He could have sworn he heard a bullet hit the airplane as he went out.

"Hans! Hans!" yelled Kaufman as he handed Kruger the handset and pointed to the sky. "Paratroopers, Hans! They are trying to recapture the airfield."

Kruger calmly took the mike as he watched the men drift slowly down under the white silk chutes. Some were already firing at the men on the ground from the air. Damn that Kueddei, thought Kruger to himself. If only he had followed the plan. Now, it was too late. He had lost too many men in the battle for the eastern sector. Having to bring in his reserves from the airfield had left little hope that the units still there could overcome the massive number of white parachutes now dotting the sky for as far as the eye could see. Slowly turning the knobs on the frequency indicator of the radio, he purposely hesitated, knowing what they were going to tell him even before he asked the question.

He flipped the last number of the Abeche frequency into

position. A voice was screaming over the mike, "Colonel Kruger! Come in, come in! We're being overrun. Paratroopers are everywhere. Come in, Colonel Kruger!"

Kruger never bothered to answer. Dropping the mike over the windshield of his jeep, he stared down at one of Kueddei's rebel officers who was serving as his driver. With his eyes still on the man, he yelled to Kaufman, "Adolf, inform our men we are pulling back to the main square. They are to tell the rebels that they are to stay in their positions until we can arrange transportation. We will not take them with us when we go. Do you understand?"

"Yes, Hans. I will link up with you in the square," replied Kaufman. He tapped his driver, and they sped off around one of the few remaining clear streets in N'Djamena. Kruger eased himself down into the passenger seat as he pointed for the rebel officer to follow Kaufman. The man nodded, then reached down to put the jeep into gear. Kruger placed the barrel of his Beretta less than one inch from the man's ear and blew his brains out. "Fuck you, Kueddei!" he yelled as he kicked the body out into the street and slid over behind the wheel. Wiping the blood and brains from the windshield, he jerked the jeep into gear and drove away.

Kaufman had what was left of the elite mercenary unit at the square by the time Kruger arrived. The leader said nothing as he stood to survey the survivors. In the beginning he had had 200 men; there were less than 125 now. They all stood or sat silently awaiting the mercenary commander's orders. The sounds of exploding artillery rounds and weapons fire came from the airfield and the eastern sector. A rebel screamed for help over the radio as a thousand Nigerians crossed the border, heading for N'Djamena. Still Kruger stood silently looking at what was left of his army.

Kaufman could sense the restlessness of the men around him. They either wanted to fight or to leave. Anything was better than just sitting there. Stepping from his jeep, he walked over to Kruger and said, "We really should be going now, Hans."

"Yes, of course you're right, Adolf. We almost pulled it off, didn't we, old friend? said Kruger in a strange far-off voice.

"Yes, Hans, we almost did it," replied Kaufman as he took Kruger's arm to lower him into the passenger seat. He got behind the wheel and started the vehicle. "Where do we go, Hans?"

"Back to Libya, Adolf. Colonel Qaddafi still owes us money. If we are lucky, we will cross the path of General Kueddei."

Kaufman swung the jeep to the north as he drove out of the square. A column of half-tracks, trucks, and jeeps followed them out of town and into the desert. They would only stop for water at the oasis with the towering palms that was sometimes used by the Kurtiwa nomads. Kaufman figured the column could be there in three hours.

Kueddei sat on the side of his half-track, staring out across the open desert. He monitored the desperate cries of his men as they pleaded for help at Abeche. Kruger had been right, he should have stayed with the plan. Now they had lost both airfields, and his army in the city was being surrounded. It could only be a matter of time before the fighters of the Zaire Air Force would start searching the desert for targets of opportunity. If nothing else, his column was now a prime target. The only good thing Kueddei could find about this unexpected turn of events was the fact that he had not heard anything from Kruger. Perhaps Allah had granted him at least one favor and the bastard was now fighting for his life in N'Djamena. How ironic it would be if his brother should be the one to kill Colonel Kruger. He decided to return to Libya to try again another day. However, they would need water before beginning the journey home. There was an oasis not far to the north that was frequented often by Habelu-Hesin and his worthless nomads. They would present no problems to him or his tank column. If they did, he would take out his rage at losing the legionnaires on the Kurtiwa.

Habelu-Hesin shifted his huge bulk on the pile of colorful pillows. Waving a chunk of goat's meat in front of him as he motioned with his hands to stress his point, he said, "My people have seen many would-be conquerors lay claim to this land; in the end it has been the desert that has subdued the conqueror. We, the Kurtiwa, are at peace with the desert because we do not try to conquer its vastness. We merely travel in harmony upon its shifting soul."

Jake and Fenelon sat on their pillows in front of the nomad

leader. They both found the man to be a fascinating character who was well versed in both the French and English languages. Changes in expression showed mostly in the leader's eyes. The old chief's eyes had at times mesmerized Jake as he related stories of the many battles he had fought against foreigners and other Arab tribes. He showed them his scars. Scars that had been won in battle and that bore the mark of the sword. For among these desert people, to do battle with the sword of Allah was still the most honorable way for a warrior to show his true courage. What honor was there in killing an enemy with a rifle. One could not see into the eyes of his enemy from so far away. Where was the honor in this? They had little respect for the modern-day weapons of the twentieth century. However, the nomads had found they had little choice but to adapt to the use of such weapons in order to survive. Nineteenth-century ideas of honor and courage gained by sword-waving men mounted on horseback stood little chance against twentieth-century machine guns, tanks, and artillery pieces that could kill from miles away without ever seeing their enemy. It was a time that Hesin longed to return to, but he knew in his heart, those times were gone forever. All that remained were memories to be shared and passed on in the tents and around the fires of the once great swordsmen and warriors of the desert.

Doc Blancher came to the flap of the tent and said that the boy was awake. His fever had broken and the youngster wished to see his father. Hesin was overjoyed as he rose to walk outside. He was greeted by the cheers of his people who shared his happiness. Cishim clasped Blancher's hand tightly in his own and praised the medic, as did Jake and Fenelon. Kurtiwa tribesmen fired their rifles into the air in praise of Allah and his divine mercy. The son of Habelu-Hesin lived. Already the women of the Kurtiwa were going out among the goat herds to select the goats that would be prepared for the great feast that would come with the setting sun. It would be a feast to honor Allah and the men he had brought forth from the desert to perform this miracle.

General Kueddei halted his column as the sounds of rifle fire were carried across the desert. Dismounting from his vehicle, he and two of his officers made their way up the incline of one of the dunes. Raising their field glasses, they focused in on the oasis that lay nearly a mile away. He was right. It was Hesin and his Kurtiwa. They were firing their rifles into the air. The rebel officer beside him grabbed Kueddei's arm and pointed to an area to the left of the tents. Kueddei shifted his glasses. A sadistic grin began to crawl across his face. There, gathered around three men, were the legionnaires. He had found them after all. Allah had played a cruel joke on him before, but now he delivered them into his hands. Slowly sliding back from the ridge, he and his officers returned to the column. Calling his men to gather around him, Kueddei drew a map in the hard-packed sand. They had been fortunate to have come this far without the dust from their vehicles being seen by those in the camp. Any attempt to mover closer with the column would surely negate that bit of luck. He still had close to five hundred men left. He would split them into three separate forces that would move on foot to surround the oasis. Once in position, the tanks would move forward and lay down a barrage in the center of the encampment. Once the barrage was lifted, his troops would attack and finish off all in the camp. There would be no prisoners.

"At least you taught him well, Hans," said Kaufman as he glanced over at Kruger who lay beside him on the ridge. Behind them sat the vehicles of the mercenaries. They had been deployed along the ridge line of the sand dunes after the first sound of rifle fire from the oasis. Lowering his glasses, Kruger smiled to himself. There was justice in this world after all. Kaufman saw the reckless look in his friend's eyes. Surely he was not thinking of extracting his revenge on Kueddei now. The rebel leader had at least 500 men with him, and there were the Kurtiwa who numbered another 150 to 200 men. They were about to be drawn into this battle unwillingly. To them, both factions would be considered the enemy.

"Hans, perhaps it is better that we go around. We can get water from Lake Chad and continue on our way to Libya. You can inform Colonel Qaddafi of what has happened. I am sure he will be as anxious to see Kueddei as you are. We can wait for him there," said Kaufman.

Kruger never bothered to look at his friend. "Tell the men to prepare for battle. I want Kueddei alive. Other than that, there are to be no prisoners."

"But, Hans, there are too many. We are only one hundred twenty-five against them all. We will be outnumbered more than four to one. Please, my friend, reconsider this. There is no need for any of us to die. Wait in Libya for this man."

"Major Kaufman, do not question my orders. I am well aware of the odds. We shall wait until the rebel bastard has attacked and wiped out the Kurtiwa. The numbers should be decreased considerably by then. That is when we will attack. Now, go! Be sure they know I want Kueddei alive. I will castrate the man who kills him." Turning his glasses back to the oasis, the Ice Man made himself comfortable as he prepared to watch what he knew would be a battle to the death for the Kurtiwa.

The sounds of tank cannons startled the jubilant Kurtiwa. They stopped their dancing as they stared off toward the southeast and the strange screaming of the deadly missiles arching through the sky preparing to rain down destruction on the unsuspecting nomads.

"Incoming!" screamed Captain York as he leaped forward pulling two small children to the ground with him. As the first of the rounds exploded near the oasis, they uprooted two of the palm trees and sent a gusher of water fifty feet into the air. People were yelling and screaming as they scrambled for their weapons, searching for something or someone to shoot at. Jake and Fenelon were lying in the sand between Cishim and Hesin. "What is it?" yelled Cishim. "Artillery?"

"No!" replied Jake, ducking his head as another volley exploded, taking out two of the tents on the perimeter and sending three nomads flying through the air. Their shrapnel-ripped bodies were deposited only a few feet in front of Habelu-Hesin. "It's those damn tanks we fought yesterday."

Handing the children over to one of the women running past him, York made a dash for Jake's position, sliding down next to him just as another series of explosions rocked the ground sending waves of sand over them. Some of the Kurtiwa were firing their rifles in the direction of the big guns. "Hesin, they are wasting ammunition. The tanks are out of range," yelled York.

Cishim jumped to his feet and ran to the men who were firing. He ordered them to hold their fire. Hesin watched as a direct hit destroyed the tent where the women and children had run to hide. Screams and cries of anguish rose from the terrified survivors and the Kurtiwa warriors who had just watched their wives and children blown to pieces. "Oh, my God," cried Jake as he watched a small girl of five or six stumble from the smoke and dust with her right arm blown off at the shoulder. Hesin screamed in agony at the pitiful sight. Pulling himself to his feet and ignoring the rounds that continued to fall all around the camp, he screamed for his men to mount their horses and camels. They could no longer sit there and be slaughtered like sheep. Cishim reached for his horse, but Hesin stopped him. "No, Cishim! You must stay. Our people will need a strong leader." Cishim started to protest, but Hesin grabbed the reins of his horse and gave it to another. "It is written, Cishim, and so it shall be," said the old man as he rode away.

Bodies of the dead and dying littered the sand. The clear water of the oasis was crimson red with the blood of the three men that floated in the center of the pool. Women cried, hugging their wounded and dying children to them while pleading to Allah for his divine mercy to end this seemingly never-ending hell that was raining down upon them. Doc Blancher came walking through a cloud of smoke and dust. He carried the shattered body of Hesin's son in his arms. He had saved him only to watch him die.

The war cry of the Kurtiwa resounded across the desert as Hesin and over one hundred of his men invoked the name of Allah as they charged toward the tanks and their fiery long-barreled guns.

The Americans and the legionnaires watched in wonder as the Arab fighters rode hell-bent across the open ground, in all their splendor, their long robes waving in the wind behind them, and their rifles held out tightly in one hand, and the reins of the pounding animals in the other. In the lead rode Habelu-Hesin, sitting astride a magnificent white Arabian stallion, waving his sword and shouting for his enemies to stand and fight like men of honor, but the rebels had no honor.

Jake and the others watched helplessly as the cannons of the tanks were lowered to point directly at the onslaught of charging nomads. "They'll be lucky if twenty of them make it within fifty yards of those tanks," said York.

"The men of this land have little hope and few choices in their lives, Captain York," said Fenelon, "but the most precious of the few they have is the right to choose the manner in which they will die. The Kurtiwa are warriors of the desert. This is a fitting death for such men."

Habelu-Hesin never looked back as he drove the stallion at full gallop straight for the lead tank. The wind whipped his face as it had so many times in the past. It was a warm desert wind; the winds of his past. His old eyes had seen all of a world without honor that they cared to see. Ignoring the fire that roared from the end of the barrel, the projectile of death hurled toward an old man and his memories.

Jake's body tensed as he watched the earth erupt in front of Hesin. The man and the horse vanished into the rolling cloud of gray-black smoke and flying sand, only to reappear seconds later still moving at full gallop. A cheer arose from the legionnaires as the old man continued his charge. Round after round of cannon fire began to explode among the charging Kurtiwa, blowing men and animals apart. Still they rode head-long into the attack showing remarkable agility as they fired their weapons at full gallop, killing a number of the rebels around the tanks. Hesin rode as if the devil himself were encased in the spirit of the stallion, 200 yards to go, 150, 100, on and on he went as if immune to the flying shrapnel and exploding rounds that hit all around him. Through his glasses, Jake could see streams of blood running from the neck and shoulders of the white stallion. He still continued his murdering pace as if inflamed by the spirit of his rider.

The hatches atop the tanks opened as the cannons fell silent. The gunners stepped up behind the 50-caliber machine guns that were mounted on their tanks. Pulling the charging handle back twice, they loaded the weapons and pressed the twin triggers. The heavy thud of the giant shells echoed in the oasis causing the cheering to stop. The men watched helplessly as the last of Hesin's men were cut to pieces. The rebels saved the old man for last. They ceased their firing and allowed him to ride past the first tank, which he struck with his sword. Pulling back on the reins, he turned his horse. He was now in the center of his enemies who swung their machine guns around to greet him.

Breathing heavily and holding tightly to his red-stained

horse that was snorting blood from his nostrils and pawing at
the ground in defiance of the men that were now laughing at
him, Hesin stepped gently from the stallion, pausing to stroke
the dying animal's neck one last time. He turned to face the
rebels. Raising his sword high in the air, he screamed, "For
Allah and the Kurtiwa!" He managed to charge forward three
steps before the 50s that surrounded him fired, consuming both
Habelu-Hesin and the stallion in a wall of lead and dust. When
it was over, it was impossible to tell which were the remains of
the horse and which were the man's.

Hesin had been blown apart. Kueddei wiped the blood that
had been carried by the wind from his cheek. Raising his
glasses, he stared across the line of dead men, horses, and
camels that led back to the oasis. The legionnaires were next.
He gave the order for his infantry to begin their attack. He
motioned his tanks and half-tracks forward. His victory was at
hand.

The momentary silence among Jake and the others was
suddenly broken by the sound of gunfire as the rebels appeared
from behind the dunes, beginning their attack from three
directions. Fenelon yelled for the men to regroup behind the
fallen palms that had been uprooted by the barrage. Cishim and
Doc Blancher gathered up the surviving women and children,
herding them into the center of the makeshift fortress. Bullets
began to strip the bark from the trees and dance in the sand
around the beleaguered little group who were determined to
fight to the end.

Kaufman lowered his glasses. "Such a useless slaughter of
men and animals," said the man with a tired voice.

"Hardly useless, Adolf, that old fool simply lowered the
odds for us, that is all. Come, now we move in behind that
bastard Kueddei. He will be caught between us and the
precious legionnaires he wanted so badly. We will position our
jeeps and tracks with the antitank guns directly behind his
tanks. When I give the order, they all must fire at the same
time. We can not allow the tankers to turn their cannons on us.
We will drive him over the legionnaires' position, and then
eliminate him and his damn rebels," said Kruger, smiling
widely as he stood. "I think I will tie each of his legs to a camel

and pull him apart at the crotch. Yes, that would be very entertaining."

The Kurtiwa women grouped together at the edge of the oasis were now chanting their death prayers to Allah. "Not a very encouraging cheerleading section, is it?" said Jake as he rolled over and slammed another magazine into his rifle.

"Can't really blame them, Jake," said York as he ducked a line of bullets that tap-danced across the tree in front of him. "We ain't exactly ahead in this game, you know what I mean?"

"Oh, shit!" said Jake. York peeked over the tree to see what was bothering the Navy SEAL. Shit was the appropriate term. Kueddei was bringing his tanks up on line, all seventeen of them. The game clock had just run out. Fenelon came over to them. "I believe the time has come for us to say our farewells, my friends. A single volley is all they will need."

The three officers flinched as they heard the first explosion, followed by a series of explosions that occurred so rapidly that it sounded almost like one huge detonation. The three were expecting a tank round to explode at any second. Instead they heard a cheer from the legionnaires. Rolling over as they looked forward, they could hardly believe what they were seeing. All the tanks were on fire or exploding as flames detonated fuel and ammunition. "Jesus, what the hell happened?" yelled York.

"Damn if I know," replied Jake, "but I'm sure as hell not going to be the one to complain about it."

Fenelon pointed to the armored vehicles and jeeps behind Kueddei's burning tanks and asked, "There! Are those Gaafar's men?"

Jake brought his binoculars up and adjusted them on the tall figure in the center of the formation who was directing the fire on the tanks. "They're not wearing Chad uniforms. I think . . ." Jake stared harder through the glasses as he said, "And they're sure as hell not Gaafar's men. The guy in charge is Caucasian, looks European, possibly German . . . Shit! They're mercenaries!"

"Brother, I don't care if it's Poncho Villa. They're tearing those rebels apart out there," said York.

"Yeah, and driving the whole damn bunch right into our

lap," said Jake as he dropped the glasses and grabbed his rifle. "Here they come!"

Kueddei's men were in a state of total confusion. Those who tried to retreat were being cut down by Kruger's men. As they turned and ran the other way, they were met by a withering hail of bullets from the legionnaires. That was the only flaw in the Ice Man's theory. The rebels could not overrun the Legion unless they did so in mass. As it was, they were hitting the oasis in small groups. The stacks of bodies building up in front of the fallen palms showed the futility of that effort.

Kueddei, his face cowering in fear at seeing Kruger, was yelling at his driver to go around the oasis and break for the open desert, to hell with his men. He knew the sadistic ways of the man who had sworn to kill him. That knowledge now overshadowed any logic or reason. The rebel leader ducked behind the armored plating of his half-track as the driver swung wide of the legionnaires who were peppering the vehicle with small-arms fire. Two of Kruger's jeeps fired their 106s at the track, but missed. "Go! Go! Faster, you fool!" For one brief fleeting second, General Hissen Kueddei felt that he had escaped. The illusion was suddenly shattered by the screaming of his driver who released the wheel as he grabbed at his chest. Kueddei stared down at the man and saw his fingers grabbing at the blade that protruded from his chest. Looking behind the man he saw the tall Arab with hatred in his eyes. Kueddei, panicking, reached for the pistol at his side, but he could not get the snap undone on the holster. The Arab withdrew the gleaming sword from the driver. Grasping it tightly in both hands, he raised it high over his head. Kueddei shrieked and cowered down in the seat as the man screamed, "For Allah and Habelu-Hesin!" The blade came down with all the force in Cishim's strong arms, splitting the man in half.

Kruger watched as the rebels who were still alive threw down their weapons and ran screaming in fear over the dunes. Two of Kruger's vehicles started to give pursuit but were recalled by the mercenary leader. He stared at the shattered camp and countless bodies that lay between him and the oasis. Kaufman informed him of Kueddei's death at the hands of an Arab. It was just as well, thought Kruger. The man had already cost him both time and men. All that remained to be done now was the elimination of those who remained within the tangled mess around the water he would need before heading for Libya. Signaling his men to surround the oasis with their vehicles, he paused to give the legionnaires a moment to consider the fate that awaited them.

Doc Blancher crawled over to Jake. Blood covered the right side of his shirt. It was obvious the man was in pain. York pulled him up near the tree trunk and checked the wound. There were two hits, one to the shoulder that had shattered the collarbone and another through his side. Pushing his captain's hand away, he said, "Jeez, Captain, here I been trying to keep that thing clean, and you go poking around with them dirty fingernails of yours . . . Hey! you guys . . . don't happen to know a good doctor in these parts who makes house calls, do you?"

Jake looked over at Fenelon. Both men were grinning. York laughed as he sat down. "You know it's so damn sad, it's funny. Hey, Fenelon, you don't happen to have another one of those harmattans in your pocket, do you?" All four men broke out in uncontrollable laughter. Seeing his men staring across at them, Fenelon repeated York's question in French. Soon everyone was laughing. The sound of that laughter was carried out to the ring of mercenaries who were waiting for Kruger's signal for the killing to begin.

"What could they have found so funny at a time like this?" asked Kaufman, seeing the same question on the faces of the men around him.

"I do not know, Adolf, but we shall see who is laughing in the end," said Kruger as he started to raise his hand and give the signal. The motion was halted by the sound of fighters approaching from the west. Kaufman pointed to the sky and yelled, "There they are!"

"And there!" yelled another man as he pointed to the east. They were F-5 French Mirages. Ten to the east and another ten coming in from the west. Kruger raised his glasses in an attempt to identify them. The planes to the west bore the insignia of the Chad Air Force. Turning to the others he was stunned to see the decal of the Nigerian government.

"Hans," said Kaufman, "I hear helicopters. They are coming from the south." Kruger shifted his glasses in that direction. Four gunships that bore the insignia of Zaire were in the lead. Behind them were twelve CH-47 Chinooks. That could only mean troops.

Tossing the binoculars into the seat, Kruger stepped from his jeep and walked to the front of the vehicle where he stood with his hands on his hips, looking at what was left of his once-mighty army. Kaufman came up to join him. Pulling two cigarettes from his pocket, the big German lit them both and passed one to Kruger. "It is finally over, isn't it, Hans?" he asked.

Kruger inhaled deeply on the smoke as he looked up at the approaching helicopters. The men at the oasis had spotted them. A wild cheer broke out among the legionnaires. "Yes, Adolf. This time, I think I should have taken your advice. Had we gone around all this, we would be safely within the boundaries of Libya by now." Taking another puff of the cigarette, he let the smoke curl out slowly from his cracked dry lips as he flipped it to the ground. Pulling the Colt .45 from his shoulder holster and checking to make sure there was a round in the chamber, he looked at Kaufman and grinned as he said, "What do you say, old friend, shall we show these legionnaires that they are not the only ones who can die with class?"

Kaufman placed his rifle on the hood of the jeep and smiled a toothy grin as he pulled his Beretta from its holster and jacked a round in place. "I suppose this is as good a place to die as any, Hans."

Kruger winked. Holding the pistol at his side, he began to walk toward the oasis with Kaufman beside him. They were in perfect step as Kruger said, "It really was a good plan, you know? If only Kueddei had stayed with the plan."

Kruger and Kaufman may have had a death wish but the other mercenaries did not. Seeing the approaching helicopters, they swung their vehicles around and began driving off in all directions. That was all the F-5s had been waiting for as they began to peel off and dive on the jeeps and half-tracks, blasting them with cannon and machine-gun fire. Neither one of the Germans bothered to look back. They knew what was going to happen to those who tried to escape, but they had made their choice, just as Kruger and Kaufman had now made theirs.

Jake and the others were standing and staring out at the two men with the pistols in their hands who were walking toward them. York looked at Fenelon and asked, "You have any idea what those two guys are doing?"

Looking down the line at the twenty-seven Legionnaires who were still alive, he answered, "Yes, Captain—they have come to die."

Jake turned to look into Fenelon's eyes, "You can't be serious! Just the two of them against all of us?"

The legionnaires locked fresh magazines into their weapons and waited as Fenelon answered, "Yes, Jake, it is a code between legionnaires and mercenaries, much like the honor of the sword was to Hesin." The helicopters were landing a short distance from the oasis unloading General Gaafar's troops and Nigerian commandos. "I will ask that you and Captain York not be involved in this, I hope that you understand," said Fenelon as he and his legionnaires stepped out into the open from the cover of the oasis.

Kruger and Kaufman stopped twenty-five yards in front of Fenelon and his Legionnaires. The men stared in silence across the void that separated them. Fenelon nodded his head slightly to the two men who responded likewise. Jake, York, and Doc stood off to the side and waited to see what would happen next. The Chadian and Nigerian troops were running toward the oasis. Jake raised his hand motioning for them to stop. They did, uncertain of exactly what was happening in front of them. York waved for them to get out of the line of fire, and they separated to each side. Doc tapped Jake's arm and pointed to the commandos. B.J. Mattson was with them. Jake waved for him to stay put. B.J. nodded that he understood. As if on cue, the wind stopped. A perfect stillness fell over the desert. Kruger took one last look at Kaufman and said, "See you in hell, old friend!" Then both men raised their pistols and fired. Two legionnaires went down, and a third grabbed his leg as Kaufman and Kruger were engulfed in a hail of automatic weapons fire that ripped them apart. It was over in a matter of seconds.

B.J. ran up to Jake and grabbed his hand, "I knew you were too damn mean to die, you Navy shit."

Jake couldn't hide the joy he felt at seeing his partner and friend as he said, "Oh, that's just great, and how are you today, Mr. Mattson?"

"What the hell was all that about?" asked B.J.

"It's a long story, B.J. Where's the general?"

Mattson pointed up at the F-5s that were regrouping to return to their base. "Up there getting a little target practice. He don't get out of the office much, you know."

"Who's got control of the capital?"

"General Gaafar."

"Who won the battle in Panama?" asked Jake as they started walking toward the choppers.

"We did."

"You were supposed to be on leave. Who fucked up and got you in on this?"

"You did!"

"Well, tell me something? Who recaptured the airfield?"

"I did."

Jake stopped as he looked at Mattson, "Damn, B.J., is that all you're going to say. We did. You did. I did. Jesus, can't you say more than two words?"

"Sure I can. You like fishing?"

"What? What'd you do? Hit your head on the door of that chopper when you were getting out, or is this little heat wave we have out here already starting to get to you?"

"No, Jake, but the general said I could go back on leave when this thing was over, and that you could come along if you wanted to. So! Do you like fishing or not?"

"Well, sure I do. Believe me, B.J., I appreciate anything that has to do with water these days. Why?"

Mattson put his arm around his friend and partner as he said, "Man, that's great! I just happen to know a sixteen-year-old kid down in Oklahoma who knows where a guy can catch the biggest damn catfish you ever saw . . ."